The Illuminated Witch

Celina has always been alone, until the new Master, Javed, draws her close. But danger and passion are never far away.

After years of struggling alone, Celina—a witchling of immense power—must find her place in the world of vampires.

But while Javed is building a new nest—the first new one in a century—and struggling to overcome his own demons, an ancient evil stirs.

Now with Celina in danger, time running out and the demands of a fledgling nest, can their love possibly overcome every obstacle?

The Blood Secrets Series

The Blood Bride - October 2020
The Illuminated Witch - November 2020
The Sorcerer's Touch - December 2020

THE ILLUMINATED WITCH

Blood Secrets Book 2

Imogene Nix

DEDICATION

*The Illuminated Witch is the second in the Blood Secrets Series.
After I finished The Blood Bride, I couldn't give up the world, as Javed
demanded I explore his story and give him a woman he could adore,
and more importantly, who would stand by him—as his equal.
To be honest, Javed's character intrigued me while I worked on The
Blood Bride so when the time came, Celina felt like the perfect foil.
She's been on her own for so long, that she only knew how to be strong
for herself.
While writing The Illuminated Witch, I joined a circle of authors who
wanted to do the best possible for their characters, particularly those of
the Wiccan and witch variety, so a vote of thanks must naturally be
extended to The Creative Cauldron for their assistance. Of course, I
also had the assistance of a practicing Wiccan to tweak the spells.
Thank you sweetie who shall remain unnamed!
Thanks to Sassie who fine-tuned as well as edited this story ensuring it
shone brightly. With the additions, changes and super fab editing, I'm
super excited to see this go live!
To my family as always and my greatest supporters - authors and
readers alike.*

I hope this re-working of the Illuminated Witch keeps you turning the pages!
Remember if you love it, tell everyone and if you see problems, tell me!

Imogene

2020

PROLOGUE

"The truth can never be known; at least not at this time. Were it known we would be hunted as fiercely as others have. That we have seen already." The dark haired woman, Jemima, spoke slowly. The other women, a blonde called Selena and the red haired, Danicka, nodded in agreement.

"Those who have killed to hide the truth could destroy all we have achieved. Everything we have hidden. The truce between the vampire nests is fragile and can easily be shattered." The three women sat dejectedly, gazing at the ancient rock in the center of the room. It exuded a power they couldn't ignore, a power that reminded them of their home, so far away. The green glow had dimmed over the centuries. But its power hadn't failed yet.

"I miss our sister." The middle sister mumbled, her red hair illuminated by a flare from the rock.

"So do I, but we cannot ignore the truth. At some point, the three we have foretold, will come together again. It will be their antecedents who will carry our power. For now, we must keep watch over the humans as the nests grow. The child of the child of the child must be kept safe and taught how to use their power.

"One will remain within the bosom unwanted, one will be alone all their life…" The red-haired woman stopped and breathed deeply, her words causing a ripple of power to spread throughout the room.

"The last shall be the key. They must meld with the vampires. Their love must be pure but tempered. They alone can fight the one who is left. And it shall be done." The oldest sister, Jemima, sealed their words as magic wove around them, stealing their breath for an instant as their eyes shone.

"Perhaps we should hide the prophecy?" The younger one sat bolt upright in her heavily padded seat even as she patted her intricately coiled blonde hair.

"No Selena. There can be no single place where it can be hidden. Not here. Not yet. There will always be those who would seek to take control of us and what we have. The only thing we can do now is destroy him. We are not yet strong enough. We need the three to achieve that. You know how the power works." Jemima glanced toward her younger sister before glancing at the other.

The oldest sister toyed with her long dark hair, lost in deep thought as she gnawed at her lower lip. None of them seemed a day over eighteen but in truth their ages were lost in millennia. "Danicka, you said the power can't be destroyed, didn't you? That it has to be gifted through birth?" Selena nestled back in her seat, waiting for the edict of the older sister.

"Well, being unable to be destroyed isn't strictly correct. Anything can be destroyed. But it will take magic which far surpasses ours. The vampires now exist because of the children's actions. Our late sister gifted her power to her one surviving offspring, as was foretold. The others, they will pass on the other powers, those lost to our family." Danicka waved her hand around the small stone room where they huddled. "Until then, the best thing we can do is hide it from prying eyes. Keep the ones entrusted to us safe. We will watch over them, ensuring they are well guarded until the correct time."

Selena, the blonde woman exhaled heavily. "So I believe we must continue the vigil then? For centuries? Until we can once more reveal ourselves?" Her voice deepened as it always did when something unsettling occurred to her.

Danicka stood then held her hand out for the book. "Yes. It will be a long and difficult journey. We will see things we would have hoped to have never seen. Things that make some vampires look tame. All we can do is protect those within the nests. They will be the key to the destruction of this book."

Once more, Selena shook her head. "But what if I'm sick of this? What if I want to be a traveler once more?"

Danicka drew a sharp breath. *Surely not!*

"Be calm, sister. It will only be until the time is right. Then we will face the danger together. Until then, we can rest. Take our time. Hone our skills."

Danicka smiled, but it was a mere shadow of her usually sunny grin.

"Now come. We must invoke the shadows. Even as the truth is written it must be hidden from prying eyes. Then a plan needs to be formulated: How to protect the descendants until the time is right to reveal them." One by one, the three sisters stood, before moving toward the stone.

Then with slow gestures, they began their task.

"Celina Worsters."

Celina grinned as her name was called out from the rostrum. She stood and carefully threaded her way through the full seating area. She'd finally done it! Achieved her degree. After years of hard work, she'd dragged herself free of the stigma of being an orphan. Always alone.

Many of her school peers had achieved their degree years before she had, but they'd been able to go to their families, for support. Instead, she'd had to work her way through school. It may have taken six long years, but she finally had the means to start the life she had chosen.

She extended her hand as they'd been instructed and accepted the scroll with a bow, carefully dipping her mortar board. "You have done very well Celina Worsters. You should be very pleased with yourself." The Chancellor's words left her dizzy from the unexpected accolade.

"Thank you Chancellor." She scurried from the stage. No one would be taking photos, no one would be cheering for her in the seats, but she held those precious seconds close to her heart, savoring the impact of her achievements.

"Ladies and gentleman, I would beg your indulgence for just a few minutes longer. We need to present the school's newest High Achiever."

She glanced upwards, wondering who in the class would be nominated as the hardest working, the most driven.

"Ladies and gentleman, if you could be upstanding. Miss Celina Worsters."

Her breath caught in her throat and someone squealed close by. *Who is making that noise?* It wasn't her, that wasn't the way she would react. At least, she didn't think so. Hands patted her and eyes turned in her direction.

She felt a gentle push at her back, shoving her toward the rostrum and she made her way on her unsteady legs. A sense of unreality cloaked her. *Surely, there has been some mistake?*

Even as she neared the podium, she waited for the correction to be announced, but the Chancellor grinned and held out his hand.

"I..." She was lost for words. *What on earth am I supposed to say?* She attempted to smile but it was little more than a grimace.

"You have achieved this on your own. No one helped you. You worked while you studied. Yes, we chose correctly."

How did he know what I was thinking?

The people in the seats stood as one and a massive cheer rose.

The rest of the ceremony passed in a blur as she was guided to a seat at the side of the faculty. Then she waited. Celina still expected them to tell her it was a mistake, but it didn't happen.

At the end of the ceremony, when everyone left the auditorium, she sat there in silence. Now there was only her, the Chancellor and a woman who'd joined them, left in the cavernous room. The Chancellor bowed deeply to the older lady before turning back. "Miss Worsters, I believe Miss Carter would like to talk to you." With a grand hand movement, he indicated she should step toward the waiting woman .

The woman removed the hat she wore, revealing a thick mane of salt and pepper hair, which married well with the horn-rimmed glasses overwhelming her face. "Thank you Chancellor," she said. As she stepped closer to Celina, her long evening gown made a loud swishing sound and the soles of her shoes squeaked.

Celina scanned Miss Carter, who watched her with vivid green eyes. "Uh, so I believe you wished to talk to me?" Her voice sounded strangled and her stomach rocked wildly.

"Yes, I have an offer for you. Now that you have achieved your degree, we have a need for someone with your dogged determination in our corporation. The Chancellor was good enough to introduce us, but I would like to discuss a proposition with you."

A small pasteboard card was pushed into her hands. Celina turned it over, before she ran her fingers over the raised type. "A bank? You want me to work in one of the banks?"

The older woman—Danicka Carter if the card was to be believed —wanted to talk to her about working in one of the banks? "Uh, tell me when and where and I'll be there. I promise."

The woman beamed. Celina couldn't help but returned it.

"Good. Tomorrow morning. Ten o'clock. The address is on the card." Then she turned and walked away.

Celina was mesmerized by her unusually graceful steps.

ONE

Celina grabbed her aching head. Just like the day before, she had another headache, but this one more violent. Her stomach lurched uncertainly and she rubbed her belly while it heaved and roiled. It was only four in the afternoon, too early to head home, but she glanced around the office, looking vainly for an escape.

"Hey, Celina? Can you cover for me tomorrow? I'm going to call in sick, 'cause I've got a hot date." Sylvia, her cubicle mate whispered excitedly.

Celina closed her eyes. *Great. Just what I need.* "Honestly? Syl, I don't know. I'm not feeling so great." She mumbled a little, knowing what Sylvia's reaction would be.

"Have you been to see the doctor yet?"

Celina swivelled her seat and cast a dark glance at her workmate. "I'm going to call—" Her words ended abruptly as the lights dimmed and went out. "Damn... This is like the third time this month. What the hell is going on?" The heat of the office swelled as the air conditioning failed. The cloying scents of a multitude of perfumes and hot sweaty bodies from the summer heat wave closed in on her.

Celina's tummy jostled once more, demanding her attention. She rose, racing unerringly to the bathroom, making it just in time to empty the contents of her stomach violently into the toilet. The clunk of the door alerted her to the fact that she was no longer alone. She sighed loudly, she knew who'd followed her. The sound of wood banging closed reverberated off the walls. The ensuing echo splintered her thoughts.

"Celina, you have to see a doctor." There was concern in Sylvia's voice and Celina shied away from it.

She leaned limply against the wall of the stall, the dim security lighting flickering in and out. "Yeah, I think you're right." She didn't want to face it, but the headaches had become an almost everyday occurrence in the past few months. She'd tried to ignore them, but with little success. Something had to be wrong. Her mind churned over the possibilities.

She pushed away from the wall and headed for the sink, turned the tap and was rewarded by the sound of running water. Celina scooped the liquid up, washed her face and swilled some around her mouth, trying to banish the sour taste. Her knees shook like wet noodles.

"Okay, I'll ring in the morning and see how soon I can get an appointment." A sound from outside caught her attention, a thudding noise, as if someone was testing the door. She wouldn't be able to hide from the problem for much longer and right now, she really needed some air. "We'd better get out there."

"Yeah. Okay." She heard the concern in Sylvia's voice, again. "Will you be okay to get home?"

They slowly made their way through the door and back into the office, where the blast of heat and the waft of body essence made her want to gag again. She struggled through one shallow breath then another.

"I'm planning on going straight home anyway." Celina shuffled towards her desk and groped around in the dark, hunting for her phone. She grasped it in her damp hand and pressed the screen, waiting for it to lighten sufficiently to see her desk. She spied her bag and opened the desk to find her keys. "It looks like these are going to be out for a while. Can you...?" She indicated the light fittings, then toward the office at the end of the row, hoping Sylvia would understand.

"I'll go tell the supervisor. You go on. Head home and take some painkillers."

With a small nod, which she quickly regretted as a pulse wavered through her throbbing skull, Celina headed to the emergency stairs. As she passed desks she saw others grabbing up their items. No doubt they obviously thought the same thing.

Finally she made her way down the fourteen flights of stairs. On the way she heard many voices, some shrill and others filled with laughter. Here and there she caught glimpses of light, probably from mobiles, illuminating the gloom.

One foot after another she plodded down the steps, her head aching viciously and finally, light glowed ahead and a breeze started to clear the stuffy woolliness from her head.

JAVED SHOOK HIS HEAD. THE MISSIVE HE HELD IN HIS HANDS filled him with emotions he hadn't experienced in hundreds of years. He knew what it was. *It was confusion.* The sense of having the carpet jerked out from beneath him. His hands felt clammy.

"So... That's your destiny, there in your hands."

Said hands shook, and the sound of parchment moving back and forth filled the air. He held not just his destiny, but also that of so many others.

He glanced at Xavier, his master, and Hope, Xavier's life mate. They were two very powerful vampires as well as his friends. "I don't know what to say."

Hope rose and glided towards him. "You don't have to say anything. We will say it all. Your leaving us on one level makes us sad, but you will be a Master in your own right. You've earned this."

Javed wanted to sputter and stop her words, but he couldn't. The intent of the letter was clear: On the night of the next full moon, Cressida would grant him his own nest. He would be elevated to the position of Master.

If that wasn't enough to accept, there was the knowledge that there hadn't been a new house in over a century.

There was so much to do. So many decisions to make and all of them would fall on him. He would need to choose a *Yeux Secondes*, the human who would oversee the financial and day to day aspects of the nest. He would also require a second, a guardian who would stand at his side. A fellow warrior, in whom he could place his trust, one who would help him build a safe haven in their nest. He would need witches to help protect the nest and followers... *Where the hell do I even start?*

"You'll need a house. Somewhere for your nest to call home." Hope grinned and he saw the lurking humor she couldn't quell. "I know of an interior designer, if you want their details?"

He rolled his eyes, remembering the problems she'd had with her parents before she'd been turned and the way she'd arranged for an entire block of units to be furnished. It had taken her one night to order and arrange for the delivery of all the furniture. Unlike the immense task her mother had proposed.

But her smile died away as her own memories must have surfaced.

"I don't know about that, but if you're offering help, then I'll accept it. I don't have a clue where to start." He moved back to the arm chair and slumped into it. "I don't usually concern myself with those types of problems." He allowed his head to drop into his hands and muttered. "I don't think I'm ready yet."

A soft touch his shoulder captured his attention. "Cressida thinks you are. Otherwise she would not have petitioned the Councillors. Now come on. You need to start planning. We have one month to arrange your investiture..."

"Cressida will arrange that." Xavier helpfully called out.

"Excellent. That's one less thing to sort out. And I don't have a clue how to arrange one of those anyway!" Hope's voice quietened and Javed knew she was trying to cajole him into a more positive frame of mind. "But you do need to pull together at least the semblance of a nest. So, what do you want to start on?"

"A house. It's no good having all those nestlings without somewhere for them to live." He lifted his head and swiped an unsteady hand over his forehead. Twenty-eight days wasn't a long time and he needed everything completed and ready. "Uh, but how am I supposed to fund...?"

"Read the rest of the letter, my friend. All that is in there." He heard the humor in Xavier's voice and glanced at the paper.

The council has allocated a funding grant to ensure the adequate startup of the new nest. Included is the purchase of appropriate housing, consisting of one main residence and appropriate housing for between fifty and eighty nestlings. Seed funding for the startup of appropriate businesses to ensure the stability of the nest and additional funding as required to furnish, employ and run the nest a period of up to five years, or until financial viability is attained.
Once that has been attained, the nest will be required to make an annual payment to the council for funding future requirements of no less than ten percent of annual gross profits of the nest.

"They have been... more than generous." He glanced at Xavier who had raised his blood wine, saluting him.

"They are. But you deserve it my friend."

"Xavier, I don't know how—?"

"You don't know how to repay the debt? Javed, my friend, it's not a debt. They believe you are able to bring a new nest into existence."

Pressure built inside of him, blooming deep within his chest. He shoved away from the table.

The broad grin on his friend's face died away. "If you really don't feel comfortable..."

Javed shook his head, trying to throw off the disoriented state that shrouded him. "Honestly? I just don't know." He ran his hand through short dark hair, felt how unsteady it was. "I certainly didn't expect this." He waved towards the parchment.

"You can deny the request, if you don't..." Hope's voice behind him made him grimace. She was so young, still so new to their life and ways. She obviously didn't yet realize it wasn't so simple to brush the will of the council aside.

"I could, but I also don't know that I want to." The words were grudging. It wasn't that he didn't want the position and responsibility. No. It was more concern that he wouldn't make it work; couldn't carry out the role effectively and protect those whose futures he would be overseeing. He stared at the ornate Persian carpet. It reminded him of his past. The one he shied away from.

"You can do it. You're ready." Xavier's words hung in the air.

He bowed. "As you wish, my master."

TWO

Home was still some blocks away as she plodded along the sidewalk. Right now, Celina regretted the decision to walk to the doctor's office... "You couldn't even see straight." Yet, right now, that was a cold comfort. If she'd driven, she'd be home already.

Her stomach had settled slightly as she reached the doorway to one of the most imposing buildings on the block and she craned her head to look up. The last rays of sunlight had died away, and she noted how the glass didn't glow in the muted reflection of the moon as it did during the day. She shivered slightly. Instead of the stifling heat, there was a crispness in the night air that only seemed to arrive in summer.

Darkness had settled during her unsuccessful wait to gain an appointment with her physician. She'd sat in the corner of the waiting room, sweltering in the oppressive atmosphere while the air conditioner buzzed and hummed ineffectually, and a vast number of hot bodies came and went while she waited, hoping for a canceled slot.

In the end, the receptionist had announced that the doctor would be unable to see her. She'd been shown the door with a "Come tomorrow morning. He'll see you before his first appointment."

Now making her way slowly home, Celina took a swipe from the drink she'd bought at the corner stall. She gratefully let the cool water trickle down the back of her parched throat as she closed her eyes, seeking a break from the ongoing ache that pulsed behind them.

"Watch out below!" The call echoed through the night and she scanned the dark sky to see a small vehicle swoop down between the towering buildings, the glare of headlights cutting through the gloom of the concrete jungle. The heels of her shoes clicked on the hard ground as the small car landed quietly where she had stood mere seconds before.

Must be someone important to be able to afford one of the air-capable vehicles, she thought. She'd seen them a couple of times and could only guess at their price tag.

The registration plates on the rear declared it was a vampire transport. In the last few years, more of them had populated the roads and skies as the nests became accepted by society. Every now and again a petition would circulate via email and mailbox drop, shared by the disenfranchised in society. The main irritation for the populace was that they, the vampire citizens, were accorded greater privileges than humans.

"Utterly pointless." She muttered as the passengers climb out. A tall man, striking to gaze upon with dark skin, hair and piercing eyes glanced around before ushering a willowy dark haired beauty before him. His middle-eastern origins had her gaping at him.

Celina heard, "Thank you, Javed," and saw the smile he gave the woman. Deep inside, she yearned for someone to care for her like that. As if she was special to them; she brushed the thought away. She'd been alone long enough to know that wishes didn't come true.

On more than one occasion she had considered applying to one of the nests, yet they took so few and her life had been such a struggle that she had shied away every time the thought struck. After all, she didn't need to be rejected again. Once more the notion bloomed, as the hunger she kept carefully banked, bit at her. *To belong somewhere, to be a part of a family...* She'd always dreamed of that.

The couple gracefully headed towards the door of the glass shrouded building before her. One of the heavily guarded nest buildings, she noted.

"Bloody vampires." A voice echoed behind her and even as she turned, someone roughly pushed past her. She shrugged then immediately regretted her action as her head ached again. A wave of dizziness passed over her and she couldn't contain the gasp that escaped. Celina stumbled heavily and would have fallen but for a gentle touch on her shoulder.

"Are you okay?"

Her stomach lurched again. The ground shimmered below her. "I'm... ah..."

Then the gray she'd been fighting all day overwhelmed her.

He'd been aware of the red-haired woman from the moment he'd stepped out of the vehicle. His eyes caught the jerky movements she made and the way she'd watched him and Hope. But he was used to being observed by humans—vampires still made enough of a splash that people gaped at them wherever they went. It was one of the reasons they lived in nests. The humans employed within the nests didn't treat them like freaks.

Her lush frame, vibrant hair and subtle scent captured his senses.

She made a sound. Little more than a groan and he'd turned away from the door. His senses on high alert, expecting trouble. The air was full of fraught expectation.

Her face was pale. In the moonlight she seemed far too fragile, while the distinct red hue of her hair glowed with warmth. He'd noted the way her eyes dilated and the sluggish way she responded to the question. Then she'd slumped toward the hard concrete.

Javed caught her as she fell, her head mere inches from the ground.

"Is she all right?"

He turned at the question, and saw Hope gazing over his shoulder. "Yes. I caught her in time."

"Then you'd best bring her up."

He nodded, his mind sluggish as he peered at the woman in his arms. His libido, rarely stirred, flickered to life as he lifted the woman's supine body. A frisson of connection worked its way through him.

"Vampires! Vampires attacking!" A voice called out in the night and he glanced up, scanning the crowd who now stepped back uncertain.

A sea of white faces stared back at him. The humans seemed frozen with horror, disbelief and something else. There was more than fear in the air now. *Malice.*

His hackles rose and the centuries-old warrior emerged. He'd been in just this position before. It was one he'd hoped never to relive again. The memories of the long distant past, one he tried to bury, rose. His heart thudded fast as adrenalin surged through his veins. He contained his instincts to fight or flee.

Hope. He had to protect Hope. She was his first priority.

His mind urged him to return to her, leave the human behind, but something, maybe the shadow of his soul told him he couldn't. Instead, he cradled the woman in his arms, holding her close while he scanned the crowd for threats.

"Get inside, Hope." He stalked backward, in the direction of the door, his preternatural senses telling him that Hope had followed his instructions, all the while his mind ran through strategic options of defence.

Hope might be a powerful vampire in her own right, but she was also the life partner of his friend and Master, Xavier. He would give up his own life to protect them both.

"He's taking the woman!" Another voice, this one shrill with fear called out as Javed moved faster, gaining the scant security of the doors which shut after he entered.

The sea of voices swelled and rose. Shouts of, "He can't take her," mingled with "He'll kill her."

Anger rose but he tamped it down with ruthless efficiency. Within the building, he freed one hand and slapped it against the emergency shields, which had been upgraded in the long months since the attack on Hope and Xavier. All security procedures and protocols had been overhauled, but he feared it wouldn't be sufficient in a major attack.

But right now, he was more than grateful for the foresight.

"We should get her upstairs. Find out if she's okay." Hope laid her hand on his shoulder.

He scanned her face. "Are *you* okay?"

Hope beamed at him. "Javed, it will take a lot more than an angry mob to frighten me." There was no tremble in her voice and for a moment he wanted to tell her that she should be frightened. But she hadn't been around for hundreds of years. She hadn't seen the ferocity of the attacks on the nests in earlier centuries. She'd never had to run for her life, the way so many of their numbers had.

He swallowed angry words and followed her to the lift, after nodding at the security guard on duty. He knew the man had made contact with the necessary authorities, overhearing his words, "... yes a mob, outside..." before redirecting his attention back to Hope and the woman in his arms.

"I think she might need to see a healer." His words sounded gruff and he winced as Hope speared him with a sharp look.

"You know, I may not be able to read your mind, but I can tell that you're angry about my comments and trying, unsuccessfully I might add, to hide it."

He closed his eyes. "I didn't mean—"

"No. I know you didn't mean any disrespect, Javed."

He breathed deeply, hearing her soft tones. He gazed out the glass elevator over the city, seeing the sparkling lights beyond while he accepted the gentle remonstrance.

"Xavier told me about the times the nests have been attacked. About the dangers older vampires have survived. I'm not being flippant." The bell chimed, cutting the opportunity for further discussion as they entered the reception area.

THREE

Opening her eyes was a painful experience. While the headache itself had finally abated, Celina's whole body still ached. Just as it had every day since the headaches began. The only difference was the severity of the ache. It increased, leaving her bones heavy and awkward.

The touch of a hand startled her and she grimaced at the cool brush against her burning hot skin. "Where am I?"

"You're safe." The words were soft, and she cracked her eyes open a little further, willed them to focus and finally the man, no—vampire—she'd seen exiting the car swam into view.

Celina blinked once then again. She noted the deep burnished, golden brown of his eyes, and the way he stared right though her. She pushed weakly at the light covering and struggled upright. Her mind worked to decipher the who-and-where of her situation.

"I'm so sorry. I shouldn't have..." *Shouldn't have what?* Her mind demanded.

He grinned, his face lightening. He went from amazingly handsome to so beautiful he'd leave the most gorgeous of women wishing for the purity of his looks.

Her stomach flip-flopped in reaction, as if a dozen tiny eels were trying to escape. "I've inconvenienced you." She knew enough about vampires. Knew enough to stay out of their way. Even as a child, growing up in a series of uncaring foster homes, she'd known the truth—learned about the world in which the nests operated. She might have toyed with the idea of applying to the nests from time to time, but she knew it was bad to inconvenience vampires.

They were a species of alpha predators. She'd heard enough of their intentions and their vast empires. Besides which, vampires fed on humans, didn't they? They saw them as cattle, to fatten, then glut themselves on. She shivered at her own thoughts, fright suddenly turning her skin cold. "I'll go now."

His lips thinned as he held out a hand, stopping her weak movements. "You will wait for the healer. Is there someone I can call?"

She stared at him, trying to process the melodic and almost caring manner. *Soft? Caring?* She placed a halt on those thoughts. Vampires weren't fluffy, caring creatures. They were hunters. The alpha's of the night time world! But even as the thoughts battered her, a melting sensation curled deep within her gut. It called out to her consciousness that maybe the stories were wrong.

"No. There's no one."

He frowned, the action marring his perfect burnished skin. She let her gaze roam over his face for just a moment. She took in the dark hair, the perfectly straight nose, his chiseled jaw line covered with a light dusting of facial hair and high cheekbones. Watched his golden-brown eyes widen slightly.

He reminded her of the old Arabian movie heroes, one of her foster mothers' had played regularly in an attempt to educate her foster brood on the classics. Her mouth, already dry now felt parched, and her hand moved of its own volition, toward him. She almost touched his face before reality intruded in the voice of a woman.

"Javed? The healer is here!" The words snapped Celina out of the trance she'd been lost in. She wrenched her hand away.

But through lowered eyelashes, she kept an eye on him, as he straightened and dragged himself upright.

"Send him in, Fiona."

A man came into the room, and she gasped, unable to contain the sound as she realized that he too was a vampire.

"It's okay, Javed. I'll take it from here."

The dismissal didn't suit the one who answered to that name. He narrowed his gaze and she stared as he flattened his lips. He bowed low and without a word stalked from the room.

"Let me take a look at you."

She scooted away from the older man's touch.

He sighed heavily. "Yes, I am one of them. But I'm still a doctor. The humans of the nests need medical attention too. Now, there isn't likely to be anything wrong with you that I haven't seen before." He placed his bag on the floor with a thud.

She gulped. "You won't...?"

He stared and her then shook his head. "No, I won't hurt you, but people don't just drop to the ground for no reason. According to Javed that's what you did, so let's find out what caused it."

Even as he reached out, her head began the familiar pulse once more, and she gasped. The doctor frowned, and reached for her forehead. As he made contact the lights in the room flickered once. Then they were in darkness.

"Oh dear." His words were soft but full of concern as he tugged his cool fingers away. The room spun, and even as the darkness overtook her again, she heard him bellow for the one called Javed. Then she let go of consciousness.

THE WORDS OF THE DOCTOR FELL LIKE STONES. "YOU NEED TO get her into a nest and get her powers under control. She's over saturated and unstable. For my money, I would call her an untrained and unknown witch."

Javed sucked in a breath at the pronouncement.

An *unknown witch* was beyond dangerous. If their powers weren't contained and used, they became unstable. Magic built within the cells of a witch where it rapidly multiplied. Eventually, the cell walls could no longer contain the charge, which would then course wildly through their bodies. Depending on how strong the witch was, the body would continue to fight it, as if it were an infection. But around them...things would happen, like lights going out.

"I've seen this before." He turned away, breathing deeply as he fought to control his response to the doctor's diagnosis.

"I would imagine you have. More than once."

Javed spun back. The truth couldn't be ignored. The body of this woman would eventually be unable to contain the magic and would simply explode. Killing her. It almost always killed those within near proximity, too.

He closed his eyes. Getting her into a nest wasn't quite as simple as it sounded. They would need to find a witch with sufficient experience to work with her. Right now, with the upheaval caused by the creation of the new nest... He broke off the thought. *Perhaps Bertha? She would be joining the new nest. She is sufficiently accredited.* He needed to get help for this woman. That is, if it wasn't already too late.

Memories rose, scents and sights he'd hoped long gone assailed him... "Xavier's household. Bertha is already there. We can find her a spot." Once more, he found his equilibrium.

"It's full to bursting right now. We have all the ones that will transfer to your nest on the full moon." The doctor glanced at Hope.

"We can't leave her free. She's a danger to herself and others." Hope was frowning as if thoughts swirled through her mind.

He turned away as memories again hammered at him. Hope was right, of course.

She spoke on a purely academic level, she'd never seen the results of the loss of control from an unknown witch. Not like he had. The carnage that was left behind when their bodies could no longer contain the magic.

In the centuries gone by, Javed had found those bodies. In the past, the remains of the unknown had been left, discarded in the sand and to the wind. Some had argued it was justified as they walked between the world of humans and magic.

He'd seen it many times both as a human and vampire, having come across more than one cadaver before his change. For many months after finding the carcasses he'd been plagued by nightmares. The scents that had assaulted him, the copper tang on the air and sickly sweet aroma of rot—

He broke off the thought far more easily than he'd done in the past.

But the memories remained. One could never forget the sight of the remains being devoured by the carrion-eating birds.

He glared back at the doctor. "We will find a place for her. I will have her join my nest after the investiture. No one deserves to die like that." And the truth was, until they could find some way to train her, she was a ticking time bomb.

"Fine, Javed. That's what we'll do. Please make the necessary arrangements." Hope spun away on her heels, no doubt concerned about the other members of the nest. He wished he could explain what he felt. But after eight hundred long and lonely years, he both questioned and respected the instincts that screamed he needed to protect the unknown woman.

He slipped his hand into his pocket, searching for the small cellular phone, and made a quick call. Javed turned back to the doctor. "Stabilize her then I'll take her to the nest."

The doctor bowed quietly and set about his task while Javed kept watch. The needle the doctor plunged into her arm, carried a sedative that would keep her unconscious until she was within an active circle. The small amount of blood the doctor drew glowed in the dim room, the lighting gradually being restored due to her unconscious state.

"See how it glows? Her magic is almost uncontainable, now. The woman must have suffered greatly in the last little while. It's a wonder she hasn't been hospitalized or at least under a doctor's care," the doctor said, as he moved swiftly, checking her over.

Javed listened to the muttered imprecations until a guard appeared at the door. "We are ready for you."

He nodded tersely. Even as he stalked towards the woman, the doctor stayed him, extending a hypodermic needle. "You need this. If she's likely to wake before you get her into a circle, inject all of it into her. It will neutralize her..."

Neutralize...? "No. I won't use it." His stomach curled wildly.

"It won't kill her, just keep her body in a form of artificial stasis. Long enough for a decision to be made or a high witch to get to you and her within a circle... before..."

Javed's mind stopped. For just an instant he imagined the situation. "It won't come to that." But he accepted the syringe without another word. He knew he wouldn't use it, though. He'd felt a subtle connection to her. An awareness he couldn't destroy. It carved his insides up, flaying him deeply. That one woman—Celina, he'd discovered her name while checking her purse—tied him up in knots like this was a surprise and a fearsome threat.

He thought longingly of Kharisma, and wondered if she would join his nest. She was a capable doctor and experienced warrior. He'd enjoyed a pleasant but recently ended interlude with her. She'd given him a sense of belonging for the short while. It had been easy going, with no strings attached. But sadly she had found her life partner causing their connection to fizzle away, leaving him once more alone. He hadn't felt this confusing sense of connection with her.

He slid the cold glass and steel syringe into his pocket then carefully scooped up the woman. She weighed next to nothing. He noticed the dark bruising beneath her eyes. Her skin was pale, as if all her blood had drained away. A sure sign the magic was winning.

"We need to get her back to the nest." Urgency rode him as he strode through the doorway.

The guard at the door snapped to attention before slipping in behind him. Javed cradled the woman, wondering what in the hell was going to happen next.

CELINA WOKE AS COLD SKITTERED THROUGH HER BODY. SHAKEN, she tried to turn. There was a roughness beneath her fingers, the indentation capturing her attention. It felt like a brick, even though the surface had a worn feel to it. Celina opened her eyes to see a dim room, dungeon-like, with high ceilings and stone which gently sloped to a wall. It was a dark room. Wherever she was, it wasn't anywhere she'd ever been before.

"Hello?" Her voice sounded thin and thready and she shook, as much from the chill as the nervousness that flooded her system.

"So, you're finally awake then." A woman's voice, stern and cold broke the silence and she glanced up. The walls were decorated with sconces, lit with small flames and a fluorescent light glowed above her head. But even as she moved, the pulse of pain slithered through her, stealing her breath.

The mechanical light dimmed and the flames in the metal holders danced but unlike the warehouse-style fluorescent lights, they remained glowing, saving her from total darkness.

A pink barrier sprang up around her, misty and ethereal. Celina tried to shift away from it but as she brushed up against it, it seared her and she flinched away.

"Stay still, silly girl." She turned her head sharply in the direction of the voice. A plump woman with gray hair sat on a high wooden stool beside the man, who had been with the doctor.

He must have abducted me. She willed her head to settle so she could find a way out of there. The need to stop the painful pulsing in her skull warred with another need. One that said she needed to find out where the hell they'd stashed her.

"Now that you are awake we can begin." The woman spoke

again, thumbing through some old book, its edges creaking as she turned the large yellowed pages.

The man gazed at her silently. His lips flattening and his eye contact remained unwavering.

"Where am I?" This time her words were little more than a whisper, yet they echoed in the cool, damp room.

"All in good time my dear. Now, the question is who are you and how long have you had this power?"

Confusion filled her... "What the devil are you talking about? My name is Celina. Celina Worsters. Now why have you kidnapped me?" She couldn't contain the fear that rose in her voice. The nerves in her body jumped and danced with every movement of the fires that illuminated the room.

"You weren't kidnapped. You were brought here for your own safety."

This time Celina threw a contemptuous glare at the woman who kept flinging nonsensical ideas at her. "Right. Like that's believable. I'm not a vampire. I don't belong to a nest, so you have to let me go." Celina injected every ounce of bravado she could into the words, then slumped spent, back to the floor.

This time the woman stood and advanced toward the pink light. She waved something that she was sure was a knife around and a section of the pink light disappeared.

Celina gulped in her fear. "What are you going to do...?" A knife. *Is she going to cut me?* "Please, don't hurt me." She tried to cower away.

The woman stared at her, then she rolled her eyes. "I'm not going to hurt you. It's an athame. Do you know what that is?"

Celina shook her head, sure her brain wobbled around in her head.

"It's a knife, used in witchcraft. As for letting you go... We can't. You're dangerous at the moment. To yourself and everyone around you. Your power is unstable. Now what do you know about witchcraft?"

Celina scooted back. "Witchcraft? What are you talking about? I'm just a regular person. Now, let me out of here. Please?"

The man she knew was a vampire pushed away from the wall, stalking towards the pink light. "Let me, Bertha." It was the gorgeous vampire she'd seen before—the one who'd taken care of her. She watched him, his walk slow and fluid. She shivered even as fear coiled within her. "Celina, you've been ill lately, haven't you?"

She nodded slowly.

"Your head, it hurts. Pulses?"

"A little." She refused to tell him anything much until she knew where he was going with this.

"We believe you are an *unknown witch*." She nearly laughed at his words, but his eyes were grave. That alone sobered her. "You are dangerous until you can either control your powers or..." His words died away.

A lump lodged in her throat. "Or what?"

He spun around. "Or until your body can no longer contain the power that runs through your veins and you die. Possibly killing many other innocents at the same time."

"Oh. Ha ha. I love a joke as much as the..."

His face hardened and fascination rose. The play of lights on his finely chiseled features caught her attention. Then she sobered again. *He believed what he was saying!*

"It's not a joke. Lights go out around you. Electrical equipment fails or blows up. Cars seize around you. It's getting worse, isn't it? The power that you can't contain, it's growing? It's bleeding out through your pores. Unless we can contain it." He stared hard at her and she could see the desolation in his eyes.

"I'll what?" She whispered the words, wanting desperately to flee from the pronouncement he was about to make. On some level she knew it wasn't good news, he was about to share, yet she stayed still.

"Then your body will erupt, causing a massive magical explosion. It will kill you and possibly hundreds of others. Just like a magical mushroom cloud."

She stilled. *Explosion?* Not quite what she'd expected.

"That's why we brought you here. It's not yet too late, but you have to learn to control it."

She whipped back to face the woman, who nodded silently. Now there was no amusement or anger on her face—just sorrow.

Celina shook her head. "No. This is a trick. Some silly thoughtless and unkind prank. You should be ashamed of yourselves." Even as she threw the words, she knew, it wasn't a trick. He knew her symptoms. Her mind laughed raucously at the ridiculous notion yet that instinct that had served her since childhood told her he was earnest.

She licked suddenly dry lips. "If and only if this is correct, then what do I have to do? How can you save me?"

"My dear, we teach you to control it. And you will have to be absorbed into a nest."

"No. No, I don't want that."

The woman shook her head. "You don't have a choice. You will be a known witch. As such, you will be subjected to the laws of our *Conclave Paramount*."

"What? Conclave Who?"

"Dear, we're wasting time. Now let's see. If I drop my casting circle, can you control yourself for a little bit longer?"

"I'll... I'll try." And she could also try to escape if it got too much.

The woman rose, stalking closer to her. Celina watched, her stomach tied in knots, as she cut at the pink barrier and stepped inside. "Now, let's see what you can do." With a few words and a quick step from the large woman the section of barrier rose again.

FOUR

The night of the investiture crept up on them, like a thief. Time ticked away and Javed remained busy, though always aware of the red-headed wraith who'd joined their ranks.

Javed had petitioned for her inclusion into the new nest and Xavier had granted his request, interceding with the *Conclave*. "I honestly don't know if I should be thankful or not." Javed's muttered words were tinged with a hint of confusion.

He'd watched her silently as she moved up and down corridors, following the high witch, Bertha. With some effort Bertha had coaxed more information out of her, including the fact she'd been a foster-ling. Each time he considered that fact, he frowned. It always amazed him that humans, with their gift of reproduction, could cast their children aside like used rags.

He steered his mind away from the negative thoughts. They'd also learned she was qualified with a business degree and had been working as an insurance assessor with one of the large banks. A skill any new nest could certainly use.

He stared into the mirror as he dressed in his traditional garb and grimaced. It had been a long time since he'd worn anything that wasn't western-centric.

He looked at himself critically. He'd already donned his *sirwaal* and *thawb* which brushed against his ankles. The white accentuating the coffee tones of his skin, but if felt alien to him, after centuries of wearing western pants and shirts.

He tugged on the *ghutra* and *agal*. "This doesn't feel like me, anymore."

"I don't think I've ever seen you wear that, my friend." Xavier clapped him on the shoulder as he stood beside him. "And I honestly still don't get how you could have fought dressed like that."

"Xavier, times were so different then. But then, so was war." Memories scrolled like faded films of long ago battles and the waves of knights he'd met. It was after the battle for Acre that his own life had changed. It was there he'd met his sire. Of course Philippe was now long gone and times hadn't stopped still. Now he would be the first master of a new nest. "It still seems so unreal to me."

He slipped on the *mashlah* and inhaled deeply. Scents of citrus and spices filled the air, stirring his senses and calling up long-dimmed memories.

"You are ready my friend?"

Javed bowed low to the one who had been his Master, one last time. Then he followed Xavier into the hall. Javed felt himself smiling slightly as the small lights shone on the steps leading to the entrance to the hall. Xavier had the lights installed for Hope before she became a vampire. When Xavier had prepared to give the order for them to be removed she'd asked him not to, so she could use it as a tangible memory of her lost humanity. Things lost would be the pattern of the night, he knew.

This would be his last time in this corridor, unless he visited as an equal. Although it had only been home for a short while, he felt the loss of familiarity keenly.

As they opened the door he started. A sharp cry filled the air and he had to stop and absorb the reality before continuing his journey toward the gardens where the ceremony would take place.

A full moon hung in the sky, a round white orb that had for centuries become the only illumination to brighten their existence. It was appropriate that major ceremonies revolved around it, he thought. Then he laughed at the touch of whimsy.

He walked briskly, the swish of cloth filling his hearing as he cleared his mind in preparation for the ceremony ahead. Each was different, planned to show the change from nestling to Master. Each ceremony included aspects of their human life and their new, vampiric life. It was, essentially, the ceremonial cutting of the ties that bound them to their past.

Cressida waited for him, dressed in a long gown of silver and blue, a circlet of flowers adorning her long and unbound, blonde hair. He focused as he approached her. "Javed of the Tudor nest, come forward." She extended her hand to him and he took it, realizing that he shook.

"Mistress of Life, I come beseeching thee for life and sanctity." The traditional greeting tumbled from his mouth quickly, she winked and the pressure building within his chest abated a little.

"You are a good and honorable servant to me and mine. What petition would you ask?" Her voice rang out.

The nest members and guests waited in silence during the ancient and powerful ceremony.

They would give their affirmation soon enough. *If they consider me worthy.* He ignored the whisper of his psyche and concentrated on Cressida. She stood on a small wooden dais, watching him intently.

"I would ask that you grant us, those who come before you, service and safety." He gulped, the power of his words rushing over him.

Her eyes shone in the moonlight while the scent of roses and honeysuckle filled the air.

Xavier strode forward, dressed in the black garb of his own

culture. With a low bow, he offered obeisance to Cressida as the most senior member of the Council and the only one with the power to carry out the ceremony. "I vouch for this servant. He is good and honorable. Above all he is loyal to those of my nest. He is deserving of the title Master."

She bowed formally to Xavier, before she removed the sword from the scabbard at his hip. It came free with a hiss, and she held it aloft so that the light of the moon glinted on the wickedly sharp blade.

A fluid motion to his left saw Hope step toward Cressida, the large ceremonial goblet of chased silver held in her hands. She winked, settling his nerves, as the moment of no return arrived. Once the goblet was transferred to Cressida, Hope took her place beside Xavier.

Cressida waited, still as a marble statue for only the passing of a heartbeat, before slowly turning to the onlookers and addressing them. "Of those present tonight, do you swear that in the tradition of honor, loyalty and righteousness to tell me true? Is this humble servant, Javed of the nest Tudor, fit to assume the mantle of Mastership?"

A ripple of magic filled the air and as one, the voices of those watching called out, "He is."

His back bowed as some unseen force pushed him to the ground at her feet.

She stepped closer, so he could only see her silver clad feet. "Javed of the nest Tudor. Rise and come to me." Her words were imbued with the same magic that had pushed him to the ground, and he gave himself up to the urges within his body. He rose stiffly and moved closer, crowding the Councillor who stood before him.

He felt the elongation of his fangs, something that rarely happened now they'd stopped feeding directly from their nestlings. The sharp sting was gone in an instant, and his awareness narrowed to a pinprick and he saw the wrist Cressida held out to him. "Feed deeply from me and accept the power that lies before you."

He frowned, fighting the urges. *Feed from Cressida?* His body urged him to do so, to embrace all the power that was there for the taking.

His mind told him that was wrong.

He wasn't there for the power. He was there for the good of their race and the nestlings.

He tore his eyes away from her wrist as pain arced through him. He stared into the crowd, searching for the red haired woman and not for the first time he felt the stirrings of desire even as his body screamed at him to accept what was freely offered.

"You have done well to ignore the call of our nature. The investiture of a house is not about power. It is about choices made to protect our way of life."

He glanced back to see a grin upon Cressida's face. *The test!* No wonder it had felt wrong. Each investiture had a test of some description, he let his diaphragm fill with air. He'd successfully negotiated that. He forced the smile from his lips. This was a sober time.

The compulsion broken, he scanned the crowd as members of the council surged forward, then knelt beside Cressida.

With a smooth action she took the sword Xavier had offered her and made a shallow slice in her wrist. Several deep red drops of blood dripped into the goblet, then one by one the other Councillors followed suit. While waiting, Cressida licked at the slice, healing the cut almost instantly. Javed observed the flesh repair itself. Cressida winked at him and shock took his breath once more.

The goblet was now passed back along the line of Councillors until it rested once more in Cressida's grasp. She stepped forward. "Drink. Drink deep and assume the mantle of leadership."

He accepted the goblet and as he drank she spoke words that he could barely hear, but he felt the effects. Power rushed through his veins, making his fingers and toes tingle. He felt stronger, lighter and faster. Once he had drained the goblet she inclined her head.

"Now you make your oath to the Council."

"I, Javed, no longer of the house Tudor, do swear and affirm that my fealty is to the council, my nestlings and my brothers and sisters of blood. I will protect them, keep them safe. Above all I will give them service. I will remain true to our ways and seek always to protect the innocents."

"Then rise, Javed of the house al bin Habbad. Accept the fealty of your nestlings."

CELINA STEPPED FORWARD. AFTER WEEKS OF LEARNING TO control her powers, the headaches had become far less prevalent. But the result of learning to control herself and the magic within her came at a cost. She'd had to agree to move into the nest, and had given up her job and apartment.

Now, here she stood in the warm night air attending an event that only rarely occurred, so she'd been informed.

Bertha, her high witch tutor, clucked her tongue and pushed her into the line. "As we are both going to the new nest, we need to give our oath to the new master." So she waited quietly, for her turn to kneel before the new master. Javed. The procession took some time so she studied those standing around, including the tall blonde woman everyone paid deference to and who'd conducted the ceremony.

The vampire caught Celina's eye and Celina smiled back only to have Bertha hiss at her. "You don't play eye tag with a counsellor. Now come on."

Truly, if she hadn't been so grateful for the help Bertha had given her she would have been royally peeved at the words. Instead she turned back to survey the procession of ducked heads and murmurings.

Finally she reached him. His eyes were now at half-mast and he indicated she should kneel. The gravel beneath her knees bit at the tender flesh, but she accepted the pain. "I promise to give service to you, Master. As well as my honor and loyalty at all times." She whispered the words but the touch of his hand on hers left her with the impression of lightning zinging through her veins. She glanced away once she finished her part of the oath, feeling the immediate effects on her body, as within her settled the knowledge that she had now given the last part of her freedom to him. It was both strangely satisfying and terrifying.

"In return for your service, I promise safety, service and protection for all your days and those of your line." When she peered up his eyes blazed. Her body tightened, a not unusual circumstance that happened around him, she admitted privately to herself.

She rose unsteadily and nearly tripped over the traditional long gown, but Javed helped her to stand and she blushed, the heat creeping over her face and highlighting the confusion. "Thank... Thank you, Master."

He grinned before turning back to take the next oath—Bertha hadn't missed the exchange. "You have to be the clumsiest witch I've ever met. Now come on, we need to go eat before the festivities begin." The woman grabbed her arm and dragged Celina behind her bulk, and she let her, knowing that the hungry members of the household had fasted in preparation of the feast. They hurried inside to find that the cold refreshments were already a hit with those attending.

The *Yeux Secondes* of the Tudor house, David, watched silently aloof from the milling people. She'd heard whispers about his history and his wife. The wife, Alexa was long gone, Celina had been told. They said she'd only married him to get at his sister, Hope.

She already knew that Hope was the life partner of Xavier, and that the relationship of brother and sister remained strained. She'd felt pity for him, but had followed the edict of Bertha who had told her he had been damaged by the whole affair and no one discussed it openly.

It seemed even vampire houses weren't immune to family politics. She snorted. "And what the hell would I know of family politics."

Bertha cast a glance over her shoulder. "Did you say something?"

"Uh no. Not really. Just talking to myself." At that, Bertha steered her to the tables spread with Middle Eastern food.

They ate quickly, circulating through the throng when the gong sounded in the ballroom and everyone proceeded to the large formal room.

The final formal part of the evening would be the telling of a prophecy, apparently it usually told of the future of the house, so everyone waited quietly while the seers lined up across the front of the stage, then there would be dancing.

Twelve people stood still at the front of the stage, a mix of old and young, male and female. Each gave the impression of being nervous and uncomfortable with the limelight thrust upon them. The room quieted and all stilled.

The oldest woman, standing at the far end, jerked slightly her eyes closing as her body tensed. She extended a hand, her head thrown back.

"The secrets of the blood must out. The lost scroll of prophecy holds the truths that only the three foretold can stop. Without these three, the secrets shall crush us all. The houses shall fall and our races will be destroyed. Be quick, though, for the secrets must be learned from the book hidden, before the next full moon."

The woman slumped to the floor, and only those closest hurried to her, fanning and offering water as she came back to consciousness. Voices chattered now, in low tones as everyone tried to assimilate the words.

"Oh dear, *our races shall be destroyed.*" Bertha screwed up her eyes. "That doesn't bode well. I can see we will be busy after tonight."

"I take it this isn't the usual kind of prophecy for an investiture?" Celina leaned forward and Bertha shook her head.

"Indeed not. At least, not that I've ever heard. My family have served for over seven generations."

A hush fell over the room as Cressida and the new Master, Javed ascended the small stage. The presentiment of doom left pockets of whispered conversations even as the two conferred. She glanced to Bertha then to the new Master. The Councillor now stepped away from Javed, raised hands in the air wordlessly calling for calm.

"I believe, given the prophecy, that our newest house has just been granted a very significant role in our future. We, as your Councillors will begin an immediate search for information pertaining to the secrets of the blood that were spoken of. In the meantime, I suggest everyone return to their homes, so that we may make immediate plans."

With those words, the festivities ended.

FIVE

Two weeks had passed since the investiture and the new nest was already finding its feet in such a trying situation. With members from other nests populating it, well, it kind of made sense, Celina thought.

Idris, a brawny dark-haired vampire and recruit from yet another house acted as second for the newly formed nest. He'd taken over the day-to-day interaction that the witches currently had with the senior vampires. Bertha suggested it was because he was interested in a liaison with Celina, but she just shrugged the suggestion away. She wasn't interested in him like that.

She watched as Idris left the basement that had been claimed by Bertha, and the other witches who were currently staying here, as their workrooms.

"So, what are you going to do about him?" Bertha raised an eyebrow at her before returning to whatever she was doing.

"He's nice enough, but not really my cup of tea."

Sure, she'd had some conversations with various guards, but their conversation either tended to be terse and to the point or suggestive on their part. Instead, she gave every waking moment over to learning the craft. She hoped that someday soon, when she had learned enough to be marginally competent she might also be given another role within the nest. Perhaps she'd even get to use her hard-won degree again.

But that wasn't now. Instead, she was relegated to the most simplistic spells and she chafed under the restrictions. She'd passed so many years living her life on her own terms. From the time of rising, to how she spent her days, hadn't been directed by others. Now even the choice of what to eat was determined by someone else. About the only thing she had control of, was what underwear she chose. "Even that would be taken, if I handed over any more control."

Celina wanted to help, but being a neophyte with little to no status sucked.

"Is there something I can do?"

Bertha looked up, shook her head, before resuming her task of searching for whatever would help them unravel the mystery of the prophecy.

"There has to be something I can do?" She winced, hearing the intense need in her voice. For the last few weeks, her world had spun out of control. From being a well-groomed and settled insurance assessor, now she was little more than a shell upon the beach, being buffeted by the tide.

"Dear, there really isn't much you can do until you learn to control your emotions and the power that runs within your veins." There was a subtle dismissal in Bertha's words.

Celina grimaced. "But surely..."

Bertha grunted, this time there was a flattening of her lips, and a distinct coolness in her voice. "If you must... The old gray book in the next room. You can try the spell for finding something you have lost... it's in there somewhere."

Celina agreed wordlessly. It wasn't much. In fact, if she didn't know better, she'd say Bertha just wanted her out of the way. But it was an opening—a way to help in the search for the prophecy. Not that Bertha expected it to work, obviously.

"I'll just..."

The woman jerked her head up. "I cannot work with so many distractions. Take yourself to the other room. And make sure you use the athame to cast a circle first."

This time Celina blushed. Her last attempt had seen her forget to create a casting circle and the consequences hadn't been terribly positive. The blackened patches on the walls bore testament to that.

Once in the other room, she moved to the bookcase, searching for the book. Each of them felt different, as if imbued with a power from their previous users. She had so many questions she wanted to ask Bertha, but given the circumstances she couldn't ask anything.

With care, Celina ran her hands over the spines, some sang beneath her touch and others made her shiver as trickles of iciness spread their tendrils through her spine.

The gray book was finally beneath her fingers. She sighed as if it were an old friend just returned home. *Could it be that this book wants me to use it?*

The pages were thick and smelled of mustiness, but it was comforting too. She slipped it from the shelf, its weight oddly familiar and she laughed at her fanciful thought.

Celina searched for the athame the older woman had given her weeks ago. The ceremonial knife lay in the open box ready for use, and she inhaled deeply.

A smudge stick sat nearby, and she swept it up and the small packet of matches that waited. *I can do this.* Even with her mental encouragement, uncertainty clawed at her.

The door creaked as she stepped through into a small anteroom that lay beyond. Celina found the old stool and hauled it to the center of the room, where she carefully laid the book on the wooden chair. It opened with a groan, and her heart beat wildly. Page after page she searched through the spidery writing.

Finally, towards the end she found the one she searched for. "To Find Something Once Lost." She breathed the words as a layer of dust lifted from the pages.

For an instant, she wondered where this book had been hidden, then dismissed it from her mind. She could always ask Bertha... later.

She swept up the tight bundle of herbs that smoked from one end, and muttered the sacred words she'd been taught. Carefully, she wafted the gray cloud around in the air. Once satisfied she'd purified the area, Celina extinguished the remains, dropping them to the chair, then she scooped up the blade. Her hands shook, and she struggled to clear her mind.

"From floor to ceiling and in-between, the circle is cast as can be seen. For all within let it burn bright, for the good I cast let it be right. Strength of will, strength of night, keep all evil doers out. And harm ye none, do as ye will. By the power of three times three, this is my will, so mote it be. And with your power, so mote it be." She proceeded around the circle invoking the four points of the compass, before carefully returning to the stool at the center.

A flare of light enveloped her, and Celina set the athame back on the surface of the stool. With great effort, she cleared her mind again as the excitement had grown, and prepared herself to begin the spell. Her fingers traced over the page. She felt the power build within her as she sought her center, detected the flare she reached for the tendrils.

"Bound and Biding, Biding Bound. See the sight and hear the sound. What was lost will now be found. Bound and Biding, Biding Bound. And harm to none, mote it be."

Once the words were said, warmth flooded her. She wanted to move, as if an unseen force tugged at her. She carefully grabbed the knife, creating a doorway in the circle, before she gave in to the need dragging her toward the doorway.

On the way out the door, she placed the silver knife on the side table and grabbed her mobile phone safely hidden in her pocket. She could leave a message to let others know where she was going, but right now she had to follow the draw before it dissipated.

Up the steps she hurried. The compulsion deep within her throbbed, almost painfully. She didn't exactly know where she was going, instead she would let her body and senses guide her. After all, wasn't that what they'd kept reminding her to do?

"And if I wait, it could disappear." She muttered to herself. It made excellent sense to her. Go where the call came from. Then let them know once she knew where.

The car waited where she had left it, with the keys still in the ignition. Once the bluetooth connected she rang, leaving a message. "I've found something and am heading there directly. I'll let you know what I've found."

Elation filled her. Surely it was great fortune that showed her where she needed to go?

Celina steered out of the drive without glancing back.

SIX

In the dark, something old stirred, stretching its awareness outside the alcove it had rested in for so long. "Who is there?" The voice was rough from disuse.

A light flared, and he hissed at the assault on his sight.

"It is I, my Liege. I call you from your slumber with tidings." He waited, holding himself very still as the servant, Jelani stepped into his view. "They have started hunting for the secrets. The secrets of how they were formed. They do not yet realize that is the path to destruction."

"How long have I rested?" He moved, grunting slightly as he straightened stiff limbs. Then he released muscles that had been locked for so long, amid loud groans.

"Three centuries, sire." Jelani bowed low and he watched silently, thinking of the changes Jelani must have seen in the world during his slumber. Just as he had, in the thousands of years of his existence.

"Did you find the one I requested?" He pinned his gaze on the quivering creature before him.

His servant was not a vampire, for the change had not been absolute. It was only after they had become aware of his *other* bloodlines that the truth had become apparent.

Others could not be changed. Instead, this one was caught in the shadowy visage of were and vampire. But he was loyal and long-lived.

"Sire, I did as you requested. But they chased him. Caught him. I managed to save him at the last moment, but then he escaped and hid for centuries. When I finally found him again and commanded him to do your bidding, he failed. He was killed seasons ago." The creature bowed deeply, and for a moment a bubble of anger rose in Attar's chest.

"Who killed him?" He stepped forward, anger coursing through his veins.

"The ones who now seek the truth, Liege. The ones who no longer live by your rule."

He waited for a heartbeat. "You have amassed vampires?"

"Yes sire." Jelani bowed once again.

"Sustenance is what I require, then teach me what you have learned. What I need to know."

The servant whirled, used to such requests. He retreated quickly out of sight and Attar shuffled to the heavily carved wooden chair that he had always favored.

He glanced to the walls of the cave, noting for the first time that the other alcoves were empty. He frowned, but another sound intruded: That of hearts beating wildly. They were joined by sounds of fear, muffled cries and whimpers.

His servant dragged several women forward. They were bound with chains, their mouths gagged. The ripe scent of fear excited him. *They will be delicious.*

One in particular caught his eye. Red hair tied back, so her throat was exposed. The pulse of a vein beat wildly, but even as he dragged his attention from the spot, her bright eyes captured him, opened wide with fear.

"Take her to the next room." He pointed to the woman, and his servant moved swiftly, showing no surprise. Hunger, of all sorts, was not uncommon on awakening, but right now his thirst raged.

The others quaked at his words. He rose, stripping off the rags that covered his body, wanting nothing to interrupt the enjoyment of feeding. He stretched, listening to the sounds of bones and cartilage finding the correct placement before advancing. His teeth elongated.

It was time to feed.

SEVEN

Celina drove, watching the needle pointing towards low on the fuel indicator. How much farther would she have to go before reaching her destination? The center of the city bustled just like any other end-of-shift weekday. She drove along, watching the workday hurry and scurry that she'd once enjoyed. But for her, it was no longer the reality she inhabited.

The magical pull kept her driving, leading her toward an older section of the city where the buildings were ratty and unkempt. Graffiti covered many walls and abandoned shells were dotted here and there, boarded up against the elements. It was a section of the city she really didn't like to visit.

"Hopefully this is just taking me to the other side." But that hope fizzled as the tug grew stronger and she turned her compact vehicle in the direction of a small art gallery.

The car park lay empty, and an eerie stillness pervaded.

She pressed the button on her phone and sat, huddled in the car. She wasn't going to go anywhere. Now was her opportunity to prove herself to everyone. *Particularly Javed.* Celina quickly banished that thought from her mind. No doubt she was little more than an irritation to him.

The silence was unnerving, as was the lack of any people around. The sun was setting, hues of reds and golds coating the sky.

"Al bin Habbad." The voice on the line calmed her slightly.

"Hey, it's Celina. Can you let Bertha know I think I've found what she is seeking? I'm at the *Day View Art Gallery*. It's deserted but..." She let the words trail off as a flash caught her attention.

"Celina? What on earth are you doing there? Hang on. I'll get Idris." She waited as the receptionist clattered the handset to the desk. She could imagine the scene in her mind.

The line clicked but now she shivered as the sensation of fear trickled through her body, icing her blood. Something was out there. *Watching me.*

She tried to shake the feeling, but the back of her neck prickled.

"Celina, where the hell are you?"

"Idris! There's uh... I think there's something here. I'm at the *Day View Art Gallery*, on the south side of the city. Can you... Can you get someone here quickly?" Her voice trembled, and she couldn't seem to get warm. She huddled further down in the car seat.

"What's there?" His voice was rough and demanding.

"I don't know. It was a flash."

A rustling sound came over the line. "Stay there. We are on our way now." *Javed.* The Master had been listening. She closed her eyes as embarrassment coursed through her.

So much for thinking she was so clever and useful. Instead, she was causing them more issues. *He must think me—* She broke off the thought and concentrated on answering him.

"I will."

Silence on the line made her wonder for a moment if he'd hung up, until the sound of breathing reassured her. "Stay safe in your car. Don't leave it, no matter what happens." Then the disconnect signal filled the air.

The flash came again, and this time she was sure she saw something that was neither human nor animal. Dark. Ugly. Misshapen.

She controlled the squeak of fear that erupted, wrapping her arms around her mid-section, hoping to control the quaking that shook her entire body.

Maybe if I stay still it will let me leave once it is ready to go?

Celina didn't even want to consider what the thing was. She wanted to close her eyes and pretend she wasn't here but the sight filled her senses. Horrified her.

She glanced at the clock. It had taken her the best part of an hour, but that was in peak hour, winding through traffic. How quickly could they get here? And would they rush, because, after all, she wasn't really useful to the nest yet... Or would they take their time?

Time passed slowly, the creature, whatever it might be, crept into the shadows, and she lost sight of it. But it was still there. She could feel it—the sense of malevolence washing over her.

The darkness deepened, and she considered starting the car, but what if she ran out of fuel? *What if I'm stranded?* A buzzing sound intruded and a light shone, growing larger. She hoped it was them. Because if it wasn't... Well, she was sure she would be in a world of trouble.

Without thought, her fingers found the key and turned it. A clicking noise sounded. *Oh no!* She was stuck here even if she wanted to get away.

A vehicle, one of the large flight-enabled cars—Celina knew by the colors of the house coat of arms, emblazoned on the side that it was from her nest—landed beside her. She clambered out of the vehicle as Javed, Idris and three guards hurried toward her.

"What the hell are you doing here?" Javed's demand was totally at odds with the emotions in his eyes.

"I... Uh... I wanted to help. Bertha told me to use the gray book, and I found the direction." She pointed to the building where she'd felt the connection coming from. But it had now fizzled away. She screwed up her face, concentrating to find some last wisp.

The guards stepped forward, and Javed turned to them, flinging out his hand to stay them. "Wait for the others."

"But what if—?" She stopped when he turned back to her.

"If there is something here, then we need to be sure of our safety." His face was a tightly drawn mask. The air around him crackled with vitality.

She couldn't help herself. She stepped closer and caught his eye. For a second, she fancied she read softness there, then he turned away.

"The others will be here in a few moments. Once they arrive we can move. Get ready to crank the shield up."

The shield. It was a new technology that he'd been working on since the attack last year, or so Bertha told her. She gulped, realizing they needed it to be magically charged. "Perhaps...?"

Javed shook his head. "No. You are not yet stable enough."

Celina grimaced, knowing he was talking on a strategic level.

"I can do it. It's one of the things Bertha's been training me for. I can help. Let me. *Please?*"

She reached out and touched the sleeve of his jacket. Calmness flooded through her, bolstering the sense of certainty. "I can do this Master. Let me show you."

"This situation isn't about you proving yourself to me. It's dangerous. We can't split the team any further, otherwise I'd have you out of here." This time, when he looked at her, there was heat. Her stomach clenched at the intensity in his eyes.

Heaven help her, she wanted to smooth away the lines that bracketed his mouth. The hunger this time came from him and joined with a twin need that coiled low and deep in her belly.

The roar of engines broke the spell between them, and they sprang apart.

She glanced away to see Idris watching her. His face blank, shoulders locked tightly. Celina bit her lip as the cars roared into the car park.

HE TRIED TO KEEP HIS DISTANCE FROM HER. KNEW IDRIS WAS interested in the red-haired witch, but for him it was pure need and possession. Each time he glanced in her direction he felt the damned *connection* between them. Growing stronger, the longer they were in the same vicinity.

This time he'd almost kissed her. Here in the middle of whatever was about to happen. The roar of engines saved him from a mistake, and he was grateful, though the primal savagery deep within him stretched out, needing to be freed.

He sensed the power, the dark and coiling anger in the shadows. It watched them. Ready for them to find what they sought—whatever that may be.

"Get the shield in place." His words were little more than a growl as he stalked over to Idris. "Have someone scout the building. Especially the perimeter."

He stalked away, alert to any movement. Keeping his distance from the woman who called to him like a siren.

The area was quiet. There was a stillness that boded badly, together with the uncertainty which gnawed at him. "Idris? Since we can't get her out of here, stash her somewhere safe.

Idris shook his head. "I don't think there's anywhere safe, right now. I sent one of the men to the back, he... Uhh, he claims there is something we need to see to believe. And it's not pretty."

Javed jerked back. "We can't split—"

"No. We can't split the teams. If she's right, we need whatever is inside that building, but we don't know what it is. Not without her. And the only one who can restart her connection to the artefact is you. That's if it's even still here."

Idris was right, of course. He was letting his emotions for her get in the way of his job. "Fine. Make sure she's guarded."

He strode off towards the back, feeling the pressure of his UV gun securely under his coat. There was no wind. In fact, the complete stillness was quite un-natural.

One of the guards led him to the back of the building, where he stopped. There on the ground was a woman—or at least the remains of one. The smell of blood, a ripe copper scent, rose in his nostrils. Red hair spread out around the woman's body. She'd been placed there. On purpose. For them to find.

He stepped forward, scanning the scene around them. The wisp of a scent teased him. It bled into the copper, making it difficult to pinpoint exactly what it was. Something that was neither human nor vampire had been here.

He leaned over the woman before rearing back. Her eyes were open. They were the same emerald hue as Celina's. Her hair was different though. Not really the red she sported he noticed, as her eyebrows were a dark brown. *Dyed.*

His mouth dried. She bore an uncanny resemblance to Celina.

His stomach lurched and for a moment the woman on the ground was, in his mind, Celina. Javed jerked back.

"Cover her and when everyone is ready, send a crew to retrieve her body. We'll want to know what did this." It clearly wasn't a vampire bite, not given the shredded state of her body. But that meant they were dealing with a whole different problem. The not knowing would put his whole crew in danger. And that was unacceptable.

The buzz of a phone sounded and he spun around to see Idris raising it. "Are we good to enter, Master?"

Javed nodded. "Yeah."

The guard who waited by the wall appeared slightly green and Javed recognized him as a newly turned warrior. "Can you cope with this?" The man clasped his gun in both hands but Javed noticed they shook. He made a mental note to raise it with Idris, and waited for the warrior's answer.

The young vampire agreed wordlessly while glancing away.

"Control is the key. Breathe lightly, but keep your wits about you." Javed clasped the man on one shoulder before heading back to the front of the building, just in time to see a young woman, a witch who had come to his nest from a distant one, lay her hands on the stone that would extend a magical shield. The stone radiated a larger version of a witch's circle.

His people congregated by the door, with Celina in the middle. He refused to think of the dead woman and how closely she resembled Celina.

He followed them into the building.

Inside the door to the gallery, Javed touched her; muttering something inaudible but it was sufficient in jump-starting the magic again. Her body tingled and she felt the jolt of power arc.

They moved quietly as she cast about in her mind seeking the item to which she had some tenuous connection.

It lay hidden within the building, but where was a mystery. Each time she thought she'd focused on it, the trail disappeared. Room by room they silently prowled. Ten burly guards, Idris and Javed followed behind her.

They trusted her to find it. Her! A neophyte witch who didn't have a clue what she was doing. By the last room, she was a mass of nerves. She'd been unable to find even a blip on her magical radar... until then.

The room was small, and in the middle was an aged scabbard and sword. Unable to help herself, she slid forward—reached toward the items, the strange compulsion tugging at her again.

Javed pushed her aside. "Wait."

One of the men brought out a scanner. She blinked. She'd nearly made a mistake... again. *Put everyone in more danger why don't you!* Kicking herself right now wasn't an option, but she was seriously tempted. *Fool!*

"It's got some kind of alarm around it, but I think I can disable it."

A man dropped to the floor, pulling a tablet device from his heavy black jacket.

Celina scanned the room. Finding it had been almost too easy. As if they were being drawn out by something unseen. She couldn't put her finger on what gave her that impression, but it was there, taunting her.

The man on the floor raised his head from his feverish work. "Try it now." Idris lurched forward and lifted the glass box from the pedestal but as he did, the phone crackled to life.

"Under attack! Get out!"

"I'll get her out of here! Idris, get the artefact." Celina studied Javed and his lips thinned. Idris grasped the items as Javed fastened his hands around the top of her arm. The grip bruising as he dragged her along.

As they approached the door the roar of battle met her—the intensity of it wild and loud. The witch at the large stone, which was the size of a bowling ball, was on her knees, sobbing and bleeding profusely, while the light of the shield kept flickering. The remains of something lay on the ground behind her. It was clear she'd been targeted, judging by the pool of blood on the ground. She was hurt but still alive, thanks to the warrior who stood behind her, a heavy blackened sword in his meaty hands.

"Oh my God!" She shrieked, staring at the ugly black creature with its dripping jaws. The savagery of the attack by the opposing vampires left her reeling.

Creatures engaged the guards and she wanted to shrink away from the sight. The scene played out before her, but even new to this world, she understood she had to do what she could to help them. To protect life at all costs.

Javed pushed her aside, moving with purpose through the door. Her mind picked out the facts in slow motion:

The length of his stride.

The way the muscles in his legs rippled.

The flat look in his face and the way his eyes glowed in the moonlight.

His grip on the gun as he raised it and fired.

One of the creatures engaged Javed, snarling as it raised a wicked curved blade. Javed lurched away, to meet it face on. Celina took advantage, rushing to the shield stone, dropping to her knees. The woman stared at her, fear and pain in her eyes. "I can't keep the shields up. I'm failing."

The shield was clearly thinning, the pale yellow glow almost gone in places. One of the nearby guards, a young male fought their opponents back, but was losing ground as he attempted to protect the witch. In that instant, Celina knew what she had to do.

The witch slumped in a faint to the ground.

With a deep breath Celina laid both hands on the stone. Her eyes closed. Then, opening her mind as widely as she could, she visualized a river, just as Bertha had taught her. The hum intensified and she worked to blank out the many sounds around her, projecting her magic into the shield. The magic flared brightly, she opened her eyes in time to see the man stumbling onto the witch where she lay on the ground.

"Get her out of here. To the car. I can hold this. But you have to get her to safety.

She didn't turn in his direction or listen for an answer, she just lost herself in the role she had assumed.

The fighting ceased to exist for her. She fed her power to the stone, only daring to peek when Javed bellowed loudly.

The stone was alive. It vibrated beneath her touch, humming and pulsing, whispering that if she continued to feed it, it would reward her.

Now, not only did she face exhaustion from the magical resource drain, she had to cope with the insidious but promising whispers from the magic. "Whoever thought of this needs either an award, or a damn good belting." Sweat trickled down her face and she longed to swipe it away but she needed both hands on the stone to keep the shield going.

"They have reinforcements coming!" Javed called out.

She nodded, shaking with her exertions. She certainly hoped so, now she was starting to feel weak.

"To me!" One of the guards yelled—she thought his name was Jordan. For the first time she heard fear and desperation in the guards voices.

No one had expected the situation to be as dangerous as it was, but thankfully the guards had been ready to employ the use of the shield. They hadn't expected the fury of the attack, or the creatures that they faced. One dog-like warrior had showed itself briefly before disappearing into the melee.

She shuddered remembering what she'd seen. The black coat, shaggy like an unkempt dog; the long snout and animalistic hind legs, were teamed with the face of a human.

"Come on." She whispered the words, as she poured more magical energy into the stone.

That this battle would continue for so long and drain the stone, and by association her, was something else she hadn't considered. At least she'd learned enough to be able to channel some of her energy into the shielding. She could give them extra time. Her teeth ached, as did her head. The longer she pushed her powers into the stone, the more she felt... diminished.

"Celina, you must stop now." She heard Jordan's voice and registered it sounded faint.

"Soon. I just need to give everyone the best possible opportunity." She glanced to the side, seeing Javed frown.

"Let it go." He indicated his agreement to the warrior.

She tried to shift her hands but was startled to realize no matter how much she might want to let it go, she couldn't. "I... I... can't." For the first time since her mad dash to the stone, panic set in. Perhaps it had been more than she could manage. Maybe she should have thought this through a little better, before rushing off tonight.

"Celina? You have to let go now. There are others here." His demand cut through her.

"It won't let me." She glimpsed at the incredulous expression on his face, her stomach curled. "I'm stuck and it won't let me go."

His face blanched and his gaze skittered to the small group of men and women who rounded the corner of the building.

"Jordan, get inside the car. Javed, you too."

But instead of agreeing, he shook his head.

"I can't leave you." The strain was evident in his voice, she could almost hear the argument that he waged within himself. Leave her here and go get the others, so they might have a chance of surviving. Or try to save her where she was stuck to the shield. But the artefact was far too valuable to be lost.

Somehow, it contained something important to the prophecy. It wasn't something that could be endangered.

"Javed, you have to get the others from inside. The shield will give me protection for as long as I'm connected." Well, she hoped it would. "Once you have the artefact safely away, then the others can get me out of here." Panic bloomed inside her chest, but she knew right now there was no alternative. If the prophecy fell into *their* hands, then the nest and those combating the evil would be exposed. In her heart she knew this was merely the first step in the journey to finding out the truth the seer had alluded to.

And she had given her oath.

"But you are in danger." The anguish in his voice tore at her.

"Get the artefact out of here. It must be protected." Celina closed her eyes and turned away from him. If these were to be her last moments, then she would be strong.

He cursed then she heard the crunching of gravel as he turned away. "I'll come back as soon as I can." Then he was gone, feet thudding away at a run.

Nearby a car rocked, but she knew the others were safe within it. The spell work performed on it would ensure their safety.

Weariness stole through her body. The last vestiges of warmth bled away.

She sucked in a deep and unsteady breath, settled her hands

more firmly against the ancient block of stone. Heat seared her where it touched and in its wake it left cold emptiness. "I can do this." Tears stung her eyes and her arms vibrated with the strain.

Several people approached. She couldn't stop from scrutinizing them. Three men and two women, garbed in leather from their highly polished boots to their molded jackets advanced. Their eyes—cold.

Lifeless.

Empty.

Dead except for a tiny silvery shine in the center.

Their skin was tinged with blue. Magic swirled around them, but it was greasy and oily.

Bad magic, her mind whispered. She shivered, shrinking from them. Horror filled her.

"Step away from the stone." One of the women stepped forward, her teeth bared.

Celina chanced a small smile. "Not on your life." Her voice was weak now, taking all the effort she could muster and her body nearly buckled with the magical onslaught as the stone stole the essence of her being. The air around her crackled and snapped.

The woman cried out as a shaft of lightning flickered at her.

"It's protecting her!" One of the males called and suppressed a small grin. "We need to get her away from it.

"I have an idea." He bent beneath her watching gaze and scooped up a handful of gravel. "Join me"

Her stomach wobbled. *What the hell do they plan on doing?* She knew quick enough as they pelted her. The protection stone attacked many of the small rocks and pebbles, making them crack and exploded, but the number of missiles were too numerous and the shield was failing.

They attacked again, this time with larger stones, and while the first lot had hurt now she was afraid of the damage the second would do.

The rattle of a car door, a yelling voice filled the air.

"Oh God, no!" She breathed unsteadily, her heartbeat racing as she understood their intent. But she couldn't protect herself with her hands firmly attached to the stone and as the missile found its mark she lost consciousness.

EIGHT

A LOUD BANG SHOOK THE WALLS, THE GROUND BENEATH HIS feet shuddered. Javed followed the others out the door, clutching the old sword and scabbard in his hand.

His heart stuttered. He'd left her out there. He turned, running toward the door and to Celina. The stone should have protected her, but fear trickled though him. It wasn't working the way they expected. He could hear Idris, trailing him. Swearing.

If what she said was right it kept her connected. "Damn it! No, I'll make sure she's safe."

The instant he opened the door he froze. She lay on the ground, her hair a vibrant red halo, her motionless body and the creatures around her laughing and advancing. He didn't stop to think, to question the reason for his intense reaction. He just advanced.

Fury coursed through him as he tossed the artefact to a nearby guard and scooped up an abandoned blade from the ground. It swooped in a wicked arc, slicing and hacking. He moved faster and faster as he surged toward her.

"Leave. Her. Alone."

The men behind him followed, but all that filled his brain was the knowledge that he'd left her alone. Even though his brain told him she should have been safe. And he'd had to protect the artefact.

The creatures laughed and the rage overtook him. He dispatched them swiftly first this one then the second attacker, their faces now projecting their fear.

"She's. Mine." Each thrust took him closer to where she lay, still and silent on the ground.

Someone brushed past him. Idris.

The other man dropped to his knees beside Celina, his face a crumpled white mask of grief. For a moment Javed feared they'd come too late. That she was dead. The way Idris scooped her up against his chest and a pain, rather like a spear to his heart stole his breath.

Now that the battle was done, they could leave. His injured guards limped from the relative safety of the building, but he ignored them. He stepped forward slowly and peered down at her white face. Her chest rose and fell. *She lives.*

He wanted to shove Idris away from Celina. He needed to take her in his arms, to hold her close against him. His fear had become a near solid lump lodged in his chest, and he scowled, hoping to keep the emotions at bay just a little longer. But the building need was so blinding that he couldn't control it. "She breathes yet." Idris spoke quietly, his words carried the power to right Javed's world.

"I'll take her." His command had Idris glancing at him, and in that instant he understood and accepted his protectiveness centered on this one human. She was, indeed his. He couldn't-wouldn't let Idris take her from him.

Idris might want her, but he was the one she needed. He knew it as surely as he'd felt that instantaneous connection the first time he'd seen her.

Idris stood, his face pale, holding the unconscious Celina in his arms and with thinning lips he advanced and slid her into Javed's grasp. Javed sighed as he touched her. He could detect the slight movement as she breathed, and it comforted him—until he saw her neck and shoulders. A deep bruise was already forming at her temple, and he seethed.

"I'll take her home with me."

Idris bowed formally. Without a word he waited while Javed made his way towards the vehicle. One of the guards held open the door, and he climbed within, keeping her close. Idris followed stiffly and took the position opposite, his face tight. Javed stared down at Celina, noting the seeping blood above the hairline. With care, he pushed the hair away and saw a cut. "She's got a nasty laceration. We'll need a healer when we get to the nest."

He heard rather than saw Idris lift the phone from the cradle and make the call. He concentrated only on Celina. The vehicle had ascended, before banking sharply. They were headed to the nest—to *their* home.

The journey was swift but silent. He ignored Idris' fulminating glare. He was Master and this woman was somehow connected to him. He glanced up as the car started to drop. "Idris, go ahead and get the door for me."

Once they landed he carried her within, along the marble inlaid corridor to the secured doorway. He watched dimly as Idris, stiff and radiating anger, entered the code. This was a problem he would soon have to deal with, he noted, then dismissed it. It was an issue for later.

The door slid open to the secured quarters, and he strode within. Unlike his previous home, which had utilized a secured basement, the core of this building was secured with lead reinforced walls. The previous owners being more than a little concerned for their safety had built it with a larger than average panic room. It had been one of the major selling points for him. In the weeks since they had taken over the property, the reinforced walls had been extended, offering them the security they required while resting.

He reached his personal quarters at the end of the hall and nudged the door open with his shoulder, striding to his own bed ignoring the lush furnishings reminiscent of his past. He flung aside the jewel toned cushions to make space for her. The bleeding from her head wounds had stopped in the vehicle, but she hadn't yet regained consciousness.

"Shouldn't she have... come to by now?" The concerned tones of Idris' voice grated, and Javed had to control the bubble of anger that inhabited his chest.

"Where's Kharisma?"

"Master, I'm here." Kharisma, the nest healer and his one-time lover, entered the room and headed for the bed. "What happened?" She squatted down beside the bed, her medical bag thudding on the floor.

He briefly recounted their experiences, and she clicked her tongue. "Well before we do anything else, let's clean her up so I can check that cut on her scalp." Then Kharisma set to work.

"Ooh." Celina woke in darkness. Her entire body ached, and her head pounded. For a moment, disorientation threatened. Maybe the weeks before had been a dream, but when a sound roused her and a light flared, she could tell that wasn't so.

Javed knelt beside her. "I'm glad you've woken."

She winced, even in the quiet his whispered words pounded through her brain. "Where am I?"

"My rooms."

She started, and the percussion instruments in her head drummed louder. A moan escaped.

"You're in pain. Let me get you something." He left quickly. She wanted to call him back. She wanted to get out of his rooms. Simultaneous thoughts came and went, but she lay still, well aware that in her current state, she was probably lucky if she could even crawl out of the bed unaided.

Javed returned, a glass of water and two small tablets in his hand. "Take these. Kharisma said they should help."

He slipped one hand beneath her, supporting her and the shock of skin on skin made her jerk and gasp at once.

"What's wrong?"

"Uh nothing. I'm just... I'm naked." Her voice wobbled, and she looked away.

"Well, not quite. Kharisma didn't think you'd be comfortable, so she left your underwear on." He nudged her hand. "Take the pills. You'll feel better for it."

Wordlessly she accepted them, slipped them into her mouth then gulped the water.

Javed helped her to lie back down. She gripped the covers tightly, making sure she was totally covered.

"Why wasn't I taken to my own room?" Her voice sounded strangled and for a moment silence reigned.

She turned slowly to peer at him and for the first time since waking, saw hunger in his eyes. "I couldn't let you go."

Celina shrank back. "Uh look, you know... I'm not easy. I don't just fall into bed with any guy. So if you could just pass me my clothes, I'll get out of your way."

No way was she going to fall into bed with him. He might be sexy, handsome, and the most perfect man she'd ever met, but she had no intentions of putting out. *Besides which, he was a vampire—a Master vampire at that. Weren't there rules about that?*

She pushed at the covers, grunting a little as the aches in her arms and shoulders made themselves known.

He stepped back to give her room as she stood with a wobble.

She remembered too late that she was all but naked, her breasts were barely covered by the lacy white bra. Celina had to stop the reflex action of curling her arms around herself, instead she gripped the mattress, grateful for the support.

But she felt her face flame in embarrassment.

"You aren't going anywhere." His softly spoken words were firm, and she felt chilled.

"I can come and go at will." Her stomach churned, and she swayed a little before locking her legs to keep herself upright.

"You wouldn't make it across the room, and none of my people will enter without my permission. And they've all retired for the day. Now be a good girl and get back into the bed."

His gaze raked her. Little fires licked her everywhere he focused. She had to hold back the moan that rose in her throat. There was a distinct tightening of her muscles, except down below where heat began to pool, softening her deep inside. She locked her legs together against the unfamiliar sensations.

"Oh, and I don't intend taking advantage of you. I only take willing and conscious women to my bed. Vampire or human."

With those words, he turned away and left her wobbling uncertainly by the side of the bed.

But her body continued to tingle, and for the first time, a sense of something missing in her life assailed her. She slumped down to the bed a hiss of pain escaped, and she dropped her head into her hands. "What the hell have I got myself into?"

He stalked out of the room. Anger warred with desire. He raked his hands through his hair. *Celina thinks I only want to have sex with her?*

Javed stilled, coping with the emotional backlash. *Well, on one level she'd be right,* he agreed. But the situation wasn't exactly cut and dried, was it? *I want more than that.*

That was the crux of his problem. He didn't really know how much more. What could he hope for? "What would she be prepared to have with me? If anything?" There were no answers for him. Not now.

In the centuries after he'd become a vampire, he'd seen the reaction of women to him and his kind. They had been distinctly bi-polar. He'd been shunned, and called everything from the devil's spawn to evil incarnate. Others had just wanted the sex-with-the-damned experience, which held no interest for him.

The last woman he'd had any kind of loving and long-lasting relationship with had run away from him. Losing his wife that way had scarred him. He'd loved Anisa truly, and she had proclaimed to feel the same. However when it had come to making a choice to stand by her claim, Anisa had abandoned him. Feared him. Hated him.

"I can't love you! You aren't my Javed. He was Allah-fearing. You are some creature wearing his skin. Evil to the core."

She glared at him with hate, her eyes glowing in the firelight. Then she threw a cup and dish at him, before she pushed through the door and ran.

Left him standing there. Alone. He didn't follow; after all, she'd said everything there was to say.

"Doesn't matter. She'd been gone a long time." Eight hundred years alone with only a casual interlude here and there was a long time. But he'd felt strongly that an eternity alone was the price he had to pay for a decision he hadn't even made himself.

Seeing Xavier and Hope together, had loosened the restraints on his hungry heart. He knew that maybe he could wish for more. He turned away from those thoughts.

The battle for Acre, all those years ago had been fierce and protracted. Dirty. Smelly but he couldn't escape the memories that cascaded.

They'd won the battle, beaten back the knights and Christians from the final part of Jerusalem. The celebrations had worn on for days, with many partaking in drink and women, lost in the high the aftermath of battle brought. Many had been uncaring that their behavior went against their own teachings.

He hadn't. Instead, he'd remained sober, helped to keep the peace. He'd protected the women who had been accosted on the streets. Rounded up the children and found them safe places to wait out the celebrations and rowdiness.

On the fourth day, he'd entered the tavern, seeking nothing more than his friends, ready to drag them away from the evils of drink.

One of the knights had hidden in the tavern when the others had left. The knight had embraced something more insidious than his violent form of Christianity. He'd learned of the darker ways. The knight was no longer human and had wrought his revenge on the invaders, slowly imbibing on those gathered there while they were lost in the bottom of their cups. Not enough to kill them, just enough to feed his hunger.

When Javed had entered, he'd seen the creature. He'd fought valiantly. But the creature had been strong and fast. Then he'd sunk his fangs into Javed, feeding. But the final blow from the vampire had weakened him. The knight-creature had torn into his own wrist and shared his blood.

No one in the tavern had survived the night. Neither had he or his soul.

He should probably send Celina away. "I can't." The words quiet in the stillness. He let them grow. Javed accepted the truth in his utterance.

He knew Hope and Xavier would be happy to take her on. But he couldn't do that. He couldn't let her go. Seeing her on the ground had made something deep within him claw its way to the surface.

Javed grabbed the phone. "Celina will need clothes in my rooms. Get Bertha to grab some for you."

"Yes, Master." Damn. Idris. Things would be uncomfortable around here if he remained. The new nest had to find its equilibrium, but the Master and his second both coping with feelings for one woman would upset that. The situation would need careful consideration.

"She'll need sustenance too. Have food brought to my rooms. Then Idris? We need to talk."

His stomach curled. The man was honorable. But they had little in common. Idris was young—eager to climb his way up to become a

Master at the next possible opportunity. But he was still little more than a pup.

With that thought came the knowledge that he wasn't young. Neither in body nor spirit. He was jaded and weary. Hundreds of years of battle and loneliness had taken their toll on him. On his spirit.

"Yes, Master." The words interrupted his introspection. Lost deep within his own mind again, never a good place to be.

He carefully placed the receiver back into the cradle and stood, waiting for the knock he knew would come. He didn't have to wait long.

After being bidden to enter, Kharisma surged into the room with a smile and a basket of clothing and a tray of food, which she laid on the table beside the door. "If I didn't know better, I'd say you've come to some kind of conclusion." He grimaced at her words. "There's the food and clothing you requested for Celina." She laughed. It was rich and throaty sound. It lightened his mood. "You know, Bertha doesn't say much. The only thing she did share was that Celina is a good woman. I interpreted that to say 'don't hurt her'."

He held his breath, unsure where this conversation was going. "So?"

"So, I would have said something similar to that. You're a good man, Javed. You deserve to be happy. Even when we were together though, I knew it wasn't forever. There was too much loneliness in you for me to fill." She coughed lightly. "I hadn't meant to say any of that, but you know me. Can't keep my mouth closed." She surged forward and clasped her arms around him. The hug was brief but welcomed. "Now you need to go to bed. And so do I. Eamon will be waiting. I'll check the patient tomorrow evening."

Then she was gone, leaving him standing in the room, focusing on the tray and basket she'd brought with her.

When Javed re-entered the bedroom, he braced himself for another onslaught of anger, but instead found her curled up in the center of the bed, crying. The bruises on her body sickened him. The purples and reds marred her pale skin.

He didn't dare study any lower. He'd already seen the fine white lace she wore. Marvelled at how the fabric made her seem so fragile but enticing. His mouth dried.

He felt helpless. What did he say to this woman? How could he put her at her ease? How could he make her understand he didn't want to use her?

"I shouldn't have said that. I'm so sorry." Her words were muffled, and they ripped a hole through the ice that encased his heart. She lifted her head, and he was struck by the shimmering emerald of her eyes. Tears had slid down her face, leaving glistening tracks

He moved without thought, sitting down on the side, the mattress dipping a little. "We all make mistakes. Sometimes we say things we don't mean to." He shrugged, feeling foolish sitting there in his stained clothing while she wore only her underwear and the marks they'd inflicted on her.

He knew nothing of soothing or settling. Nothing of calming, after all, he was a fighter.

He was a warrior. In life, he'd been a soldier for his ruler against the incursions of the Christians. As a vampire, he was still a warrior. He fought for the Council and the protection of the innocent.

He released a frustrated sigh, realizing he couldn't give her the softness she no doubt craved. Javed made to rise.

She reached out then grabbed his wrist.

"Don't... Please don't go." Her voice carried pain and fear and right now all he wanted to do was take her in his arms. She was in pain and still she apologized. He closed his eyes, and she released her grip.

"Oh God! I'm making a fool of myself." He heard the whisper and even as she jerked away, he carefully took her hand.

"No. You're not making a fool of yourself. Please, be peaceful. I should have known better than to bring you here. But I can't let you go, not yet. It's daytime, and the secure quarters are locked down until nightfall. If you will get back under the covers, I'll bring you the food that has been prepared."

She watched him as she swiped at the tears on her cheeks. He felt as if he was being weighed and measured. *What would she find?*

"Thank you."

He turned away and heard her moving, slowly. She had to be uncomfortable, but he didn't know what to do for her. So he waited as she scrambled back, huddled beneath the sheets. When he was sure she was covered he headed to the other room to collect the tray and clothing.

On his return, he noted that she had the bedding tucked firmly under her arms. It strained across the bountiful mounds of her breasts, and the pumping of blood through his veins took on a louder quality. The rest of his body also reacted. He breathed deeply, hoping to calm his need, instead he could smell her scent in the air. His body hardened further.

"Here is the food." He moved slowly and carefully lowered the tray to her lap, concentrating on her face. She blushed slightly, the pink tinge cresting her cheeks. Her breathing sped up, and he could hear the thud of her heart beat. It was racing.

"Thank you, Master." She whispered the words before she ran her tongue over her lips as if they were sandpaper dry.

The moisture in his mouth evaporated. He wanted her.

She grabbed his hands as he made to shift away. "You saved me from them. I saw you."

He chanced to gaze into her eyes. "I did what I had to do."

She nodded, and averted her eyes. *Damn!* It wasn't right that she should glance away. "I... Yes. I understand that."

"I saw what they did to you. I left you alone. To face them." The rage grew once more, chasing away the desire.

"The stone should have protected me."

He clenched his teeth so hard they ground together. "But it didn't. And you are damaged because of it."

She must have heard the self-recrimination in his voice because when she looked back to him, there was shock on her face. Her eyes widened. He was entranced by her beauty. The clarity of her eyes and the fine purity of her skin intrigued him. "But you are the Master. You must ensure the protection of everyone. And I should have been okay."

"No!" The word burst forth. Unable to withstand the caustic rage he felt at himself, he leaned in. "I. Should. Have. Protected. You."

Close. So close, he could taste her breath. He gave in and lips touched—a glance of flesh on flesh.

NINE

He tasted so damn good. Her mind couldn't concentrate on anything else, except how he invaded it. The touch of his lips against hers was amazing. They were soft and gentle. They didn't plunder and demand.

He touched her shoulder.

She moaned and flinched a little at his touch, and he pulled back. "Forgive me." The shock on his face would have been comical if she'd been able to think. "I didn't consider your feelings."

Celina frowned. "I don't... Uhh...Yeah." Her face flamed.

She felt the heat of it and turned away, but she'd seen his anger at himself. Somehow she had to explain. It was wrong that he thought she didn't want his touches. "I wanted you to kiss me."

"You don't have to..." He sounded confused and cross.

Damn! She'd have to spell it out. "You didn't upset me. I wanted you to kiss me more." She flamed, embarrassed to have make the admission. "Now... Maybe I could dress and eat my dinner? Then we should probably go to bed." She made a strangled sound, realizing what she'd just said and how he might take it. "Not in the same bed, but we should sleep." She closed her eyes, breathing deeply, hoping to ignore the embarrassment crawling through her. "Look can I just have my clothes?"

This time he smiled, though the worry still lurked in the back of his eyes.

He held out a basket and quirked his eyebrow. Men and relationships had never been really high on her agenda, so she was at a loss with how to deal with the sensations that she was experiencing. She reined in the thoughts, realizing he was still standing there, observing her.

"Uh, you can leave now." Her words must have startled him because his eyes widened and with a stiff bow he retreated.

She dragged the light pants and top from the basket, ignoring the fresh underwear, and shimmied into them, remembering once more that her body ached. Funny how it hadn't seemed so bad while he was there, touching her.

Celina shook her head. *I'm a prize winning idiot. Even considering getting into something with a Master vampire is foolish.* But even as she spoke sternly to herself, the insidious voice in her mind whispered that, maybe it would be okay this time. Surely with him she might find somewhere to belong, be part of a family.

"Bah humbug to you too." She muttered and slid back under the covers. *I'll eat later. Right now, I need sleep. It's sleep deprivation that's causing these ridiculous thoughts.*

Celina closed her eyes, tried to clear her thoughts. But it was a long time before she slept.

THE AIR WAS HEAVILY PERFUMED. HUMID.

She moved and felt the whisper of silk on her skin. A jingle came from outside, and she rose on one elbow. "Who's there?"

The words were quiet, and her stomach clenched tightly. She rubbed her hand across her exposed skin, touching naked flesh. She glanced down, and shock invaded her system.

The clothes were so unlike anything she owned. Crystal tones of pink and blue edged with gold embroidery. They were almost translucent. She hunted around for something to cover herself with. Cushions, mounds of cushions were everywhere, and she scooped one up as the sound of moving material caught her attention.

Celina peered up. Javed stood in the doorway. The white of his traditional clothing contrasted with the tones of his skin. He looked in control. Comfortable. Peaceful.

Her mouth dried. "Javed?"

"Yes, Celina. We are here together." He inched closer, removing the headpiece and dropping it to the floor. His dark hair glistened damply in the low light of lamps scattered around the room.

"Where are we?" She clutched the cushion to her breasts, her nails digging into the fibers.

"At an oasis."

The sounds of horses, jingling harnesses and voices intruded for just a moment, and he smiled. "I have sent the others away. It's just us here. In our own private hide-away."

He reached out to a carafe that sat on a low table. She hadn't noticed it before. Javed filled two goblets and handed one to her. She observed him, sipped on the drink, finding it pleasantly refreshing. Then she put the goblet down on the small shelf beside the divan.

She took a deep shuddering breath. "Why?"

This time his eyes twinkled. "So we can be alone." He advanced slowly on the bed of cushions, and the sinuous motions left her weak. Her body betrayed her.

The way he moved was so sexy and fluid. So alpha male and she wanted him. "But... But..."

"No regrets. Celina, tonight you are mine. I will love every inch of this body. Your bountifully full breasts, your lush lips all will be worshiped. I will feast on your rounded stomach and glory in your taste. Tonight, nothing is forbidden." He sipped deeply from his cup before placing it on the floor beside the bed.

Javed dropped to his knees and leaned into her, sliding his arms *around her waist. They clung together as he touched his mouth to hers. He slipped his tongue between her lips, and he tasted good. The kiss was hot, turning her inside out at the power of his desire. Her passion raged hot and wild.*

When he finally shifted away, she panted for breath.

His eyes were glassy, and she extended a trembling hand to caress his cheek, but she tugged it back before touching him. "How do you do this to me?"

"Because of the connection we feel." He stopped and gazed at her as if seeking her very soul. "No one else has ever made me experience such emotions."

His words filled the emptiness she hadn't realized existed within her.

She took the goblet he'd offered before, needing a moment. The nectar was tart but refreshing, and she drank deeply. He sipped from his goblet while her mind whirled.

Her body was betraying her. She desired him, true. But never before had she experienced this intense need that came from being around him. She tingled, and couldn't seem to find her way back to reality. She seriously doubted it existed right now, and couldn't make herself care.

When he held out his hand for her goblet it was automatic to give it to him. He put it beside his on the floor and shifted up onto the cushions beside her.

"You are magnificent in that." He indicated the clothing she wore, and for the first time she realized she'd dropped the cushion. Now he could see her. His face was tight, the planes of his cheeks taut. Her nipples puckered below the light covering. He saw her reaction, the heat in his gaze blazed.

Unable to stop herself, she caressed his cheek, felt the warmth of his skin. He leaned in and nuzzled. The most secret recesses of her being heated, dampness gathered at her core.

Celina clenched her legs together just as he shifted closer. This time when he towered over her she didn't care. He cupped her breast through the soft material, rubbing gently over her nipple and she mewled.

His lips feasted upon hers, and she opened to him. They slumped back to the cushions...

AWAKE! AWARENESS FLOODED HIS SYSTEM. SHE MUST HAVE woken because there was a sound, the opening of a door. What could she need? He couldn't help himself, the primal reaction to the dreams made him shove the covers on the sofa away. His body ached as desire rode him—desire for Celina.

The sound of movement within the room left him frowning. *What if she needs me?* He rose and stalked to the bedroom. The bed was empty, mussed as if she had shared his dream. Thoughts of the oasis, the tent and the passionate embrace notched his need higher. His cock was hard and ready for her sweet flesh.

He could still taste her. The heady scent of Celina and nectar mixed.

A door opened and she stood there, mussed and soft. Pink riding the tops of her cheeks and her eyes flushed.

It was clear something had occurred. "Celina?"

She glanced up, and he caught a momentary glimpse of shock. Unable to help himself he swooped, taking her lips with his. She twined her arms around his neck as she leaned in and he felt her softness through the light layer of her top against his chest.

The kiss was hot—fervent and hungry. It almost stole what was left of his soul. He jerked away. *My soul? Who am I kidding? I don't have one. I'm a damned vampire! Hasn't eight hundred years been enough to prove that to me?*

"Javed?" Her voice was lost and uncertain and he cursed himself anew.

"I shouldn't have done that." His voice was hoarse as if the screaming in his head had been released. Inside his heart told him that it needed her and the connection between them, while his mind warred, telling him he was unclean and unfit for her. He couldn't do this. "I have to go."

Javed didn't dare turn back, instead stalked away, every footstep stiff as he kept himself tightly controlled. If he didn't, he'd reach for her. And that might just break him.

He heard her breathing hitch. In his chest, his heart thudded wildly while he wished for the one thing he couldn't have.

He left the room. The sound of footfalls filled the air as he gained the sitting area. In the room beyond there wasn't a sound. Nothing. He stilled and waited. Knew that his internal examination of the situation did nothing to help recover his equilibrium.

Every second of silence damned him. Eventually, she shifted. He heard the soft sounds. He also heard the sobs that she fought to contain. Every sound another knife plunging into what was left of his heart.

Celina woke, the sleep hadn't refreshed her. But at least there was no more dreaming of Javed. She surveyed the ceiling. Her body ached. Not just from her injuries but from unrequited passion.

She lifted her arm, and inspected the horrible bruises. They were a nasty red and purple against her pale skin. "Good thing I live in a nest, otherwise people might get the wrong idea."

She rose, her muscles still tight, but she didn't ache the way she had the night before. As she headed to the bathroom, she chanced a peek through the door to the sitting area. Empty.

Celina didn't let her mind settle on whether she should be pleased or not. Right now she needed to visit the toilet then get out of here. She scurried through her ablutions then carefully vacated the area, creeping to the door and back to the sitting room. She spied the basket where it lay on a table and snatched it up. She could ask about her other clothes later. Right now she just wanted out of this area.

She snatched the door open, unsure where it would take her, but it was the only one in sight, so naturally it must lead out of the master's rooms, she theorized.

"The master would like to see you." She stopped, shocked to find the healer Kharisma on the other side of the door.

"I didn't..."

Kharisma glanced at her. The strands of her blonde hair glowed under the artificial lights shining from the ceiling. The healer was toned and tight. If she was a size eight, Celina would eat her hat. In fact, she felt downright frumpy in her own size sixteen frame against this amazon of a woman.

"Uh, can I go change first?" She spoke stiffly.

The woman observed her. "Relax. He doesn't even know you are awake yet." There was amusement in her voice, and Celina wanted to grit her teeth. "You know, he's a good man."

"I uh... I really don't want to discuss him." *How embarrassing! Does everyone in the nest know I have a thing for him?*

She made to head up the corridor, but Kharisma stopped her. "He doesn't need to be hurt. If you want something with him, then you need to be honest. Both of you."

"Look, I'm really not sure why you think you had to say something. But he's made it pretty clear, he's not interested. So if I could just get out of here?"

Kharisma pointed to the door. Even as she headed for it, the woman called out to her. "Honesty starts with yourself."

Celina almost stopped, but with her emotions jumbling inside her, she might have said something she'd regret, so instead she laid her hands on the door and opened it.

A breeze wafted through the open door and Celina gulped gratefully before hurrying up the steps. The house itself had four levels and from the outside appeared boxy and more than a little ugly, but it was large enough to accommodate a fledgling nest.

The interior could best be described as, a 'warehouse chic theme' as Bertha had termed it, with stark whites and polished chrome. Even the flooring of polished concrete had a coldly impersonal appearance, but that was offset by the heavily padded seating areas in jewel tones and the banner like wall hangings. It should have jarred. But it worked, Celina thought as she hurried toward the large metal staircase and clattered upward.

She'd been allocated a room on the top floor, so by the time she'd reached it, her legs ached unmercifully. Of course, she could have taken the lift, but she needed time to decompress. "Decompress my backside. You just wanted to avoid talking to anyone."

She flung her shirt on the bed as she started stripping, then headed for the small personal sanitation unit. As for the decorating in the nestlings' rooms, it bordered on utilitarian. The glass and chrome married with rippled iron to complete the effect of spartan efficiency.

Standing beneath the spray of water, naked, there really was nothing but honesty. She'd made a major mistake in kissing Javed. The sheer fact that he wanted to see her in his office made that clear.

"He's going to send me away." The thought did more than just hurt her pride. It didn't even just sting. No, it felt like someone had picked up a stake and thrust it through her heart.

Tears leaked and mingled with the water as she leaned against the wall, both hands outstretched.

Celina wasn't sure just how long she stood there, it couldn't have been a long time, but the heaving of sobs had quieted. She had to face facts and accept her fate.

She grasped the taps and turned the flow of water off, stretched and hunted for a towel and dried herself, all the while avoiding the mirror. No doubt she had a pink nose and watery-pink eyes, and he'd see that too. But she wasn't going to look. "Why make things any worse than they already are?"

In the bedroom, she hauled on panties and bra, opened her wardrobe and found a casual shirt and teamed it with old well-washed jeans and her favourite boots. Her hair she tamed into a ponytail and decided against makeup. "This is as good as it's going to get."

With a heavy heart, she headed downstairs. But when she reached the door to his office, it swung open before she could even knock.

Idris, Javed's welsh second, stalked out and stopped just in front of her. "Don't let him steamroller you into bed." In his eyes, there was turmoil and anger. His stiff movements held her stock-still as he gripped her arm painfully and dragged her close.

He kissed her before she could shift away, but she didn't want it. Didn't want him and she shoved against his broad chest, trying to make him back down. It was unsuccessful.

A roar of wrath sounded, and Idris was gone. An incandescently furious Javed pinned him against the wall.

"Don't. Ever. Touch. Her. Again."

Her heart thudded like a freight train, and she panted as sensible thoughts fled. She'd never seen Javed enraged. He was scary. His eyes glowed and the length of his teeth and nails married with the wall of anger, nearly stole her breath.

Idris had paled, in fact, he appeared sick. "I won't. Never again, I promise, Javed."

With that, Javed flung him away and he collided against the metal walkway with a bang and thud. Idris slid to the ground. "Get out of here. Never return."

His words carried power and a palpable ripple moved through the room. She watched as Idris picked himself up off the floor and scurried away. Silence reigned as those waiting nearby returned to their tasks in silence.

Javed growled, impatient and ill-tempered as Idris fled. The altercation, if he could name it something so tame, hadn't been pretty. No second liked to be dismissed, but for this second in command, it was a significant loss of face. And Javed still didn't have a *Yeux Secondes*.

Seeing Idris kissing Celina, had tripped the switch on the rage. It had surged through him during the run-in. He'd been unable to contain the fury when he saw her push against him. She hadn't wanted it. Not his touch or his caress.

"Shall we?" He indicated the room.

She nodded and preceded him into the office.

He fought to contain the memories, but they tumbled around him. He'd heard the bastard's words. He clenched his fists and ground his teeth while he waited for his body to settle. The pounding of heartbeats slowed as those who'd witnessed the scene returned to their tasks and finally, sure he was in control, he turned.

He castigated himself for a fool. He should have controlled himself.

Celina remained in the same spot she'd stood in when he'd wrenched Idris away from her. He didn't know what the emotion on her face was.

Fury? Not really. Fear? Perhaps there was a fair dose, but it was something else. Not for the first time, he wished he could read what went on inside her head.

She was stiff, and he could still see the red bruises and welts on her face and scowled. "Do you feel any better?"

"What?"

"Your injuries. Are they any better?" When she finally glanced into his eyes, he read the confusion.

"I... Uh, yes. A little." He could see she'd showered and changed. The scent of her filled his nostrils, and he inhaled deeply. "Look. Just tell me where I'm going and I'll be gone as soon as I can pack." The words tumbled from her lips, and he was shocked.

"Leave? You aren't going anywhere. I called you here to tell you that I was asking Idris to leave." He shifted closer and gazed at her shocked face. "I told you, I can't let you go."

"But he's your second."

"No. We wouldn't work well together. It's not uncommon for a new nest and master to go through several seconds before he finds one he is comfortable with. I have already contacted Cressida." He followed Celina with his gaze. "But please, take a seat."

He shook his head at the confusion he saw on her face. *How the hell had it got this complicated?*

"I will be making an announcement later. But, I wanted you to know first." He rubbed the back of his neck as he turned away. When he swung back, Celina was still standing, waiting for his announcement. "Kharisma is to be my new second."

The shock on her face would have been amusing if the situation wasn't quite so trying. "Kharisma? But wasn't she…?" Celina broke off. He could read the thoughts running through her mind. Kharisma had been his lover, something he'd never hidden.

"She was. But we are friends. I trust her. And there are few who have the range of skills she does. Strategically she's brilliant. She's also an excellent fighter as well as healer."

Celina stepped back. "So why did you want to tell me?"

"Because I had to. I felt, under the circumstances…"

She hunted for a chair and sat down heavily. "I don't get this." The whispered words betrayed her feelings.

"I don't either. All I know is I can't let you go. And I need someone I can trust in my corner right about now."

"So where does that leave…?" She spread her hands.

"I don't know that either."

TEN

Attar paced the length of his grotto; Jelani had been gone for hours. He'd slaked his initial thirst before renewing himself, locked deep within the body of the red haired woman. He'd enjoyed the result, then had fed deeply before casting her body aside. Jelani had suggested using her to draw their quarry. So he'd allowed the removal of the remains to who knew where.

It had been the remarkable resemblance to his youngest sister that had drawn him to the woman, to spare her initially. He, together with his sisters and brother had enjoyed their peculiar union for many years, until they had drifted apart. Of course, they were Gods and Goddesses who walked among the humans. Even the Babylonian ruler Psamtek, had bowed before him after his invasion of Egypt.

Over time, his brother and sisters had found lovers, unlike him, claiming they no longer felt their relationship was appropriate. He'd stayed true to their nature.

Of course, then she, his youngest sister had begot a child.

That was strictly forbidden, his mother had been most clear on that. They might make servants of their vampires, something they had all eagerly embraced, but they were strictly forbidden from passing on their abilities and bloodline.

He'd regretted the necessity of destroying his siblings. He missed them. The bond between them had been deep and satisfying of all his needs.

His hunger roared to life once more. "Where is Jelani? I require food." His mind cast about, seeking the servant he had made so many centuries before.

"Master!" His servant hurried into the cavern. "I bring food and news."

He stilled his motions and waited for Jelani to speak.

"They have found the artefact which would show them where to find the tomb, telling of the others. It was foretold at the investiture of this new nest that they must find it. Sire, what would you have me do?" Jelani got to the floor and effaced himself, while anger seethed within Attar.

"Do? You must find the receptacle. Kill whoever took it. They must not live long enough to uncover my secrets." Surely one new nest could not be strong enough to keep him from the secrets hidden within the vessel. Had he not spent centuries guarding his secrets?

But I lost the sword to Estersham. The murmur inside his head reminded him of the last time he trusted someone wholly unconnected too much. The last time had resulted in the loss of the *Sword of Vengeance.*

"Master, the nests are not as they were. They are now living openly. They are protected and strong."

"Openly? What untruth is this? Humans cannot live with vampires. The same as they cannot live openly with other. That was the edict from my maker." His voice echoed through the cavern and Jelani quaked before him.

"Come. First sustenance, then you will do my bidding." He waited for Jelani to bow and retreated to his chair. There were other things, far more important, right now, to consider.

ELEVEN

C ELINA THUMBED THROUGH THE BOOK IN FRONT OF HER. S HE suppressed a yawn, still unused to working during the night and sleeping through the day, but she'd been told it was the way that some nests worked. *What I wouldn't give for a coffee right now.*

Bertha had become standoffish in the last few days, and she half understood why. Idris had been sent away, she'd disappeared without warning Bertha or anyone else and nearly got herself killed then spent a day sequestered in the Masters rooms.

She'd also found the artefact.

No neophyte was supposed to do anything like that. Or so Bertha had informed her.

"So now I'm stuck here practicing warding." Bertha had given her specific instructions to practice erecting wards on the items in the rooms they used. After they were up, she would try to break through the spell work. It was an attempt to work out her strengths and weaknesses but Celina chafed. "I'd rather be doing something useful."

"Warding is very useful. If done correctly it will keep the uninvited out of our living quarters. And believe me, I remember the torching of the manor all those years ago. So don't whinge. Just do what you are asked."

"Torching of the manor? What happened?" She leaned forward hoping to learn more, but Bertha just shut her mouth and refused to say anything. In disgust, Celina took another look at the book and snorted.

Celina picked up her athame and prepared her circle, then cleared her mind. Her slow and careful movements assessed by Bertha, she knew. Celina called upon the light, something she'd already shown an affinity for. This time the energies flowed easily as she raised her arms and imagined a dome settling over the dolls-house she'd been given to start with. The flare of pink light no longer surprised her. She kept the energies pouring down until she was certain they were complete, then finished her task.

As Bertha stepped forward, Celina dismissed the circle and hovered against the wall, watching in silence.

Bertha cast a circle and set to work. But no matter what she did, Bertha could not break the spell she'd wrought. Eventually, her mentor stepped beside her. "I don't know how you've done it, but you've created a ward I cannot break. So let's go outside and practice on something larger shall we?"

Celina and Bertha had just emerged from the basement into the corridor when the noise began.

She hurried quickly to the doorway, to find it barred. "What's going on?" She could hear the anxiety in her own voice. But dammit, she needed to know.

"We are under attack." Javed's terse words stopped her. She inhaled deeply understanding that this, the place where they existed wasn't as safe as she'd thought.

"What?"

"Attack. Now stay inside." He brushed past her and out through the door he'd cracked open.

She wanted to stop him, but knew it wasn't the right thing to do.

Her stomach roiled as the sounds of fighting filled the air. Cries and clangs married with thuds. Screams rent the night, and she shivered.

Javed. Shouldn't he have stayed inside? As he was the Master, surely the nestlings were supposed to protect him? But even as the thoughts surfaced, she squashed them. He was a fighter. She'd already seen that in the way he walked. His body loose and with a long vicious looking curling sword and the UV gun strapped to his side. She'd seen the way his attention had zeroed in on whatever was going on outside. In his eyes there was a flat distant look.

"He'll be fine."

She shivered at Bertha's words. "How do you know that? You can't be certain."

Bertha laid her hand on Celina's. She squeezed her eyes shut, hoping to stop the hot sting of tears.

Celina had to hold herself still as the sounds of the battle raged. She needed to know he was safe, but also understood she had nothing to offer the nest, during this time. Her heart continued to race as the adrenalin kicked in.

How long the skirmish went on for, she couldn't honestly say. Minutes and seconds flowed and ebbed, yet the battle felt as if it was outside the regular flow of time. She knew Bertha stood beside her, working as her hands twitched. She felt the magic filling the space around her and hated that she had nothing to do. No way to either protect or help those battling outside. Not like at the gallery. In that instant she knew, if and when this happened again, she would have skills to offer.

A stray memory seeped... "The stone? I can use the stone. Let me out there." She turned to the vampire guard at the door, but he shook his head almost apologetically.

"The stone would be no good. We would need to get it outside, then have both camps separate. Which isn't how battle works."

The small feeling of usefulness melted away. "But—"

He shook his head again. "You just need to wait."

The sounds of the battle grew dim, less distinct until it stopped totally. She made to step to the door, but the guard held out his hand. "Not yet."

She gulped. What else could be happening? The air was thick with tension, so thick breathing became hard. But still, she waited.

Finally, the door opened and some of the nest vampires carried the injured within, before heading to the secured zone. She peered into the gloom, discerning some small movements. She curled her fingers into the palms of her hands and she took a tentative step forward.

Even as she reached the door, he was there. "Javed!" His face drawn and tight, but infinitely welcome to her.

She flung herself forward, needing to touch him. To assure herself that he'd come through intact. He *oompahed* as she launched herself, then slid her arms around his waist, holding on tightly.

He felt warm and comforting and she sank in to the embrace. Now she allowed herself to experience the desperation that had zinged through her while he'd been outside. "I was so scared."

He grunted.

She frowned. "Javed?"

He made a sound and for the first time she felt something wet, trickling against her arm. Then he slumped, and she grappled to hold him. "No!"

The guard was there dragging him from her arms before he slumped to the ground.

Horror filled her as she watched him being swept away while she stood, frozen in place as the guard carried him from the room. She hadn't been able to miss the dark, damp patch blooming on his back.

Awareness came slowly. "The nest?" The rasp sounded unlike his usual voice, and he frowned, hoping it was only a temporary weakness.

"Safe."

His first thought was of the household but swiftly on its heels came concern for those who had recently joined him in the newly formed nest.

Now he knew the nest hadn't been breached, but he feared for Celina's safety.

His last memory had been of her launching into his arms. He cracked one eyelid open and hissed as the overhead light seared his vision.

"Back with us, are you? A good thing too!" The dry tones of Kharisma were imbued with relief.

"What happened? Where's Celina?" He closed his eyes and concentrated on listening to her answer while his body ached. In particular his back burned. Javed felt the descent of his teeth and breathed deeply, hoping to dispel the hunger for blood that now ravaged him.

"Well, in case you didn't realize it, you took a nasty slice along your back." Her voice had settled into the matter-of-fact cadence he was used to. "Celina is fine. And the rest of the nest too, so thank you for asking."

He grunted, smelling blood nearby. A goblet was thrust into his hands and he sat upright, drawing it to his mouth before greedily gulping down the contents. "More?"

A laugh met his request and this time when he glanced up Kharisma was smiling at him. "Here. This should sate your need for now."

The goblet was refreshed and he took his time, letting his mind whir into action.

"So... Was the artefact the reason we were attacked?"

Her grin died away to be replaced by a thoughtful expression. "It could be, but we haven't yet found what the secret could be." She sank to the side of the bed. "No one in the nest seems to be able to find the importance of the item, even though we've had the human nestlings working on it since we retrieved it. The only thing that has come to mind is..." She stopped and grimaced.

Inside Javed a niggle of suspicion formed. "What?"

"Well, I'm wondering if she... Celina, could've been wrong about it?" Kharisma glanced away.

For an instant a spurt of anger rose in his chest. "No. I don't believe so." He controlled his temper, but when she turned back he could still read doubt on her face.

"But no one can find..."

He groaned. "Has anyone contacted Cressida?"

Kharisma backed away. "Hey, that's your job. But if it's any consolation, I did contact Xavier."

"And?" He closed his eyes, looking for some internal strength in the face of his first significant hurdle.

"He said if you didn't come round before dawn, to let him know. Thankfully you weren't out for that long."

He pushed off the bed, the blood having done its job. It had begun the healing process and while he wasn't fully healed, the pain was little more than a dull throb now.

"What do you think...?" Kharisma made to push him back to the bed, but he waved her away.

"We need to find out what the hell we are dealing with. Now, where did you store it?" He could tell that she knew what he was talking about.

Kharisma grimaced. "Where else would I put it? In the safe room."

Javed stood, wobbling slightly, but was determined to show everyone that while he might have been down, he had no intentions of staying out. "We need to sort this. Meet me in my office with it." He left the room and headed for the private work suites.

He padded through the open areas while the nestlings watched him, open-mouthed. He ignored their stares as he entered his work area. The room itself was as soulless as the rest of the house. The pale tones of white and cream sat at odds with the butter-colored leather of the seats and the wood furnishings. He wasn't really comfortable with the house or the furnishings if he were honest. The only room that held his stamp was his private quarters, but it was the best option he could find in the tight timeframe he'd been given.

He let his mind cast over what they knew about the sword and scabbard. Perhaps there was something on the blade?

Even as Kharisma opened the door and entered, he was still trying to consider the options.

"Here it is."

She placed the package carefully on his desk. He unwrapped it, lifting the sword first then running his fingers over the iron of the hilt. But while it was old and engraved with *herr Jesu Christ der du der Guender heiland* on one side and *Führer durch deine Barmherzig zeit anno 1603* on the other, there was nothing unusual about it, except it was clear that it was an executioner's sword.

With a heavy sigh, he placed it on the wood and turned to the scabbard. It was old, covered in decaying leather, but even as he ran his fingers along it, he could find nothing to give him a clue as to the secrets it hid.

"Kharisma, would you ask Celina to come here?" He murmured the words, sliding the blade into the scabbard and while it didn't slide well, it did eventually slide within partway.

When Kharisma called her on the internal phone system she shook a little. Did this mean Javed had recovered? Had he decided she was more trouble than she was worth? Or... Was he humiliated by her over eager embrace?

Even as she hurried down to the office, her stomach quivered, but she refused to give in to the worry that stripped her confidence.

Mouth dry, she reached the door and knocked softly.

His "Come in," was muffled

She gulped, and with a push the door open and she entered. He sat, uncomfortably, his face tight. "You called for me?"

He indicated the items on his desk. "You found these in the

gallery, but I need to know if you *feel* anything that will help us to work out their importance?"

"I... I don't know." She touched the blade, then shivered and slid her hands quickly away. "I don't like that."

His laugh was discomforting.

"What?" She spoke sharply.

He stilled. "It's an executioner's sword."

Celina couldn't contain her gasp. "Oh God! You have to be kidding me!"

Javed thrust the scabbard into her hands. "What about this?"

She ran her fingers over it, grimacing at the negative emotions swirling in her mind, being so close to it wasn't pleasant. She traced a pattern of something unseen, seeking something hidden. It was on her third pass, at the throat of the scabbard, that she felt it: a slightly raised roughness. She frowned. "There's something here."

Celina pressed a nail into the leather. "Right here. There's something hidden." She couldn't explain how she knew, just that something felt out of place.

Javed took it from her hands. "Are you sure?"

She stilled for a moment before nodding. "Yes."

He tugged a small dagger from his boot.

She quirked an eyebrow. "A dagger in your boot?"

"Old habits die hard."

She laughed as he sliced into the leather. It came away in strips, revealing the metal below and... "What is that?" A piece of parchment fell to the desk.

He lifted his head as she reached out. "Wait!"

He used the dagger to carefully turn over the brittle item and she grimaced. She moved forward and so did Kharisma. Without touching the parchment, he stroked the blade over it and flattened it. It creaked. Celina held her breath, not wanting to damage what they had found.

They could see the writing on it, though the edges were jagged and clearly torn. "Can you read that?"

He shook his head. "Kharisma we need to get someone to look at this tomorrow."

The sound of rattling blinds filled the air. "Dawn is nearly upon us. We should retire."

She waited as Kharisma backed away. "I'll leave you."

Celina turned and watched as the woman left the room. Now alone with Javed, Celina stomach was tied in knots, and she didn't know what he was going to say. Instead, he rose in silence and prowled around the desk, and she couldn't ignore his presence.

"You are unharmed?" His gaze pierced her to the core, and she shivered.

"I'm good. And you?"

He smiled slowly. "I'm quick to heal." He held out a hand, her tummy flip-flopped as nerves quivered inside her.

"That's... That's good." She curled her fingers into a fist, wanting to reach out and touch him. But she couldn't, could she? But he appeared as ill at ease as she felt and she didn't know what to do, for the life of her. *Should I go? Should I wait? Should I—*

"Celina..." He broke off with groan, grabbing her to him, his motions jerky and urgent. He kissed her, and the sensation was electric.

The fiery kiss ended when she pulled away, needing oxygen. Black stars formed in her vision, and she panted as if she'd run a marathon. Their bodies tightly mashed together.

"Celina will you..."

"Javed, I..."

They both laughed, their words halted, and for an instant she gloried in the sense of lightness in her being. But she sobered again quickly.

"Join me? Spend the day with me?" Javed's quiet words filled her with warmth.

Can I take this step? Even as she questioned it, she nodded. "Yes." One simple word, yet it carried such promise.

He curled his hand around hers and together they headed to the secure apartments.

"Wait!"

He glanced at her.

She reddened before him. "I um... I'll need fresh clothes."

He grinned and her stomach curled at the heat she discerned in the depths of his gaze. "Well, will you need them during the day? But yes, tomorrow you will need something fresh."

She gulped. "If I just run up—"

"I'll come with you." With those words, they turned companionably and headed to the stairs in silence. When they arrived at her door, her throat felt stuffed, and her mind spun.

One day. He's offering me one day. Will it be enough? She honestly didn't know. But she'd take what he offered right now.

He entered the room behind her, and she hurried, snatching up the first small overnight bag she found in her cupboard. In the bathroom she grabbed toiletries then headed back to the dresser for fresh clothing, jeans and top, bra and panties. She didn't look at him, otherwise she feared they wouldn't make it downstairs. She knew he'd tested her bed, laying one hand on the coverlet and pushing down before grunting his satisfaction.

"It's bare. Are they all like this?" His words stopped her quick actions.

"I don't know."

He nodded in silence before holding out his hand. "Let's go."

TWELVE

His hands shook as he touched the key panel on the wall. Never before had he felt with this intensity. Wanted so much.

Celina stood beside him, and without effort turned him inside out. Right now, she was there, with him. She wanted him as much as he wanted her. Hell, he could smell it. Her scent of desire flared and his mouth dried.

He stabbed the keypad and waited for the green light to glow. As soon as it did, he tugged her within and closed the door. "Come with me."

The hallway was empty.

Silent.

Unable to contain himself, he dragged her close again and leaned into the wall, let it support him. He touched his lips to hers, and she sighed into his mouth.

He sipped at her lips, hungered for the taste of her while sensations exploded within him. Hot and warm. He ran his hands, up and down her spine, each pass dipping lower until he gripped her butt. He hauled her close against him.

"Can you feel how much I want you?" He spoke roughly, and she moaned deep in her throat. "Today you are mine."

She cupped his shoulder before twining her fingers in his dark hair.

He nibbled his way down to her jaw-line and she arched back, granting him access to the sweet spot beneath her ear. For a moment vertigo assailed, as the pound of her heartbeat and the whooshing of blood filled his senses. He shoved aside his inner predator with difficulty, all the while sliding the point of his tongue against the soft skin of her neck.

"Javed." Her moan turned him white hot.

"Not here..." He lifted her into his arms, her bag falling almost forgotten to the floor. He scooped it up and prowled to the door of his rooms. Once inside he dropped the satchel on the floor and continued to the bedroom as she clasped her arms around his neck and dotted tiny kisses on his skin while the primitive being within remained firmly leashed.

Javed stopped at the bed and let her slide down his body, knowing she felt the heat of his erection, from the way she sucked in her breath. Her eyes were glassy and her color high. Deep inside he felt a greater flush of pleasure to see her as needy as he was.

She watched him, as he reached for the buttons on her shirt, carefully slipping them through the openings one at a time. Finally it hung open, and he slid his fingers under the light material, pushing it from her shoulders.

"I want you Celina. I want to feel your heat. Tell me you want it as much as I do." He needed the affirmation.

She nodded. Then she tugged one of his hands to her breast. "My heart is racing, knowing that we..." She groped for his belt and tore at the buckle, licking her lips while she continued her feverish activity at his waist. "I have never wanted anyone like I want you, right now." Her eyes blazed, and triumph roared.

His belt dropped from her fingers as he hoisted her up and onto his bed, her red hair billowing around her head. It looked right. The thought paused him for a moment, before he followed her down, crouching over her supine figure. He caged her body with his arms as he leaned in for another scorching kiss which started at her mouth then trailed down her neck and to the top of one soft mound. She shuddered beneath him, her hands dragging at his shirt.

"You need to take this off…" Her mutter ended on a hiss as he opened his lips over one peak, hidden below the soft white lace of her bra.

She pushed on him and he shifted, sitting upright. "Take. It. Off."

He laughed at her demand, but dutifully removed the shirt, throwing the garment over one shoulder, then reached for her. He marvelled at the flash in her eyes, her pouty red lips. He stared down to her full breasts.

She stretched behind to the clips.

"No, let me."

She sucked in a deep breath, her softly rounded belly tense as he found the fasteners. Javed slid the bra away from her. Her breasts were full and tipped with plum-colored nipples, dark and ready for him. He bent and tasted her, and she moaned again.

"Please." She bucked below him, and he could smell her arousal scenting the air. It made his own desire burn hotter than before. His body trembled with suppressed desire.

Javed propelled her back to the bed, unzipping her jeans before pushing them away to reveal white panties below—a scrap of material that covered her intimate recesses.

His dipped his fingers beneath the thin elastic, but she stopped him.

"Take yours off first." Her voice was thin and reedy.

He smiled. "Fine." Within seconds, he had stepped away from her, toed his shoes off and removed his socks. Next he stripped pants and briefs away, so he appeared naked before her.

She hooked her fingers under the lacy edges of the elastic. She arched her hips off the bed and his mouth dried.

Now she was bare in front of him as she kicked the material free of her feet.

Her body was ivory perfection all the way down to her toes. She moved sinuously like a siren and the thatch of red hair which covered her mound was like a neon invitation to him. He stumbled back to the bed, dropping to his knees. "Perfection."

She grinned at his words, her eyes were heavy. "Come to me Javed. Fill me."

They touched, she dragged him to her, while she parted her legs. This time, he had no will power. He couldn't stop.

Javed touched her, caressing and searching, and finding her hot wet core. Her breath caught as he slipped his fingers within. She writhed and cried out as he feasted on her; first he sucked at one breast before sharing his attention with her other.

He was rock hard and so ready that when she captured him in her hand he nearly exploded. He couldn't contain his cry as she pumped him with exquisitely torturous touches.

He grunted, eyes closed as he fought his own nature. The sensual beast within was barely leashed.

"Stop. You have to stop."

Her movements stilled at his entreaty.

He squirmed away from her caress. With a swift motion he seated himself at the cradle formed between her legs. "This time... This time we do it right." He panted, breathless while sliding his fingers from deep inside her body. With infinite care he slid his cock within.

The wet thrill of her surrounding his erection was ecstasy. Never before had he felt so complete—so at one with himself and nature. He flexed his hips and she sucked in an unsteady breath. He caught her gaze. Tried to hold it. But she shut her eyes as he continued the slow advance into her body—inch by inch. "Don't. Open your eyes. See how much I want you."

Then he was totally enveloped by her. He stilled, letting her body adjust. She was so tight.

Slowly, so very slowly he began to thrust, little more than the tiniest of actions, but each shift was electric. He felt alive. She moaned as he nudged, and it ratcheted his own need higher. His body tightened further, and he gripped her hips, holding her close while he kissed her. It was deep and carnal.

When she wrapped her legs around him, his body went supernova. The intimate embrace letting him know wordlessly that she felt the pleasure he yearned to share with her. All the while she pulled at him, tugged him close while their bodies danced.

The tremors started deep within her. The sensation of ripples that grew as she neared her orgasm, he groaned, wanting her to have her climax before he took his own.

"Javed!" She arched, lost in her orgasm.

Too much! Fire erupted in the form of his release and he held her close to his heart.

SHE LAY WRAPPED IN HIS ARMS, STILL HUMMING IN THE aftermath of her orgasm. Her body tingled all over, a sensation that she could honestly say was totally alien to her.

She ran her fingers up and down his back while she studied the ceiling. Now that they had been intimate, how would it affect their-whatever it was? She shied away from using the term 'relationship'. He rolled off her, and she felt the loss. She contained the cry that rose in her throat.

"Extraordinary." His words were lost as he tightened the embrace. "Thank you." His lips claimed hers and even in her confusion, she melted a little.

He slid away. "You are a truly beautiful and caring woman. Now you should sleep." His voice was rough as he tugged the covers over them both.

She felt him move, using the remote to dim the lights, and his lips touched her cheek. *"Num jayidaan ya eazizti"*

She tensed, waiting to hear more. But as moments ticked past he didn't speak again.

"What did you say?"

But he didn't answer, so she lay in the dark listening to the sound of his breathing, soft and rhythmic before she finally dozed off.

CELINA WOKE TO AN EMPTY BED. SHE COULD SEE THE indentation on the pillow, but she was alone. Her heart clenched.

Slowly she inched to the side and around. When she was sure no one was there, Celina slipped her feet over the side, taking the top sheet with her and winding it around her nude body. *If he's had second thoughts, I don't want to embarrass him or me.*

The urgent call of nature couldn't be denied, so she headed in the direction of the small bathroom. As she opened the door a voice called out. "You're awake then?"

She stopped. *Javed hadn't left her!*

He ducked around the corner and stopped, taking in the sheet and no doubt the shock on her face. "Where you planning on going somewhere?" His voice held mirth, but he searched her face.

"I uh... I thought you'd gone." Her voice held the husky vestiges of sleep.

He narrowed his eyes. "I see. So..." He stopped, and she waited. "After the loving we shared, you thought I'd gone?"

Her soul shrivelled a little at the coolness she detected in his voice. "I... No..." she drew in a breath. The need to stop, reflect and focus on the question warred with fear. "Look, I've never been into one-night stands. I don't..." She glanced away briefly, overcome with shame.

Whatever kept his back steely straight seemed to flow out of his body, and he nodded. "I shouldn't have acted like that. I apologize."

Celina shivered. "I had heard some vampires liked to have fun then disappear. To be honest, I didn't know if I'd done something wrong though."

He raised his hand to cup her cheek. "No, my love. You have done nothing wrong. Now, if you wish to get back into the bed, I will fetch you some sustenance."

She blushed, the heat radiating from her face. "I need..." She waved towards the bathroom.

He laughed a little. "Go, and your breakfast will be ready when you return."

She dragged on the fine cotton that swathed her before retreating. Celina avoided peering in the mirror as she washed her hands and finally, unable to think of any other way to avoid the moment, left the questionable safety of the bathroom.

He'd tugged the comforter up over his lap, and for a moment she wished he hadn't, but she tugged the sheet closer.

"Do you need that?"

She dipped her gaze and blushed once more. "Well, I don't make a habit of wandering around naked in men's bedrooms."

He grinned. "So you just make a habit of being undressed in men's bedrooms then?"

She shook her head. The sum of her lovers had numbered two and that included Javed. "I don't do that kind of thing."

He sobered. "I don't intend to hurt you, Celina. So come and sit down. Break your fast and tell me about your life."

Celina gingerly lowered herself to the bed.

"And you could dispense with the sheet." She could see he was controlling a laugh.

With a last quick glance at him, she took the plunge. She found the edge of the white cotton and unwound it, baring her body to him. He raked her up and down, a slow curl of warmth invading her belly at the smoky look in his eyes.

"Come. Eat." His voice sounded slightly hoarse, and she allowed herself a moment of pure feminine triumph.

Over breakfast, Celina explained about her background. She'd been abandoned as an infant at a hospital. They'd been sure she was only hours old when a woman had come in looking harried and handed her over to the staff. Her formative years had passed in a series of cold foster homes. He'd held her hand as she shared her battle to complete high school and gain a scholarship to the university. The hours she'd worked over six long years until she graduated.

"So when I finished I was offered a position in the bank. It was great because I managed several promotions during my time there."

"Do you miss it?" The words escaped him, and he wanted to call them back as she glanced away. "Celina, I..."

"No. It's fine. Yes. I do. I miss being able to make decisions for myself. To be able to help in some way. I've been on my own for so long that... I don't know how to let someone make decisions for me." She turned back, but now he understood what had driven her to investigate the situation at the gallery.

"You're a nestling now. You'll never be alone again." His words sounded pompous even to him and she giggled before sobering.

"Sometimes you can be alone in the middle of the maddest crowd. It's something that can't be fixed quite so easily." She lifted her hand to his cheek, and he covered it with his own. "I'll get there. But giving up the sense of being... I don't know... Just me against the world isn't that easy to throw off."

He couldn't understand that. In his human life, he'd been the feted son. He'd been wanted, pandered to. Even his wife had fussed over him until the day she ran away. Then the Master who made him had stepped in, brought him into his nest.

In the last centuries, he'd never really been alone. He'd had comrades and lovers. Friends and servants. Unlike Celina, who'd been alone for most of her life.

His emotions must have shown on his face because she leaned in and whispered to him. "Don't fret about it. That's how my life was meant to be. I've come to terms with it. If I hadn't...it probably would have buried me. I couldn't let the loneliness beat me. I fought, and I won. I made myself who I am. What's more? I like me."

Javed pulled her against him, hugging her close and promising himself she would never be alone again. Never again would she be without a home and family.

Celina lifted her head and peered into his eyes. "Javed, you can't fix this. Please. Just let it go." She grabbed another strawberry.

For all her calm words and bravado, he couldn't grasp how she might ignore her solitary past. "You're sure?"

"I am." She popped the sweet fruit into her mouth, and he let her go, leaning back against the brightly colored silk cushions.

"You do realize, now that things have settled, we need to complete your blood profile." She stiffened in his arms.

"Why?"

"It is a tradition, based on the blood sacrifices we give. Now, we map all members of the nests so that we can offer appropriate medical intervention, especially for those with rare blood types. It allows us to take all necessary steps to have supplies of blood products on hand. It also means that those who become vampires who are lost have living blood sacrifices to be given at the time of their passing." He didn't say more, but surely with the many nest members who'd been mapped, there would be a match somewhere in the system? A long lost member of her family...

Javed stopped the thoughts. They weren't appropriate. That wasn't what the blood depositories were for. He heaved a sigh as he caught sight of the clock. Seven had come and soon he would have to emerge from the haven of his rooms.

Tonight he would be meeting the candidates for the position of his *Yeux Secondes*. Traditionally, they were the humans who took over the day to day running of the nest, liaised with the human world and ran their businesses.

"So tell me about how you came to be the Master instead of anyone else."

THIRTEEN

Bertha came hunting for her once the sun went down and found her in the communal kitchen-dining area drinking coffee.

"Where have you been?"

She'd blushed scarlet as Javed had come up behind her, wrapping his arm in a casual embrace around her waist.

"Good evening Bertha. I was hoping to find you tonight. I need your services and those of Celina. The candidates for *Yeux Secondes* will be here soon. I would like both of you to sit in on the process. To represent the witches of the nest."

Bertha's mouth opened then closed without a sound. If it hadn't been so embarrassing, it would have been quite funny. She herself squirmed, but he pulled her tighter, and she noticed the assessing gaze Bertha flashed at his hold.

"We will be there, Master. What time will you require us?" Her stiff words concerned Celina, and she made a note to talk to her mentor later.

"In the next hour. Now, I'll leave Celina in your capable hands." But before he withdrew he dropped a careless kiss on her cheek.

She turned to watch him leave, his gait jaunty.

"You need to be careful. Falling into relationships with vampires is tricky enough, without it being a Master." It wasn't censure she heard but concern.

"It's not really like that..."

"Did you sleep with him?" When she didn't answer, Bertha nodded knowingly. "Then it is like that."

"I didn't look for it." She had to make sure Bertha understood. She hadn't stalked Javed. Hadn't gone out of her way to entice him into bed.

Bertha touched her shoulder. "No. You wouldn't do something like that. But you were interested. Intrigued. I should have spoken before. Most nestlings don't get involved with their Masters. Many nests forbid it, because there is a power imbalance that eventually breaks even the best of unions, usually causing disharmony. Humans and vampires don't go the distance because you will age. He can't."

Bertha's harsh words hurt, even if they were meant in kindness. He hadn't promised her anything, and it wasn't like she'd spun any fairytales. But the truth ripped away the sense of wellbeing that had filled her.

Bertha's right. We are incompatible.

"Now we'd better get some work done if we have to be in the Master's office within the hour. And I'd like to run some tests..." She stopped as Kharisma joined them.

"Good evening, Bertha. I'm wondering if I could spirit Celina away? Just for a while?" The blonde vampire smiled.

Bertha frowned. "What on earth do you need her for?"

"Blood sampling. Because she is joining the nest as an adult, we need to ensure we have the necessary information." Kharisma cocked her head to one side, her bright blue eyes piercing as she watched Bertha. "Of course if you have—"

"No. That's fine. We need to meet with the Master within the hour anyway." She spoke with a frustrated tone, then she turned and walked away leaving Celina with the view of her retreating bulk.

"She is not pleased? Have you done something untoward?" Kharisma now focused on Celina, who squirmed slightly.

"Beside spending time with a Master?" She dipped her head so Kharisma wouldn't get the gist of her feelings.

"Oh. That's a problem if she's upset about that. Okay, come on then, you can talk to me once we get to the clinic."

Surprise flashed through Celina as Kharisma threaded her arm through hers. She held the mug of coffee tightly in one hand as she followed the vampire to the other end of the house and into a small room. It was fitted out with clean white walls and industrial brushed metal shelving. The bank of lights overhead were turned off, but she supposed they would be bright, like she'd seen on television, when needed.

The area itself was compartmentalized with retractable walls, and fitted with washing zones, a seat and desk, computer, and in the back of the office was a large slab, which she guessed was where surgery was undertaken.

"Amazing." She placed her coffee on the desk. "What a fantastic layout."

"Yes. Javed let me have free reign to make sure this was set up exactly as I wanted it."

Celina stared at her. "You were..."

"We were. But it's long over. Now sit down and roll up your sleeve while I get everything together."

FOURTEEN

Kharisma entered Javed's office. "I think you may have a problem or two brewing."

He glanced up and scowled, running one of his hands through his hair.

The reports in front of him made no sense. The words like *gross negative return* and *facilitation of corporate branding* swam before his eyes. "I hope you plan on saving me. I don't get half of this." He waved at the masses of reports that littered his desk.

"No. I don't do that either. That's what the *Yeux Secondes* does. Thank heavens. No. I'm more concerned about the outcome of any relationship you plan on having with Celina. Bertha is walking gingerly around her, and it's already been noted that you have a partiality there."

He stilled. "Are you asking me what my intentions are?" He observed Kharisma as she sat down on the other side of the desk.

"Yeah. I guess I am. What you decide could affect this nest. You need to be sure about what you hope to achieve before it occurs."

Javed pushed the chair back and rose, stalking to peer out the windows. "I don't know. I mean... She's like a ray of sunshine in my life. When I'm with her... I feel like I can do anything." He shrugged. "But then I remember I'm over eight hundred years old, a Master vampire with the safety of a nest on my shoulders. And that I've never managed to keep a relationship together for longer than several months since my turning."

Flashes of light cut through the night time gloom as he continued to gaze out over the driveway. He knew Kharisma saw through to his inner turmoil.

"I can't tell you that this will work either. But you need to decide if you want to be with her or not. You need to talk to her. She is bound by rules too. The rules of the nest and her oath to the *Conclave Paramount* are very clear. She has as much to lose as you do. Maybe even more."

He turned at her soft words. "What do you mean?"

"She'd be on her own. If she's removed from a nest, then she is back to where she was. But this time with nothing to fall back on. The *Conclave* might turn their back on her."

He stared at her, surprised.

"She'd have no career. No job. So if you plan to take her for a lover, then consider what will happen if it all ends." Kharisma inhaled deeply as if clearing away the topic then continued. "Your candidates are here, too."

His mind whirled. He hadn't really considered the consequences, and he would certainly have to think long and hard about what he was going to do. But right now he had matters of the nest, not the heart, to focus on.

Kharisma looked uncomfortable.

"Send in the representatives, please Kharisma."

"What?" She gaped at him. His mouth flattened as he watched her reaction. Kharisma blushed slightly. "Well, did you mean to include her in this?" She picked up the small pile of blue files at the edge of the desk.

"Yeah I did. Along with every other member of the panel."

Kharisma nodded without a word and walked to the door, before casting one last look at him.

"I hope you're doing the right thing." She slipped through the exit.

He stood there. He knew what she meant. He'd settled on a casual and inclusive structure for the nest.

Was this really the way he wanted to go forward? The answer was there, though. *Yes. I want this nest to be free of the restrictions that nearly tore Hope and Xavier apart. I want my people to be able to have their say. I want them to feel equal and valued in a way that other nests do not.*

Nervous energy filled him, and he thrust his hands into his pants pockets and leaned against the desk, fighting the urge to tap his foot.

The door opened and in filed the nestlings he'd chosen to participate in the choosing of the *Yeux Secondes*. Two witches, two nestlings, two of his vampire guards, Kharisma and the one shifter who lived with the nest.

"Thank you for joining the panel. Tonight I am talking to the candidates for the position of *Yeux Secondes*. Each of them has various skills and abilities. But because this is a new nest, we have the opportunity to make our own rules. Tonight I want you to talk to every candidate. Kharisma will hand you a folder; within are details of the candidates. I want you all to choose the three you think would best fit into our nest by mingling with them. Later tonight, we will shortlist, then meet with the top four candidates."

He stared at the people gathered before him. They were a motley crew, but everyone was picked by him to represent their position in the nest. "Any concerns or queries, ask Kharisma."

He had decided on an informal meeting tonight, a barbeque outside so all the members of the nest could see them and interact. Normally the position was hereditary, but that wasn't what he wanted for his nest. He'd seen the havoc that could be caused when people didn't acquire the role on merit.

Everyone filed from the room and he stood in his empty office, watching the door close. He would talk with each one privately and draw his own conclusions. But first he should go meet them.

A knock came at the door, and he frowned. "Come."

The door opened, and Cressida entered. He rose and moved toward her. She was smiling broadly. "So, I finally get here, and you are hiding in your office?"

"Councillor Cressida, it is my pleasure to formally welcome you..."

She waved away his words and embraced him. "I am so pleased to see you. And don't bother with the Councillor nonsense. I count you as my friend. It's time we found new ways of doing things." The knot he hadn't realized was there, loosened a little in his chest.

"Then you don't have any objections?"

"It's your nest. You have to make choices and decisions that feel right for you. The Council does not and will never tell you how to run your nest." She gripped his hands hard, ensuring he understood what she meant. "Now, let's go meet these candidates."

Celina received her blue folder from Kharisma. "Thanks."

Kharisma gave her a long look, then winked.

Thoroughly lost as to what that meant, Celina hurried through the door and opened the folder, checking the listed candidates. There was a mix of men and women from a range of nests and each had a sheet, noting their strengths and how it might work with the nest. It also included details of their family status.

She wasn't totally sure how she felt about being one of those who would whittle the list down, but Javed had shown his confidence in her, and she had no intentions of letting him down.

Out in the garden she could hear voices and smell food cooking, so she headed in that direction, but not before she noticed the cool blonde Councillor who orchestrated the investiture had arrived. The woman walked into the office after knocking while Celina watched. The door shut, and Celina turned back to see Bertha watching her.

"Come on then. Let's go get something to eat and see who we can find from the candidates."

Trailing behind Bertha was no mean feat, for a larger lady she was quick. Celina had to hurry to keep up.

The first of the candidates stood by the door, appearing to observe the nestlings mingling. Her face betrayed indignation at what she saw. She'd dressed impeccably in a smart slim skirt suit and matching pumps of blood red and the peek of a lace camisole hid whatever assets she might have. Her dark hair was fastened up and back severely, though, it did accentuate the pale pearls at her ears. The way she clutched her bag, nails digging into the highly polished leather betrayed her discomfort.

Mentally Celina crossed her off the list. Javed had talked about how he wanted to set a new standard. That it should be democratic and welcoming. This woman didn't feel right for his vision. All this was formulated quickly, but when she glanced around Bertha had disappeared into the crowd. "Great. She's gone." She muttered as she swung around.

Instead, Celina headed for the bar, deciding a glass of white wine was in order. As she stepped up, a man bumped into her. "Sorry."

When he turned to apologize, shock stole her breath. His hair was the same red as hers and his eyes... They were the same green. She'd never met anyone else with the exact same hue as hers—emerald. The thought discomforted her.

"Hi, I'm Daniel. You must be from the nest." She couldn't detect any shock in his voice, just a genuine interest. She accepted the hand he held out, and shook with an odd formality.

"Hi Daniel. I'm Celina. Welcome." She waited for his reaction, but he just grinned.

"Would you... Would you like a drink?"

She nodded, unsure of how to progress the situation. He was exceptionally friendly, but was it because she was holding a folder?

Was it because he knew she was one of the panel reviewing the candidates? Or was he naturally like this? There wasn't a sign of anything hidden in his open gaze, a gaze which exuded honesty.

"Sure. A chardonnay would be fantastic." He slid around her and returned quickly, icy cold glass in hand. She peered at his soft drink

He shrugged. "My mother... She was an alcoholic and left my father when I was seven. Just took off. I can't face alcohol... You don't need to know all that though." He smiled uncertainly.

She mentally put him onto her 'keep' list.

JAVED WALKED WITH CRESSIDA INTO THE GARDEN, MARVELLING at the work his nestlings had done in preparation for the night. Lanterns were hung with fairy lights winking inside them.

A small bar had been set up outside, and nestlings laughed and chatted happily. This wasn't the way the other nests operated, but it seemed to be working for his. It felt right.

But even as he mingled, he kept searching for Celina. When he noticed her talking to a slight red haired man his stomach clenched. The predator deep inside wanted to go over and drag her to him—to kiss her and lay his claim. "You are very much interested in that witch. What's her name?"

He heard Cressida's words, keeping an eye on Celina while she nodded at something the man was saying, he answered, "Celina. Celina Worsters." He curled his fingers, and he had to calm himself.

"She's very beautiful. And I feel, very powerful." Her words had him turning.

"What do you mean?" He glanced over his shoulder.

"I see an aura of light. It's pulsing. She's exceptionally witrong. Or she will be, one day."

Javed frowned. "I don't—"

Cressida laughed lightly. "No. You have yet to embrace your

power fully. It will come in time. Then you will see some of what I do. Now come, let's circulate before you begin the formalities."

They circled the area, meeting many with a quick, 'hello, how are you?'. He allowed himself to scan and listen, though his awareness was always partially on Celina.

She'd disengaged herself from the man and had been introducing herself to others, yet her face betrayed none of her thoughts. Eventually, it was time to retreat to his office. Cressida retired on the grounds of other places and meetings to attend, and Javed felt strangely relieved.

This was a decision he had to make, with his nestlings. He appreciated her appearance, but once she'd left they could lay the foundations for their own ways.

He caught Kharisma's eye and she nodded, understanding what he required. From then on the night was long as he met and interacted with those who they'd decided to interview. One after the other, some he felt wouldn't fit the nest, some he doubted could even fulfil the role. Then there were those who felt right.

Kharisma tapped on the door not long after the last left. "Do you want to see everyone together or one at a time?"

He understood she meant those from the nest. "Send them all in... And I would like to talk with Celina at the end."

Kharisma inclined her head.

He flushed a little under her knowing gaze.

Once everyone trooped within he called them to order. "We need to decide which ones are suited to our nest. Did you all get a chance to meet with everyone?" The chorus of 'yes' pleased him.

One by one, he ran through the names, pleased to find that the majority of the nestlings agreed with his thoughts, though he did drop another from the list by the end of the meeting.

"Thank you for your participation. This being the first new nest in a century, we have an opportunity to make it what we want. Tonight you have all played your part. I thank you."

Hearing the implicit dismissal in his tone they all exited the room, except Kharisma and Celina. He grinned seeing the way Celina nodded at Kharisma. Then Kharisma too left, leaving the two of them alone.

"Sit down."

Celina quirked an eyebrow at him but sat on the chair.

"You were deep in conversation with the one man. Daniel?"

"Uh, yeah. He's had an interesting life so far."

Javed bristled slightly. *She'd had time to find out about his life? Just how long had they chatted for, then?* He castigated himself mentally knowing his attitude was over the top. *But dammit! She's mine!*

The thought startled him for an instant before he accepted it.

"You'll move your things into my room tonight."

She stared at him. "What?" Her voice rose.

He flattened his lips at the question and tone.

"You're moving into my room tonight." He stood and walked toward her.

Celina rose, her face dark with anger. "One night and you're ordering me to move in with you! Until when? You change your mind? Then what? I'll get ordered back upstairs, or out the door?" She laughed, and the anger he'd tried to bank rose. "Pigs bum, I will!"

In that instant, he realized he'd gone about it wrong. Remorse filled him and he made to touch her hand but she tugged away quickly. His gut churned. "Please. I shouldn't have ordered you... Will you please stay with me?"

She glowered at him. "Look Javed, just because we spent one night making love... having sex, doesn't give you the right to order me around." She stalked to the door.

"No. It doesn't, and I didn't mean it, at least not the way it sounded. Please Celina. Don't leave."

Celina rested her hand on the door knob as she glanced back, indecision clear on her face. "Why?"

"Because I'm asking."

CELINA WOKE SLOWLY, STRETCHING MUSCLES THAT HAD STIFFENED *in her sleep. The night air brushed a cool caress over her burning-hot naked skin and the rustle of silk captured her attention. Slowly she turned over.*

Javed lay beside her, his breath fanning the warmth that spread through her limbs. "You are so beautiful."

He leaned forward, his lips grazing hers so softly and the whisper of his breath musky and warm as it fluttered over her. Her insides felt like they were melting and she concentrated on the moment. She experienced a sense of all being right and completion in his presence.

Celina reached out, brushing a lock of hair from his face as the net curtains above them swayed in the breeze. Sunlight dappled his skin. "I have never wanted a man as much as I want you."

He stilled for an instant before she noted the way his eyes blazed. "You honor me." His movements were slow, languorous even as he gathered her against his firm chest. Her nipples were crushed against the smooth satin over steel.

She traced her fingertips over his shoulders and down his arms, lightly playing over the muscles that she found.

He nibbled at her neck, the touches both sensual and reverent. The rasp of day-long growth scratched at her, heightening the sexual tension that fizzed deep in her veins, like quicksilver winding through her body. Will I ever get enough of this man?

As if hearing her thoughts, he laughed, the throaty sound filling the air. She slumped back to the pillow, waiting to see what he would do next. Slowly, he cupped one breast, plumping it with a smile. "You have such beautiful breasts. They are full and ripe. Ready for me to taste." He lightly pinched the distended bud and a sharp sensation shot all the way to her womb, stealing her breath, before he lowered himself, and opened his mouth just over the aureole. He blew and she arched as a million tiny nerve endings quivered in response.

"Ooh!"

Carefully, he brushed his fingers over the curve of her belly. She stopped him and he looked up, laughter evident in the crinkled lines at his mouth and eyes.

She levered up to his chest and kissed the silky smooth skin. Laved his nipple and he groaned.

With care, she spread her fingers over his hard stomach and circled the tiny indentation she found.

He clapped a hand over her shoulder. "Come to me." He rolled onto his back, and a wicked thought took hold. Celina pushed to her knees and opened her lips to close them over his cock, then slid slowly all the way down. He bucked, and she let go, a small pop filling the air.

Javed's grasped her hips, lifted her...

Bang! Celina woke with a jerk, her heart racing, and she was unbearably aroused. Her legs clenched against the urgent need, and she was hot. *So damned fired up!*

The t-shirt she slept in had tucked itself around her middle, and she was naked from the waist down. Sunset had arrived, and she shivered, wondering what Javed's reaction would have been to her unbelievably erotic dream of him—of them.

She didn't want to rise, and she wondered for a moment if she was late getting up, would anyone notice? Celina slid her shaking hand down her body, but she stilled it. *Is that really what you want?*

If she were honest, the only thing that would satisfy her now was Javed, moving deeply inside of her. She released a strangled moan. "I doubt he'll want anything to do with you after you told him no last night." The words ended with a wail and she slumped back on the bed, her eyes on the ceiling.

The crash of her door opening startled her. There stood Javed. His face a mask of fury, and she gasped. "What are you doing here?"

"I've come to you."

FIFTEEN

Attar watched his servant pace and mutter, waiting for his orders. Jelani had retreated back to the cavern, injured and bleeding, and it had taken every ounce of Attar's willpower not to rip his throat out and gulp down the red liquid that spilled on the floor.

His hunger had raged fiercely until he had contained it with the cattle Jelani had supplied. He'd fed deeply, then rested, gathering his strength. Now the need filled him once more. It was always like this after he'd hibernated.

"Master, you are hungry. Let me get you sustenance." Jelani's voice carried a wheedling tone.

Attar indicated his agreement.

Jelani scurried from his sight, but once gone Attar frowned. This nest that had the artefact was much stronger than he'd been led to believe. They'd had it for days now. Had they found what was hidden?

Estersham had been tasked with retrieving the sword after he'd lost it in a game of chance, but he had failed. Now, after hundreds of years it had reappeared without any warning.

"Jelani should have known." Attar bit the words out as he glanced around him.

For now he was reduced to hiding, living in a cave. The vacant booths mocked him in their emptiness. He studied the inscriptions etched in the stone above each niche.

Perhaps Jelani had become a liability? "Maybe he has outlived his usefulness?" He let the words echo in the cavern while he waited. His thoughts swirled as he considered his current situation. His memories had started to resurface clearly now and he chafed at being hidden away.

He'd been treated like a God in the fertile valley of the Nile delta. Now he was reduced to hiding from the world. *Hiding! Me! A God!*

Jelani had told him of amazing things. Metal ships that flew through the air, horseless carriages that moved swiftly. It seemed unbelievable and he'd told Jelani so. Jelani had insisted it wasn't magic but the evolution of humanity that had wrought these changes. But Attar hadn't seen it yet. Soon though, he would leave this cavern. He too would experience the wonders of this modern age.

"Once more I will decide what will survive." He enjoyed the sounds of the humans being herded, the scent of them filled the hall. "Food." He rubbed his hands together. Once he was sufficiently ready he could make his appearance and once more humanity would bow down before him. *Just as they did in the past.*

Jelani appeared in the doorway, dragging the human cattle with him. "I have reached a decision. Listen carefully..."

His servant blanched then waited as he began to outline his plan.

SIXTEEN

Javed wasn't happy. After Celina had refused to spend the day with him, he'd endured a highly erotic dream. Of them. *Together*.

Once he'd woken he made his way to her bedroom, and when he'd entered it he could smell her arousal. It had been too much to bear. Her come hither look had just about sealed the deal. He'd pulled off his clothing in record time while she jerked her t-shirt over her head, revealing her form. Unable to wait, he'd crawled onto the bed with her, running his hands over her body while his cock strained, needing the hot wet glove of her core surrounding him. Then, his phone rang.

Clambering off her heaving form and away from the tangled sheets he found his pants then grabbed the phone. He'd checked the caller identification. *Kharisma*. With a silent oath he punched the glowing green button. "This had better be good." His heart still pounded, and the warm flush of sexual hunger heated his body.

"Well, Cressida is on the phone, so yes. I suppose it is." Kharisma laughed.

He ground his teeth in frustration as Celina scurried from the bed and headed to the small bathroom with her t-shirt in one hand.

"Why? Did I interrupt something?"

He growled.

"Okay, I'll put her through now." A click sounded then a voice trilled.

"Javed, I just needed to ring you to see how you went with short-listing the applicants for the position of *Yeux Secondes*? I'm not ringing at an inconvenient time, am I?"

He rolled his eyes but kept his voice steady. "Of course not, Cressida. We have the list down to four and I hope to meet with them, and my team later tonight to make a final decision." He waited, sure that wasn't the only reason for the call. The silence on the line was excruciating while he stood here naked, his erection slowly ebbing away. Celina remained out of sight, engaged in whatever she was doing in the room beyond. He'd purposely made no attempts to listen.

"I also need to present an update on the artefact. Have you managed to get any further information?"

He swore under his breath. "Yes, we have. May I call you back, later? I need to check some facts."

He had the uncanny sensation that she realized he wasn't focusing totally on the conversation with her, "Of course. Ring my private line when you are ready."

Even as he hung up, Celina opened the door to the bathroom, her t-shirt firmly in place. He wanted to curse. "I'm sorry..."

"Look Javed. We really need to talk. But to be honest this isn't the place nor am I dressed for it. Could we...?"

Her bosom heaved as she inhaled. She was clearly agitated by his naked nearness. "Can we do this later?"

He could read the storm of emotions in her eyes. He ran tightly clasped fingers through his hair and exhaled. "Of course. I need you to come help with the artefact anyway." He turned away and grabbed his discarded clothing, tugging them on with greater speed than finesse. "When you're ready come down to my office."

He turned to see her nodding, then without another word, he left.

The team gathered around the table, engaged in a robust discussion, now that the last of the final four candidates had left the office. The candidates would wait in one of the communal seating areas, but Celina was pleased she wasn't one of them, waiting for the news. She sipped her coffee and scanned the people sitting at the heavy white marble table. The chairs at least were comfortable, she thought.

"I didn't like the woman. She didn't mix at all last night, and I thought she felt we were less of a nest because of the casual structure we have chosen." Bertha shook her head. "I can't see her working at all well here."

Celina sat quietly, surveying the group. Javed had been watching her. She could feel his gaze like a palpable entity, and she had to suppress a shiver.

She needed him. She wanted him.

She just couldn't have him. Pain pierced her heart at that thought.

Celina curled her fingers, welcoming the bite of nails in the palm while she fought for internal control.

Another piece of paper was shelved, leaving them two possible options. One was a man in his late forties but something about him felt wrong to Celina. The other was Daniel. He'd been personable, interested. Not at all buttoned up—something she strongly felt would be in his favor. He'd made his way around the group of nestlings, shaken hands and chatted freely.

"Celina, you haven't said much." Javed's voice broke into her introspection. At his words, all eyes had turned to her.

She jumped a little before blushing. "I don't think I have much to offer to the discussion right now." Her words sounded lame, even to herself, and she wanted to shrink under the table. The others at the table shook their heads at her words.

"You've been asked to participate, Celina. Your thoughts will be taken into account." Bertha nudged her in the ribs and Celina grimaced. She just hoped Bertha hadn't worked out what any of her errant thoughts were about.

"Well for my money, I think Daniel had the most in common with the members of the nest, and Javed said he wanted it to be democratic. I felt he was open to others thoughts and ideas. I liked him, too." She finished her words quietly. Javed's lips thinned as if her final admission angered him. The situation had become so fraught that neither was keen to rock the boat. Yet it was clear he didn't like where her thoughts were going, even though she was sure he knew it wasn't in the least bit sexual.

The others agreed, and another voice piped up from the end of the table. "I felt that too. It was something in the way he met our eyes. He actually talked to us, not at us, and showed an interest in what we wanted and not just what we do for the nest. The others didn't seem to do that. I felt like they were sizing us up."

Javed nodded, and Celina scanned him from under her eyelashes. He turned to Kharisma. "Your thoughts?"

"Well, I don't think either would be a negative influence on the nest. Gerald patently has more experience in the business aspects, but I have to agree with the others. Daniel would fit into the nest better. It really depends on how you want the nest to function, but you must make the final decision."

"Then that's it. We have a decision."

Javed pushed the older man's information sheet to one side. "Let's go welcome the new *Yeux Secondes* to the nest." They rose, and the intensity of emotions was palpable. The group broke up, but the grins on the others' faces showed that the nestlings agreed wholeheartedly.

As they were leaving the room, a hand caught hers, and Celina stilled. She tingled at the touch and knew who it was.

"Celina? After this, we talk." Javed's lips were so close to her ear she could feel the whispering caress of his breath. This time nothing could stop the shiver that wracked her body or the pulsing warmth that pooled down low, urging her to turn and kiss him.

He growled low in his throat. She had to stop herself giving in to the urge. She fought it, eyes closed. She refused to look at him. *If I do...* She moved fast, uncaring whether he followed or not.

THE EVENING WORE ON, STRETCHING HIS NERVES TO NEAR breaking point. His proximity to Celina, and yet his inability to touch her was playing hell with his libido. He was also aware that Kharisma noticed his distraction.

They'd joined the candidates where they waited and the decision was accepted good-naturedly. He noticed that Daniel smiled broadly at Celina and he'd had to contain the sound that rose in his throat.

She's mine! The primal roar remained unvoiced.

Something must have telegraphed in his stance because Kharisma leaned over his shoulder. "She's not interested in him. You do know that, right?"

"I'm not discussing this with you." It was private, between himself and Celina. Some boundaries still existed. This was one that he was marking clearly.

Kharisma might've been his friend and second, but it wouldn't be right to talk about their relationship.

He glanced over his shoulder as Kharisma shrugged and laughed lightly.

"You've got it bad, haven't you? Okay!" She lifted both hands, stepping away. "I won't raise it again. Unless it interferes with the running of the nest."

He nodded soberly, cutting the discussion off as he observed the tableau unfold before him with a mixture of satisfaction and concern. *What if he offers Celina something I can't?*

Celina was human. Daniel was a human. He was a vampire. A

Master. Daniel could give her children. The insistent uncertainty gnawed at him. Once most of the nestlings walked away, He gritted his teeth and strode forward to shake Daniel's hand.

"Welcome to the nest. How soon do you think you can make the transition?"

Daniel frowned. "Well, so long as I can bring my father with me. That was in my application?" Daniel cast a glance at him, and Javed agreed wordlessly with a simple tipping of his head. "I believe I can relocate within the week."

"That is acceptable. I'll have Kharisma allocate you both rooms. We don't have apartments in this nest, so that's the only private area, apart from your office."

He turned, away realizing he needed to talk to the other candidates—to thank them for their efforts. He didn't want to, though.

What he really needed was to take Celina in his arms, with everyone and everything melting away. But that wasn't going to happen. So instead he made small talk with the people who had been unsuccessful, shook their hands, and wished them well.

Celina had wandered over to Bertha and they talked quietly. Bertha cast a glance in his direction and gestured. They both left the room, and he gave his full attention to the people who were ready to leave. "Thank you so much for applying," he intoned to each unsuccessful candidate, softening the words with a handshake.

Javed walked with them to the door and waited as they climbed into vehicles in the gloom of night. Lights cut through the darkness as engines roared. The crunching sound of gravel filled his hearing as they drove down the long drive and through the imposing gateway.

He turned and headed inside. There was still plenty to do, and Celina had promised to talk to him before she retired.

SEVENTEEN

The artefact and the piece of paper sat on the table between them. They hadn't examined it yet. "I've asked Cressida to send over someone who knows more about such artefacts. But to me it looks as if it's come from a book. A very old book." The paper was yellowed, brittle and sported a tattered edge. He wasn't quite sure if he should touch it, so one of the nestlings had acquired an acid free box to keep it safe. It bothered him that time was leaching away; there was only one week until the new moon.

"Cressida said she was sending someone tonight to inspect it." The email on his computer instructed them to leave it in the box until the professor arrived from the local university. He was already on the way. Javed checked the timestamp. The email was over an hour old. "They should be here any minute."

"What if it doesn't answer the question?" He heard the concern in Kharisma's voice and screwed his face into a frown.

"Then it has to be a clue. A way to find where the answer is hidden." At least he hoped so. Doubts and concerns assailed him. He felt so out of his depth. Xavier never seemed to have these issues.

But Xavier's nest was established when he'd arrived. There were already structures in place.

He knew that on an academic level, but it didn't help. He had nearly fifty humans, his guards and all the others to assure the safety of the location.

The hot bubble of frustration rose inside his chest. He wrenched his gaze from the screen, swivelling the chair to glare out the window. He cleared his mind and settled his thoughts... until a knock on the door broke the silence.

"Javed?" Kharisma reminded him that he needed to give the order to enter. She called out to the person waiting outside. He faced the door once more.

A short and paunchy man shuffled in. Light shone off the bald spot on his head and he seemed out of place in his immaculate gray suit, clutching an aging briefcase.

"Counsellor Cressida requested me to attend you, Master Javed? I am Professor Junat. My specialty is Print Culture."

With a squeak of the chair, Javed rose and extended a hand to the academic. His grasp was cool and slightly limp. Javed was pleased when he retreated a few feet. "This is my second, Kharisma. We need to know about this." He indicated towards the box on the table, and the professor squinted at it.

"Hmm. Just let me grab my gloves." He glanced around and carefully placed his case on the long marble table with a clatter. Two clicks opened the locks and he delved inside, before holding up two white cotton gloves and a piece of material, which he spread on the table. The professor's movements were precise as he opened the box and pulled the contents out and carefully laid the paper down for inspection.

He reached back into his case tugging out an eyepiece before inspecting the paper with a grunt. "Without radiocarbon dating, it would be difficult to say if it's truly as old as I imagine, but my gut says two or maybe even three hundred years old, judging by its fragility and the tell-tale hints in the ink. It could even be up to four hundred years old."

"Damn." Javed swung away, ignoring his second's searching glance. Celina had been right. This was indeed significant. Now they needed to find out what the book was. He glanced back. "Can you tell me what book this came from?" It was a vain hope, but he had to ask.

"Oh well, as to that, I can make an educated guess. It's from a study of the Lost Queen's Pyramids." He placed the sheet back into the box then sealed it. Next he stripped off the gloves and dropped them back into his briefcase. He grabbed a tablet device and tapped on it.

Javed waited in silence. "Yes. That would be correct. There are only six copies of that title left in existence. One is missing this particular page. I would say that is key to whatever you need to know."

The man stared at Javed, a question in his eyes. Javed rolled the known information over in his mind before he nodded. "These pyramids. They would have hieroglyphs?"

The professor beamed. "Oh yes. They are truly amazing. I visited there last summer with Professor Anderson. She's on staff with the university."

Javed moved reflexively. "She can read hieroglyphs? She's here, in town now?"

The professor stopped with a frown. "Yes. She can. And she is here on contract until the end of winter."

Javed ignored the question in the man's eyes. "Kharisma, make arrangements."

Her face tightened. "I'll get right onto it."

Celina stepped into the office, tiredness dragged at her, and she feared the confrontation to come. She shook and repressed the tears that threatened to fall. *Damn it. It's not fair!* She'd not done anything wrong. But the relationship that could grow between them couldn't happen, either. Bertha had told her that most of the nests forbade it because it was unfair to the Master. They had to watch those they loved wither and die. Such relationships had been outlawed because of how it negatively affected the vampires and nestlings.

In her whole life, she'd walked alone. Been unwanted.

Her parents hadn't even kept her, instead leaving her at some hospital like a superfluous package.

Things had just started to fall into place. She felt like she belonged here, but she didn't know if she could remain, seeing him every day. Wanting him. Unable to be with him. *It will be the cruelest form of torture imaginable.*

He waited, and in his eyes she could already see the smokiness of desire. She gulped and clasped her fingers tightly together. "I'm here, Master. Just like I promised." She damned the huskiness of her voice. How could she make him believe she didn't want this if she couldn't even control her own reactions? It left her feeling weary.

She pushed the door shut and waited for him to advance. He didn't. He kept the distance between them. She squirmed inside, wondering what he had planned. How would he react to what she had come to say?

All the phrases she'd carefully memorized and rehearsed fled. She stared, unable to tug away from his magnetic pull. Hunger flared, but she tamped it down. She shoved it into a corner of her mind to reflect on, in the empty years that stretched before her.

The force of her emotions crashed upon her. The pain of leaving and never seeing him again finally made sense. This wasn't a mild interlude. It had never been mild. Not even at the beginning.

This was bigger, all-consuming. She realized she'd fallen for this man. Her resolve quavered as she absorbed the blow, swaying for an instant before struggling to control her reactions.

"I won't let you go." His quiet words broke the spell.

Her eyes burned in response. As if he knew what she'd prepared herself to say. "You have to. We can't be together. You're a Master. I'm a nestling." Her heart shattered as she said the words aloud, "I won't let you suffer. I won't. It's wrong that for my happiness, you have to experience loss. I can't do that to you. To us." She advanced without thought. "I won't let you see me wither and die. You have to let me go."

Her voice splintered as tears dripped down her face and she noted the twin of her anguish on his, the flattened lips, and drawn face as he pulled her close. "We will find a way. Just believe in me. In us."

She shook her head and pushed against his chest. "Please let me go Javed. Please."

His eyes closed at the entreaty in her words. "There will be a way. I just need time."

She laughed even as she cried. "You have time. I don't."

"No. Those are old rules. We can make our own. New nest, new ways. Please don't do this to us, Celina. Please."

She squeezed her eyelids together. Her resolve weakened. "I don't..."

"Give me time. I'll find a way. I promise."

Her snicker was tense. "I don't want to leave. When I'm old you'll still be perfect, though. The man I..." She stopped short, swallowing the words that nearly escaped.

"I'll be the man you...? You didn't finish." His soft words lanced her, and the last ounce of will power seeped away.

"The man I love." She whispered as his mouth closed over hers.

He slid his hands beneath her legs and lifted her up to his chest. Her words, the fact *she loved him*, hammered into his brain, filled his chest to bursting point.

Javed had to show her just how much he wanted her. Needed her.

Emotion threatened to overwhelm him as he strode toward his

rooms. The passage of time seemed impossibly long as she curled into him. The tension wound itself tightly in his gut. But once within his quarters he kicked the door shut. He loosened his grip and she slid down his body. He hissed as she brushed past his urgent erection.

He devoured her in an open-mouthed kiss. Her taste left him heady as he feasted. He tugged at her clothes, the sound of ripping cloth filling the air.

He stopped and she gasped for air while he feasted on the sight before him. Her eyes, puffy with exhaustion were still watery and pink. Her face was flushed and her lips were swollen from his kiss. She was beautiful. He placed a shaking finger to her mouth, and she gazed at him, then sucked the digit within. She played the tip of her tongue over his fingertip while sparks flew within his body.

Her actions were so innocently erotic. Celina's hair had escaped the usual fastening and lay free around her shoulders. A red-gold cloud of silk and he wanted to reach for it. With a pop, he tugged his finger away.

Javed knew she found his intimate perusal of her arousing, so he let his attention roam. Her shirt lay on the floor, torn off in his urgency, so she wore only a white bra.

"Javed?"

"Shhhh..." Slowly he traced his fingertip over one of the straps, barely grazing her skin. The pulse point in her neck jumped and quivered like a mad thing, while he continued his slow caress. His body craved the taste of her, the essence of the woman in his grip exotic and alluring to Javed.

Her eyes closed and she moaned in the silence. His heartbeat sped up, but he refused to rush this time. He needed to show her how good it could be. What she would be walking away from.

With great care, he leaned forward, laying tiny kisses on her collarbone. She shivered beneath his touch as he stretched behind, finding the clasp. The bra opened, releasing her breasts. He cupped her, feeling the weight of them in his hands.

"So damn beautiful."

This time when he raised his eyes he observed the tinge of red that suffused her skin, the way her nipples had pebbled beneath his touch and the blaze of desire in her eyes. "Always mine."

She fumbled with his shirt, but he brushed her hands away. "Not yet. Soon my beauty."

Javed ran unsteady hands down her sides, his gentle caress leaving her arching beneath his ministrations. Down to her hips he slid, carefully skimming inward and back up to her ribs. Her skin was silky and smooth. He knew it tasted divine, and a flare of desire flashed within him again.

He slid his lips to hers, gentle and soft while she parted to allow him access to the moist cavern of her mouth. He told her wordlessly of his passion before pulling away.

"Javed!" Her needy cry sounded breathless.

Once more he caressed her breasts.

Her exquisite nipples were tight buds that he needed to taste. Javed didn't stint as he suckled, working them to tight beads.

Celina's breath came in gasps as she writhed beneath his caress. "I need to feel you, Javed."

He lifted his head and with a wordless movement shucked the shirt he wore and let it drop away.

She ran her fingers over the muscles of his chest, sliding over his sensitized flesh. For a moment or two he allowed it, before stopping her.

"Come with me." In the silence, he held out his hand, and she glanced from it to his face.

With a silent nod, she accepted the touch and followed him to the bedroom.

They entered the room and Javed started to strip off his pants and underwear, his gaze on her.

Her heart thudded madly as she fumbled with the snap and zipper before she slipped her jeans over her hips.

The scene felt surreal as they shed their remaining clothing in silence. She sat on the side of the bed removing her boots and sockettes quickly, while she avoided glancing at his engorged cock.

His smoldering focus burned her, as it roamed over her naked body. For an instant she wanted to cover her well-endowed flesh. He moved forward and her muscles weakened, loosening in readiness for his sensual assault. Deep within, she burned and melted. The need to touch and kiss him overwhelmed her.

"I want you Javed. I have since the first moment I saw you."

He smiled and she had to lick now dry lips. The emotion in his eyes was pure hunger. Her senses working overtime.

"As I have wanted you."

She made to stand, but he shook his head, instead taking one foot in his hand and raising it to the bed with slow measured actions. Then he did the same with the other. But this time, instead of letting her go, he kneaded the flesh then kissed along the bared inches of skin, hot carnal kisses that scorched her.

Her breath fled. "What are you doing to me?

Javed didn't answer. He continued kneading and kissing, moving down to her ankles. She discovered there were pleasure points she'd never before been aware of. Celina slumped back letting him explore while she twined her fingers in the sheets.

With great care and attention he found the back of her legs. Celina opened for him.

Unable to concentrate, she let her eyes flutter shut as he wove his sensual spell. He whispered words she couldn't understand. *"La asta-tee'a an a'aeesh bedonak."* She heard the emotion in them, and trembled.

A warm breath whispered over her intimate skin, and she ached unconsciously as he touched her. He parted her folds.

"Javed? Please!" Her broken cry must have spurred him on. He dipped his finger within. "Oh. Please!"

He slid against her, tightening the spell he wove around her. The precipice of orgasm loomed. The thrill of his touch, seeped deep into her pores. She moved wildly, ready for the flash of pleasure she knew was just out of reach. Then he stopped. "Not yet. *Nhabek.*" He watched her, taking control of her will. "Do you understand? I love you."

Celina sat up, pulling him to her. "I love you. I always will." Now as they kissed, there was desperation. They used their lips and he dipped his tongue within. He bit lightly while he worked his hands feverishly over slicked flesh.

She dug into his shoulders while he gripped her, lifting her in preparation before slumping to the mattress. Celina shifted, straddled him, more than ready for his penetration. She glanced at his heaving body lying beneath her, slid her hands down his pectorals to his trim waist. For an instant she stilled, and his stomach muscles clenched.

With a wicked grin she trailed her fingers down, found his cock and caressed it gently. Velvety softness covered his hard length. She shivered again.

"Ride me. Ride me fast and hard."

She eyed him hungrily before crawling her way up his body. His gaze settled on her breasts as they swung to and fro, feminine triumph filled her. With slow and careful motions she positioned herself above him. Inch by glorious inch, she lowered herself down.

He filled her.

The sensation of fullness amazed and awed her.

Her breath caught.

She started to rock, undulating over him. He caught her hips and dug hard fingers into her flesh, she covered them—let him guide her.

The heat that built deep inside roared to life.

"Oh God! Javed!"

The grip of his hands at her hips tightened as his thrusts became deeper. Faster. Wilder.

The sound of slapping flesh and the scent of sex permeated the air.

She couldn't breathe, her mind lost in the whirling vortex of sensation crashing around her.

Her body broke. She splintered and cried out.

He rocked faster, taking his pleasure as she held frozen, lost in the clasp of orgasm then he stilled. His shout loud in the near silence.

She fell into his arms, which closed around her.

EIGHTEEN

"You'll come with me?" He couched the words carefully and was rewarded with her confused look.

"Where to?" She lay on her back, her head turned toward him. She appeared like a siren, with her billowing hair fanning out on his pillow. Her lips still swollen from his kisses, and she'd tugged the sheet up to cover her nakedness in a very maidenly fashion. He fought and lost the urge to grin.

He realized he hadn't shared the information about the page. It left him light-headed. "Professor Junat met with Kharisma and myself tonight. He believes the paper is a page from a book dealing with the Lost Queen's Pyramids, and was going back to the University to check. It seems like I may have to pay a visit to Egypt."

She frowned but remained quiet as he continued.

"I had Kharisma chasing down a Professor Anderson, who is an expert with hieroglyphs from the same area as the book. She is with the University on a limited tenure. Hopefully we should be on our way within a day or two. We're running out of time."

She looked thoughtful and bit her lip. "I'd love to, but I don't have a passport or anything."

He laughed, which drew a questioning glance from her.

"You don't need a passport. As a member of a nest, you just need a letter of passage from myself and Cressida. We can arrange that this evening."

"Oh. Is that one of those 'reciprocal government arrangement things' vampires have with the human government?"

There is still so much she needs to learn about nests. It occurred to him that the basics of vampire government, their relationship with humans and rules were unknown to her. Perhaps, once things settled, he could ask someone to talk to her. School her in their ways. Maybe Kharisma? Or perhaps Hope?

"Yeah something like that." He cupped her face, marvelling at the softness of her skin. She leaned into his caress, nuzzling against his hand. Satisfaction filled him. The woman of his dreams was here, in his arms. *Perhaps the Gods are finally smiling on me. Maybe I can get this right.*

Sleepiness was creeping like a fog through his body and he dragged her close against him, snuggling her in the crook of his arm. "Now sleep, *houbi.*"

A soft giggle filled the air. "What does that mean?"

He snickered, about all he could manage in his restful state. "It means we should sleep."

"Not that. The other word. *Hoobee?*"

"It's *houbi,* and means *my love.*"

She became very still and quiet. He thought she might have drifted off to sleep. "Is that correct?" Her voice sounded strangled and not for the first time, he wished it was simple to deal with their relationship. Right now he wished they were both human so that these entanglements and restrictions between them disappeared. So they could be together freely.

"It is true. I do love you. *Bahebek.*"

She sighed, and he grimaced at the sound. "What's wrong with that?"

Celina rolled onto her side. "Saying the words doesn't fix this mess between us. All we can say for certain is at least one heart is likely to be broken." The despair in her voice clawed at his insides, stripping away his sense of well-being.

"I'll do anything to keep us together. You know that, don't you, Celina? Anything."

She nodded, snuffling a little, then yawned. He stroked her hair, realizing nothing could be done right now. "Sleep. We need rest and to be honest, I don't think we can fix any of this in one day. We have to find a way around it."

He'd already considered the simplest way to move forward with their problem and examined it. He could turn her. But there wasn't time to broach the subject, to explain everything. Not with them only having a week to find out the meaning of the prophecy. To have any hope of that option working, he would need her agreement.

Turning took planning and time. Long nights and days for the transition to take place. He would need to seek permission from the Council. She'd need to learn to deal with the hunger and training to feed without damaging a host, or killing them. No, it was better he consider all the pitfalls, find a time when they could discuss it logically. Calmly. Had time to gain her acceptance and approval.

He congratulated himself on his plan as he dozed off.

Professor Anderson turned out to be a wiry older woman, with a no-nonsense exterior. She was clad in old fashioned tweed suit and wore traditional metal rimmed glasses. She felt vaguely familiar to Celina, though as hard as she thought, she couldn't place her.

It could have been her turn of phrase or her piercing gaze. But even as she searched her memory, Javed ushered her up the stairs and into the private jet where it waited on the dark airstrip.

Celina shook her head as she took her seat. *Who knew that the Council had a jet for just these types of situations?*

She snorted at her private thoughts. Like she knew much about nests and the Council anyway. She still hadn't managed to get a handle on the *Conclave Paramount* and her responsibilities to them.

Her stomach wobbled a little as the young attendant came over to them and gave instructions about the belts, emergency situations and where to find all the amenities. She curled her fingers into the arms of her seat. The seats resembled large armchairs, but with seatbelts. The whine of engines filled the air, keeping her mind busy.

Javed frowned at her. "Are you okay?"

She felt like a fool now. "I've never flown before." She cringed at little, realizing her words must've surprised him.

He grinned at her, crinkling his eyes. *Obviously he'd not thought of that*, she assumed. "Then we'll have to make it memorable."

She chanced a look at Professor Anderson, but the woman was engrossed in some dry tome she'd brought with her. Celina blushed deeply, knowing what he meant.

"Uh, is it safe?" She leaned forward to whisper to Javed. "I mean... Can you actually do that on a plane? I've read about it." Her skin burned hotter, and she gulped.

"There's only one way to find out."

She was both scandalized and intrigued. "But what about...?" She indicated with her head to the professor.

"I don't think she'll be too worried."

"We shouldn't." Celina shook her head, and he beamed.

"Well if you're sure. Since we can now get up and walk about."

Celina glanced out the window. "We're in the air? When did that happen?"

"While we were talking." His tone was imbued with amusement.

She fumbled with the buckle and he reached over, placing his hand over hers. "Let me help." Javed lifted the clip and it released.

Celina breathed deeply, pushing away the ever present arousal. "Maybe you could show me about?" Breathlessness overtook her, but she was keen to see everything possible. He took her hand and indicated towards the back of the plane. The two bedrooms were comfortable but by no means luxurious. "I thought they'd be bigger."

He snorted "No. This isn't a status ride. It's more about getting us to places quickly and safely."

She understood what he meant. After all, they wouldn't want to be flying a commercial airline during the day. He'd burn to death, from what she understood.

A small meeting room sat at the very back, she noticed there was room for ten. "How do you fit that many in here?"

"We use it on the tarmac for meetings when we are visiting other zones. It gives us a neutral venue." Celina pondered his answer as they headed back to the main sitting area. The hostess was placing a platter of nibbles on the table for the humans and decanting a drink for Javed from a bottle.

"How long should the flight take?" She popped a small canapé into her mouth, savoring the taste. "Hmm. We should do this more often."

"Fly?"

"No. Get the food catered in."

Javed snickered at her comment as Professor Anderson wandered over to join them.

"I do hope I don't seem rude. I was doing some research on the site we will be visiting. It seems the tomb of a younger pharaoh's sister might be the one you are searching for. It's a little out of the way but has the most fascinating hieroglyphs."

She held the book out and Javed inspected the color plates. "I don't—"

"Not to worry, when we get there I can explain what you are seeing." Her tone was absent as she glanced back at the pictures.

Celina frowned. Something about the whole situation was skewed. A sense of uneasiness filled her, but she shrugged it away.

The flight wasn't long. They touched down several hours before dawn.

"Do we go straight there?" Celina's voice sounded strained, as they climbed into a waiting car.

Javed shook his head. "No. We don't have enough time. We're to be met by a guard from a local nest and they have arranged secure accommodation for us."

Celina stared at Professor Anderson. "Will she be staying with us?"

"Yes. But she will remain with the nestlings." She frowned but he smiled again. "I gave orders that you were to stay with me."

THE EVENING AIR WAS REDOLENT WITH SCENTS AND SOUNDS that called to Celina while Javed ushered her into the waiting vehicle. "We must hurry, the helicopter is waiting to take us to the location. We can be back on the plane and heading home before sunrise." His words were terse, and Celina noted the concern and worry on his face.

His meeting with the Master of the local nest had imparted information he wasn't happy about.

Celina shrugged. Not for the first time, she was glad she'd packed jeans and a cool shirt. The air was close, with heavy clouds building. If she didn't know better, a storm was brewing. It wasn't something she looked forward to in a helicopter.

"What if... What if there's a storm?"

Javed glanced out over the horizon. "Not yet. It's coming but a few hours away."

Their transport was dark and sleek, carrying a body of guards who immediately ushered the three into the center. The engines whined and whipped the sand up into the air. They donned helmets as they'd been instructed. Before she had even strapped in, the helicopter was lifting off the ground, moving over the desert sands.

"Javed, is everything okay?" She placed her hand on his. Fine lines of strain were evident around his mouth and eyes.

"Everything will be fine. There've just been some strangers seen around the pyramid in the last week. Abdullah had his people guarding it since we made contact."

His tone was dismissive, but after the intimacies she'd shared with him, she knew there was more to the story. It was clear he wasn't going to share his concerns. Whether it was because they were surrounded by others or another reason, she didn't want to consider.

So she waited in silence, twining her fingers around his as the Egyptian nestling brought the chopper down. She marvelled at the sites. The view illuminated by strong lighting awed her. She couldn't contain her gasp... "It's amazing."

He smiled at her. "Yes, I guess it is. I've been here before. Long ago."

She stared at him, surprised. "You've been here before? How long ago?"

This time his grin held little warmth. "Three hundred years, give or take."

She gulped. *Way to make a girl remember your age.*

Javed gripped her hands and they followed the human Professor and guards to a small entrance at the rear of the pyramid site. "We will go in this way. It's more private and it will take us directly to the room where Professor Anderson thinks we'll find the information we need."

"Why do you need the Professor to read it?"

He grunted, "Not all were taught to read during the time of this script, I have been told. Very few vampires were made. Of those who were, there was none of the nobility among their ranks. So the ability of reading the glyphs was lost to vampires and it has been these humans who've been able to decode what we will read."

Celina kept pace. They descended down a narrow stone stairway. She breathed deeply, staring at the walls which were marked here and there with what she assumed was a mix of ancient and more recent graffiti.

Once underground, the passage became a long corridor. It was well lit but unmarked, yet the Professor strode along the passage quickly. Her actions calmed some of Celina's nerves. She'd seen the amount of stone and sand above and thoughts of them crashing down on her head nearly overwhelmed her. *What would it be like buried in here?* She couldn't contain a shudder, though Javed queried her convulsive movement silently with a raised eyebrow, he said nothing.

They came to an entrance and the Professor stopped. "In here."

They entered a small, but ornately carved and painted room. The colors on the wall were still vibrant and Celina marvelled at the tones. When she gasped, the sound echoed.

Professor Anderson laughed, the sound reverberating. "Yes. Just as I remembered." She started with the north side first, scrutinizing everything carefully before shaking her head. "Not this one." She inspected the next surface just as carefully but, as before, she turned away. The third side stopped her.

The professor pointed to a single row of glyphs. "Here. This is where the secret is hidden." She sat down on the stone floor then took out a notepad and tablet device, before she began drawing the pictures and making notations.

Javed and Celina waited in silence as she kept working. The air grew close and a little dust filled the air. Celina felt excitement fill her, she wanted to ask what the professor had learned, but one quick glance at Javed, who silently shook his head, told her it wasn't the time or place. So she waited, scuffing at the sandy floors with her feet and listening to the sounds of scuttling bugs.

Eventually, the professor stood, dusted off her skirt and faced them. "I have what we need."

They hurried back through the corridors and up the stairs, along the sand and into the helicopter. It was only when they were back in the air that Celina had enough breath to ask, "Why are we hurrying? And what did she find?" She was tired and struggled to comprehend their actions.

"We can discuss it on the way home." His words were final and Celina frowned. Why come all this way, if not to learn what was written on the walls? But then, it really wasn't her place to ask, she reminded herself. Instead, Celina gave in to the tiredness that had dragged at her in the last few days. She placed her head on Javed's shoulder and dozed off.

JAVED FROWNED, CONCERNED BY THE EXHAUSTION HE COULD SEE on Celina's face. Deep blue bruising sat under her eyes, and the skin of her cheeks was chalky white. There wasn't much he could do right now, but when they got home he'd be sure to get Kharisma to check her over.

He turned away and headed for the cabin. Professor Anderson waited for him, her brow furrowed as he sat down opposite her. Every blind had been dropped to keep the sun out of the living area. He was uncomfortable travelling during the day, the primeval pull of sleep called, but he had things to do before he could curl around Celina's body and take his own rest.

"Have you discovered anything?" She glanced up, he felt a shimmer ripple through him. This woman had power, which he hadn't sensed before. For a moment the predator inside him roared. He pushed it back down and waited.

"Well, yes and no." With a single finger, the professor pushed the metal bridge of her glasses higher up before exhaling dramatically. "It depends on exactly what you want to know."

"I need to know where I can find the prophecy." He couldn't control the small hint of frustration.

She smiled. "Well, that's actually really simple." She turned the tablet device to face him. He realized she had photographed the carvings on the wall. "See this?" She pointed to a particularly long sample of glyphs.

"Yes."

"At the beginning there were four of them. *Four with the power of Gods. Four Gods the Egyptians bowed down to.*" He understood what she meant, but was unsure as to the importance of her words.

"There were also three women, High Priestesses, if you will. Filled with magic and knowledge. They came to the Princess, told her of their fears, but she was smitten by one of the Gods. Yet another wanted her."

She muttered again to herself as she peered down to the notebook, flicking through pages. "His name isn't clear. But what is, is that she rebuffed his advances. The Priestesses had warned the Princess, but she continued to ignore them, taking one of the others as her lover. He died. He was murdered before the child of their union could be born. There is no record of the fate of the child, only that it was born. It was a girl child. Here, we can see that the vengeful God came searching for her. He claimed that the child was evil and had to die. Unable to find the child, he killed the Princess. Tore out her throat and bathed in her blood."

The Professor shrugged, her face pale and his uneasiness grew.

"There is one small hint if you check here." She pointed to another spot. "There is a scroll, given to the strongest and oldest. It gives instructions on how to defeat the evil God. It was given to one of her protectors, placed there on the Princess's demand. Find that and you will find the truth. From what I am seeing here, that is the key to your prophecy."

Javed's mind whirled. The oldest. The strongest. That would now be Cressida. Their overlord, Gianna, had utilized her in the centuries past as her personal warrior and guard, until Cressida had petitioned for her own nest. No one was actually sure how old Cressida was. In fact, he wasn't even sure that was her original name. Over the years many vampires had changed their names to hide the fact that they didn't age. They just passed their items onto their heir, which was always them, in another guise.

He needed to contact Cressida, but she would be asleep. It was noon at home, he calculated, glancing at his watch. Right now there wasn't much else he could do.

He stood, and turned back to the sleeping cabin. He needed to think everything over.

"Professor, if you would excuse me. I will retire."

The professor inclined her head. "Of course. The daytime must be extremely draining for you."

He avoided her comment instead peering at her. "Please, make yourself comfortable. There is a sleeping room available for your use."

"Thank you, Master Javed, but I do not require that at this time. If I need anything, I will ask the stewardess."

He bowed low and left her.

He closed the door to the cabin where Celina slept, setting the security lock on it. Thoughts crowded his mind. A child was born. *The child of a God? Was there such a thing?* Eight hundred years ago he would have said yes. Back then his faith had been firm. He had never heard of *Vampires* or *Others*—just the scourge of the Christian Knights.

Over the years his fundamental beliefs had wavered and fallen away as he'd seen and participated in battle after battle. Each one stealing another bit of his soul until he'd felt empty inside.

He stripped off his clothes, folding them neatly and placing them on the chair in the corner. "Unlike the rest of my clothes since Celina came into my life." His lips quirked at the humor. Since Celina, his divested clothing ended on the floor a lot.

Javed lifted the sheet and crawled under, frowning once more. She didn't move. He reminded himself that he would talk to Kharisma about that. It felt unnatural. He tugged her closer, welcoming the warmth of her body and closed his eyes.

THE PLANE CIRCLED THE AIRSTRIP AS DUSK FELL. CELINA WAS pleased to be home. Travelling was exciting, but there was nothing quite like her own bed, especially when she was feeling as tired as now.

She smothered a yawn. "We'll head home first?"

Javed held her hand, and she shivered. He was a truly inventive lover. Her body still tingled from the way he'd woken her, his desire urgent. Her face flamed. She could see that he knew what she was thinking about, in the way his gaze settled on her body; the hooded desire was present. Her body had reacted as it always did, the pulse of passion beginning to throb once more. She saw the flare of his nostrils and knew he could smell her desire.

When he glanced away, she felt the break of the sensual connection between them. It left her feeling empty.

"Yes. There are things that need to be done before we head over to Cressida's estate. Papers that must be signed and I have a meeting with Daniel." He frowned a little. "He was very quick to transfer to the nest."

Celina snickered quietly. "Maybe the restrictions of other nests got in the way of his romantic inclinations?" Instead of lightening Javed's mood though, her words were met by a deeper frown .

The plane landed with a soft bump and Celina gazed out the window. The familiar sights of the city entranced her. "And so we're home." The air temperature in the cabin dipped. Her warm breath on the window fogged it up and she felt a childish urge to draw a heart. The thought passed quickly as she heard Javed unfasten his seat belt.

The plane taxied to a halt outside the large hangar and the Professor collected her bag. "It's been a fascinating trip, Master Javed. Celina, I hope we get to meet again someday."

The door was opened as the steps were wheeled into place. Celina clutched her bag on her shoulder. Javed squeezed her hand as she clambered down the metal stairs. The big, black car he seemed to prefer waited on the tarmac. She climbed in before him.

The trip to the nest was silent. Javed looked out the window. She didn't doubt there was a lot on his mind. He hadn't yet told her what conclusions Professor Anderson had come up with. Instead, she concentrated on the list of things Bertha had told her to practice.

In the last few days, each time she had searched for her magic, it had been pale and insubstantial. Her stomach jittered thinking that she might have somehow used it all up or damaged it. So much had occurred in a short period of time and she had no frame of reference.

They entered the grounds, sweeping up the pebbled drive and the house shone like a beacon in the dark night.

Groups of people milled around, arms waving urgently. It was clear something negative had occurred in their absence. She chanced a quick glance at Javed, his face was set in lines of anger as he leaned forward. His eyes shining the golden color she had learned to fear. "Javed?"

Her voice shook and she extended her hand toward him.

"Stay here."

The words were implacable—icy cold. She shivered.

He left the car and surged forward. Kharisma met him halfway, her face drawn. Celina gripped the arm of the car seat, wanting to be there. She needed to know what happened.

When Javed turned back, she saw an unfathomable emotion in his gaze. It captured her attention, freezing her bones. The news was bad. It was clear in the set of his shoulders.

Celina shook as he made his way toward her. She opened the door and climbed out. "What is it, Javed? What's wrong?"

His eyes were now full of sorrow, and she felt it like a punch in the gut. "I'm so sorry, Celina."

"What happened? Just tell me?" She gripped his arm painfully.

"Tonight the nest was attacked. Whoever it was, took Bertha." He swept Celina into his arms just as his words hit home.

Bertha! Her mentor and first friend in this new world. "How?"

"Someone rang. Whoever they were, pretended to be you. They said you needed her at the airport. It was just on dusk. They took her by force as she was heading for her car."

"No! That can't be true." She pulled away as denial coursed hot through her veins. "We have to find her. They can't have her. She's my friend."

"We will. We'll find her and bring her home." But no matter what Javed said now, Bertha was still gone. *In the hands of their enemies.*

NINETEEN

Anger boiled in his gut. One of his nestlings taken from her own home! It was unacceptable. He clutched Celina close to him and hustled her inside. No telling who remained out there, observing them.

Kharisma flanked Celina, her face hard and cold. Her eyes a burnished gold. He'd be willing to bet his were the same. Right now his hands itched to grasp his scimitar and gun.

"Do we have any clues yet?"

Kharisma shook her head, as she marched beside him.

"Not yet. I'm about to send a crew out. I've already contacted Xavier and Cressida. They too will put out feelers through their own channels."

Celina was crying silently. Once inside he cast a despairing glance at Kharisma. "I need you to check Celina."

"Javed, we need to find Bertha first. I'll see Celina later." The exasperation in her tone angered him. *Yes, we have to find Bertha, but right now we don't have another witch capable of any kind of warding. The witch who'd been injured at the gallery, had chosen to return to* her family. They would need to call on other nests again, *a wholly unacceptable situation*, he told himself.

"No. If we need wards, we need Celina to be able to erect them. There's something wrong with her." She was slumping in his arms. Fear coursed through him. *What if it's something serious?*

"Javed..." She spun on her heel, staring at him but she acquiesced, her face showing a pained acceptance of his request. "Fine. Come on Celina."

Celina let go of him and staggered. Kharisma flashed him a shocked glance. "What's wrong with her?" She grimaced and scooped Celina up in her arms. "All right, you go and I'll get her to the clinic."

Javed watched as she strode off. His stomach roiled and he felt torn. He had responsibilities to the nest, but his connection to Celina screamed that he should be with her as well.

He headed for his office. The phone rang as he settled in his seat. He picked up the call.

"Javed? Cressida here. What happened?" Her voice was calm. It settled him as he slumped in his office chair.

"Celina and I just arrived back from Egypt. As we drove to the nest, we could see everyone on the lawn. Kharisma informed me that the nest was attacked and the assailants took Bertha, our senior witch."

He searched the empty white walls, hoping for a hint of assurance that he was doing his job well. Responsibility rode him hard. "I wasn't here, Cressida." Everything inside him ached. *How can this happen?*

"Javed, it's the price we pay when we lead. You have done nothing improper. Indeed you were following the directive of the Council." She spoke soothingly, but a fierce gush of anger overflowed from him.

"I wasn't here. One of my nestlings is out there, somewhere. In the hands of someone who would rip her away from where she belongs. We don't even know what is happening to her. It's ...." He felt at a loss for words.

"That's what makes you a leader, Javed. You care. Now, I have my best teams looking. Can your other witch find her?"

He dropped his head to his hands. "She's sick. There's something wrong with her. Kharisma is checking her out now." He ran his fingers through his hair as he listened to the silence on the other end of the line.

"You're in a relationship with her?"

For a moment, he wanted to rage, but now wasn't the time and he tamped his reaction down. "Yes. I am." The silence drew out again. He scrubbed a hand across his aching eyes and glanced up as the door to his office opened.

"I'll send a witch over to you immediately. But Javed? You're going to have to make a decision. You know the consequences if you don't."

The line broke and he was left with the beeping. He replaced the phone in the cradle and turned to Kharisma as she reentered the room.

"I'm sorry to say, I'm about to add two more things to your plate." Her face was grave as she handed him a folder.

He took it and opened the sheet. "I don't get... Kharisma! Just tell me what the hell is going on."

"Turn to the next one, Javed." She waited as he opened to the page she requested.

"So?" He didn't have time for this right now.

"Read the report." She indicated to the papers and he frowned. *I have to read this now? Fine!*

"*... it is the view that this patient shares biological and DNA markers with Daniel Markham, lately of the House Godetski. It is clear, however that Albert Markham, father of Daniel Markham, is not the biological father of Celina. This finding is based on the lack of genetic markers.*" He stared up at Kharisma, more confused than ever. "What the hell does that mean?"

"It means that your Celina, is in all probability the half-sister of your new *Yeux Secondes*."

"Oh..." His brain seized with the information he'd just received.

"Yeah, my point exactly. The results only just arrived as I sat down to check her over."

"Is she okay?" He leaned in, needing to hear some positive news, but Kharisma shook her head.

"I don't think so. To be honest, it's almost as if she's starving. I'd guess at the very least her magic is waning because it's not being recharged."

"How..." He had to stop and close his eyes. He needed something positive right now. "How does she recharge her magic?"

The pounding in his head grew because he knew what she was about to say...

"Through sunlight. It's like she has a Vitamin D deficiency. She needs to be out during the day." He opened his eyes.

Daylight. When I can't protect her and only humans can be awake and outside.

Kharisma led Celina to the communal eating area.

Her knees shook violently. "I'm sorry to be such a pest. I honestly don't know what's happening to me. I'm not usually... I don't usually fall apart like this." She cringed at the wailing tones.

Kharisma helped her find a seat. "I'll grab you some water and food. Then we need to talk. There's a few things I need to discuss with you."

"Really? Can't you just tell me now?" She bit back the bubble of panic and hunted for her equilibrium.

"You need to eat, and I need to think over how to explain it."

Kharisma left her sitting at the table. Celina laid her head down on the molded table top as she closed her eyes. Exhaustion had overtaken her after the desperate spurt of adrenaline on hearing about

Bertha. Her eyes teared up again, as she remembered. "Oh God! Bertha, I wish you were here."

She blew her nose on the tissue crumpled in her hand then dashed away the tears that continued to course down her face. She wasn't a weakling. It was her physical condition that was causing this. She knew that, but hated it nonetheless.

Kharisma returned with a tray, loaded with water, juice and a sandwich. "You need to eat."

"I can't." She raised her tear-stained face to Kharisma, the woman who was well on her way to being her best female friend, apart from Bertha. The thought had her tearing up again, she moaned. "I'm not normally a watering pot. I'm not!"

Kharisma patted her hand. "I know you aren't. It's just your body getting cranky with you."

Celina let out a watery snort of a laugh. "Oh fabulous. I can't even laugh without sounding like a wet sponge!"

She dabbed at her face with a fresh tissue. Kharisma gave her a mock glower. She drank the juice slowly, her eyes scanning the people working. Everyone had a role to play right now. "I should be helping. I can ward..."

Kharisma's head shake stopped her in her tracks. "No. That's part of your problem. Eat and I'll explain."

Hunger had fled, but she knew she wouldn't get her answers until she did, so she took a bite, chewed the sandwich and swallowed, then repeated the action while Kharisma watched. "I know Bertha was working with you to find what fired your magic. Do you remember what she said?"

"Umm, Bertha said it was light that was my affinity. That was why, when I couldn't contain it, the lights blew around me first." Celina picked up the next sandwich and chewed while she thought over what she'd said. *Light. I've been inside for weeks. And when I'm awake, it's night. Unnatural light.*

"Your mind is ticking over. I can almost see it." Kharisma gave her a weak smile as Celina swallowed.

"I need natural light, don't I? That's what has caused this... this weakness, I suppose you'd call it."

She was rewarded with a nod. "So I need to go outside during the day. Well, that's simple enough." She smiled, but it faded as she noted the frown on Kharisma's face. "What?"

"Our nest is night focused. We have guards, but..." she turned away and Celina felt physically ill.

"Javed is a man of the night. My magic is of the day. They don't mix."

"Not easily, no."

If someone had driven a stake through her heart, it wouldn't hurt half as much. "So... So when do I have to leave?" She whispered the words.

"We can't arrange it right now. Not with the state we're in, but soon. It has to be, otherwise you will collapse totally. We need to make arrangements with the *Conclave Paramount* to find you an alternative home."

"Can I say goodbye to Javed?" The pain stole her breath.

"I don't know if that's wise."

Celina nodded. Kharisma was right, of course. But it didn't make the truth easier to accept.

Cold seeped into her pores, taking over her body. Her brain refused to think of any way to reject the information. It was frozen with the truth that she had to go away. *Far away. Never see Javed again.* The thoughts spiked through her brain.

She pushed from the table with a jerk. The chair fell to the ground. Celina ignored it and on shaky feet left the eating area. If she peered around, she'd see Kharisma watching after her. She'd probably also see pity. "I don't want pity."

Pushing past anyone in the way, she made for the lift, depressing the button when a hand caught her shoulder. Spinning her. She didn't know the older man, but recognized the emotion on his face —animosity.

"Where is she?"

"Sorry? I don't—"

The man loomed closer. "You're not... You're not her. You look like her. You act like her, and share some of her mannerisms. Where is she? Where is Farrah?"

"Wha. . ?" She wanted to run away. To tell the man to leave her alone. He was old and frail but his words harsh, just like the emotion in his eyes. Her head ached again and black bled into her vision.

No more! Please don't... Then she crumpled to the ground.

"WHAT THE HELL DID YOU THINK YOU WERE DOING?" JAVED couldn't contain the rage. Too much had happened in such a short time and now that Celina had collapsed, there was no way to stem the tide of rage that roiled in his belly.

"I told her that you were incompatible. She's day, and you're night. She needs daylight. You'll die in it. Who will protect her if she's out there on her own?"

Kharisma stood toe to toe with him. Celina was resting in his room, he'd been informed. He was thankful they had at least made it to his office before he exploded.

"That wasn't your decision to make! You're my second—"

"*And your friend.* You're tearing yourself apart. And in the process she is dying. You can't keep her like this. It's cruel to both of you."

He shook his head. "Do you think I don't know this? I thought I had time! I was going to ask her to change." He jerked away, needing space.

When he stared back at her, she seemed strained and shocked. "You never said!" There was accusation in her tone and he cringed.

"I didn't have to. It's between us. Something I can't and won't discuss with you."

Kharisma shook her head. "But you are going to kill her if you don't do something soon. Her body will shut down, organ by organ."

Her damning words stopped him cold. "That's not what I want. I just... I can't let her go. Not like this." He turned away and covered his eyes with one hand. "But I won't let her die either." His guts churned. "I don't know what to do, Kharisma. I just..." He shook his head, blinded by his fear. "In my head there's so much..."

Kharisma grabbed his hand. "You have to talk to her. You're almost out of time. You both need to make a decision and you need to do it tonight, my friend. Her body was weak when she came to us. She hadn't fully healed. Now it's under pressure again."

She left him there staring blindly into the corridor. How could he go back to her right now, knowing that his intractability was doing this to her? Kharisma had told him he had to make a decision. He hastened up the stairs and along the corridor, through the doorway and sat down beside the woman on the bed, twining his fingers through hers.

He noted the way her chest rose and fell, slowly, the red of her hair against her pale skin. The bruising beneath her eyes hurt him. The knowledge that he was the cause of them being there tore at him.

In his mind, he played over the vision of the woman he had first met. The exquisite curves of belly and breast. Her eyes had flashed fire and captured his attention. Now they were faded, as if her light was dimming.

She moved, her hand twitching just a little and he turned back to gaze into her eyes. They opened slowly. "Hi there."

"Hi, yourself." His heart beat a slow and steady rhythm. "We need to talk."

She pushed up carefully onto one elbow. "I think this has gone beyond that Javed. Everything Kharisma said is correct. I can't stay because I'm damaging your ability to think. It's time to let me go."

"I can't." He inhaled deeply. "I'll find a way. I just need some time." He knew he was pleading.

"You need to find me somewhere else to go. Once everything is settled..."

He hated the weak and strangled tone in her voice. Until they had everything under control he couldn't ask for anything else. When she changed he would need to be there with her. Right now his attention was splintered. He didn't like it, but he could send her to Hope and Xavier. They would protect her. Not a perfect outcome, but it was a temporary fix. One he could live with, in the short term.

"Kharisma said you weren't alone when you passed out. I'm thankful for that."

She groaned, her forehead creasing. "I don't know who it was, but they weren't at all impressed with me for some reason."

"You';re sure you don't know them?"

She shook her head, hair flying around her face. "No. It was a man."

Someone new in the house. Someone older. It could only be the father of his *Yeux Secondes*. "Are you well enough to rise?"

"Yeah. What are you thinking?" He lifted her against his chest.

"We need to talk to the man who scared you."

Celina was silent as he strode down the stairs and to his office. He entered the room and placed her down on a chair.

"I can walk you know."

He winced. "I know. But humor me."

She nodded and he picked up the phone, calling Daniel's room. "Daniel can you and your father please join me in my office?" He waited for the answer before hanging up.

Within minutes, the door opened and Daniel entered, followed by his father, Albert.

Albert's gaze flitted automatically to Celina. "You! Who are you?"

His voice chilled the air, Javed bristled. "She is a member of the nest. In good standing. If you have a problem with a nestling, you tell me."

The older man, with faded blue eyes and gray hair, must, at one point, have been tall and well built, but that had melted away leaving him spare framed. In his late sixties, he was stooped as if carrying the weight of the world.

"She looks just like Farrah. My wife."

He heard Celina's intake of breath. "But she isn't," Daniel spoke quietly.

"No. But you look like her." The tone was warmer just by mere degrees. "Do you know where she is?"

Celina huddled, as if lost, and he knew it was time to step in.

"Celina doesn't know. But she is related. She's your wife's child. She's Farrah's daughter, it's true." He challenged the older man in front of him to deny his words.

Albert's gaze burned with a cold fire. "She's not mine?"

"No. But she is your son's half-sister."

Celina wasn't in any way sure of how to deal with this latest problem. What the hell was she supposed to do with a bitter, angry and twisted man who just wanted to yell at her? And how had Javed come to by the knowledge of who her mother was?

"Look, I don't know what you are searching for, but this Farrah? I don't know her. I don't even know where you got the idea Daniel is any relation to me, Javed. I honestly don't want anything to do with this."

She rose on shaky legs, but Javed took her hand. "It's correct. He's your half-brother. The only reason we know that is because the blood tests came back. They always cross reference the DNA against existing nestlings, it seems. "

"Javed, I don't know anything about any of this. I just want to go. Please?"

She needed to escape the anger in Daniel's fathers face. She wanted to be somewhere quiet. Free of any upheaval, because, right now, it was too much. "I can't do any of this. I thought I could, but I need to get away. Please arrange somewhere now."

Javed blanched. "Fine. I'll have you transferred to Hope and Xavier's nest. But this isn't over."

She turned and made her way to the door, refused to look back. She had been out of her depth for as long as she'd been involved in the whole vampire world. She needed reality. *So why does my chest hurt so damn much?*

The walk to the lift felt like it took forever. By the time she arrived at the bedroom, the tears streamed once more, but this time they were of anger and betrayal. That Javed had kept this from her, hurt. If he'd kept *that* a secret, what else hadn't he told her?

She grabbed her bags from above the cupboard and threw them down on the bed, before she thrust clothing into the suitcase. Then she emptied the drawers and headed to the bathroom for her toiletries. She'd already got rid of everything that had no particular meaning to her. Her small stash of photos and books were still in storage, so she had little to pack.

She hurried through the door, seeing one of the men of the nest. "Joel, can you help me?" He gave a terse bob of his head, indicating his acceptance, though he looked surprised. He carried her bag downstairs and out to the car without a word.

Good thing Joel isn't a talker.

She was pleased no one intercepted her. A burst of adrenaline coursed through her system and gave her the boost she needed to keep going. But it would soon run out and she wanted to be far away from here when that happened.

For an instant, she regretted her outburst, but drew strength from the knowledge that the ordeal would soon be over.

She refused to consider that it might just be the beginning of the end for her. Once her bags were loaded into the car, she turned the key without a glance in the rear-view mirror.

Celina slewed onto the road and hadn't gone far when she was flagged down by another motorist. The woman seemed pale and lost as she waved madly for Celina to stop.

She pulled over and cautiously wound her window just a small way as a woman hurried in her direction.

"Can I help you?"

A bright flash of light flared and Celina fell into the darkness.

Javed paced the floor of his office after Celina left. He knew he should have told her, but he hadn't expected her angry response or the fact that she would leave the room.

His anger had telegraphed to Albert who settled into the seat heavily. "Forgive me Master, but... She looks so like Farrah. My wife..." He turned away, and for a moment Javed felt a seed of pity for the man. But it quickly dissipated.

"But, she's not. She is your wife's daughter, not yours." He saw Albert flinch, and almost instantly felt a flare of guilt at the man's reaction.

"She... Farrah took off when Daniel was only seven. I don't know where she went. She just left the nest abruptly one day and was never seen by anyone who knew her ever again." Albert leaned forward. "But you are sure she's not..."

A shake of his head had Daniels father releasing a sigh and Javed hardened his heart.

Albert had been willing to yell at Celina. Demand what she knew of Farrah. He would have taken his anger out on her for something she had nothing to do with. One thing she would always be totally innocent of.

"I didn't mean..." His words stopped, and Javed stood, anger radiating from him.

"No. But you were willing to blame her, even for an instant for being Farrah's daughter. I have asked Cressida for assistance in finding Farrah. If she turns up dead or alive, the researchers will find a record. But never again will you address this situation with Celina. She doesn't need the angst that goes with it."

In his mind, a whisper of doubt argued that he couldn't ask that of the man. Instead, he quelled the concern that came with his decision firmly.

Albert shrank back into his seat. "No, Master. You are right." His head hung low and Javed nodded. *Perhaps now I can find some way to salvage the situation with Celina when I'm done here. Offer that knowledge so she'll see I meant well.*

"Fine. Then if there is nothing else?"

As soon as Javed indicated there were no other issues, Albert stood and left the room. Javed breathed deeply before turning to Daniel, who waited, perched on the side of the couch. "Your father must earn his place in the nest, as does every other nestling."

Daniel had been silent during the earlier exchange but showed his agreement with a quick bob of his head. "I will make sure to discuss it with him."

Then he cleared his throat, and indicated the stack of files in front of him. He wasn't totally sure of his new *Yeux Secondes'* reaction to his announcement. He wasn't unmoved, but he also assumed a business-like manner quickly.

"If you have a few minutes, I'd like to talk to you about your proposal."

With a wave of his hand, Javed signalled towards the large meeting table and Daniel stood, making his way over and laying the files on the marble top.

His thoughts fractured for a moment and he inhaled deeply. Business had to come before pleasure, but for an instant he wondered where Celina was. What she was doing? How she was coping? Once the meeting wrapped up, he planned to go searching for her.

"I have quickly read through the reports you sent. To be honest another day or two to familiarize myself with the operations you are considering would be welcome. However, I have made some notes."

Daniel waited in silence, his face drawn and pale. But there was an air of determination about him. Daniel handed him a file, and Javed flicked through it, reading the detailed information his new *Yeux Secondes* had prepared. They included conceptual outlines, and the basics of a business model.

"In all honesty, do you see the ventures as viable?" The council may have allocated funds sufficient to seed his business idea, but he had to get it off the ground first.

It was up to him, and his nest to ensure that the business turned a profit as quickly as possible while ensuring its long term ability to provide for the nest.

"Yeah, I think a meat processing plant is a great idea. The added benefits of utilizing the blood products is, I believe, inspired."

Daniel glanced at him and for a moment he wondered what the nestling was thinking. "I am a little unsure about the concept of the Blood Sorbet dessert though. I can see that drinking blooded wine must get a bit wearing and while I can see the benefit in a Bloody Russian drink, I'm not so sure about some of the animal blood based products you are suggesting, but the majority I think will be financially rewarding. I'd like to run some modelling, once you have a sample of the products in hand."

Javed nodded. This kind of planning had always been the problem of the Master of whichever nest he had belonged. Now it was his.

At that moment, the door to his office was flung open and he spun, hand at his hip expecting an attack.

Kharisma stood there, her face red and tight. "She's gone Javed! Celina left while you were in the meeting. One of the nestlings just informed me."

He pushed away from the table, papers flying. "What do you mean?" He advanced and was nearly out the door when Kharisma caught him.

Her fingernails dug into the flesh of his upper arm. "She left. Packed her bags and took her car. I didn't know until too late." Her chest heaved, and her blue eyes swam. "But Javed? The guards found her car not far from here. I think..."

His heart stopped beating. Suffocating emptiness filled him. He didn't need to hear her words, because, inextricably, he already knew.

"I think she's been taken."

TWENTY

Dull lights shone overhead and Celina shivered in the cool air. She slumped against a cold metal wall, and the contact chilled her to the core.

She wondered how long she'd been out of it and where the hell she was. She tugged experimentally on her hands, but they were fastened tight; burned the skin of her wrists.

She was bound to a wall, and though she had some small amount of movement left and right, she couldn't escape the pervasive cold. The ache of her bones and screaming muscles warned her that she'd been here for some considerable length of time.

Celina bit back a moan.

Had they realized she was gone yet? Had anyone raised an alarm? For the first time, she realized that she'd been hasty in her flight from the nest.

A door slid open and she caught a flash of twilight sky, the dimming glow making her flinch, and her eyes sting.

Her sight cleared and she gasped at what stood before her: A hairy humanoid creature. It had a human-like head, sitting on a dark shaggy-dog body. Long misshapen legs traipsed towards her.

She shrank back. It reminded her of a monster from a nightmare. It twigged a long forgotten memory of her history classes. Anubis? That's who it reminded her of. *Of course, it couldn't be*, her mind screamed in denial. That was the stuff of mythology.

"Awake! Excellent, the Master will be satisfied with me again!" The high pitch screech made her want to cover her ears.

She tugged again on her bonds, but found there was no slack. "Where am I?"

The creature cackled. "In a safe place, of course. My master has been waiting to meet you."

What the... ? His Master? Who is his master, a vampire? Her head spun and her mind pounded out its rhythm. Celina's stomach revolted, she had to close her eyes against the sight. She breathed deeply, hoping the nausea would pass.

Footsteps echoed and she cracked one eye open. The creature had come closer, the stink of rotting flesh filled her nostrils and she tried to scoot backwards.

It crouched and for the first time she got a view of the teeth and the golden eyes.

"Oh God!" Fear left her mesmerized and unable to drag her wavering gaze from the sight before her, because that dog-like body had the eyes of a vampire. *Surely not?*

"Dear me. Do not be afraid, for I chose you as a gift to my master." It spoke with a heavy, odd accent. It reached out and grazed her arm with a single long claw. "But I think, first a taste." That claw sliced through her flesh and she cried out. Blood welled, rivulets dripping down her arm to her shoulder.

It sniffed the air cautiously then a long pink tongue peeked out of its mouth and slid over her skin.

Cold. Slimy. It's breath fetid.

"Please. No. Don't touch me." She whimpered, but the creature continued. Each pass of its long tongue pressed slightly harder.

The creature finally pulled away, but it was panting hard. Its eyes were glassy as if her reaction had excited it. The chill of the room together with her fear raised goosebumps.

The creature pushed at her clothing and she tried again to jerk away, tugging against her bonds and breathing heavily. "No. Please, no."

"So soft. And you taste so good." The mutter froze her insides, and she knew how this scenario would go. A thrum started echoing around her. She felt the fear bloom stronger than before.

"Let me go. Please." She panted and jerked but the rope cut off the blood flow in her hands. They quickly turned numb while she pushed at the creature with her feet, scrabbling away as it panted and lunged at her.

Adrenaline coursed wildly in her veins, giving her the strength to continue fighting. Celina managed a quick, awkward blow. Her heel hit a vital part, she was sure as it grunted and stilled.

Then it howled. The sound reverberated, and her hair stood on end. She could see the glaze of hunger and something else melt away, replaced by anger. "No..." Her scream of fear and fury mixed with the rapid spoken words by the creature. She couldn't understand most of them as they were spoken in some language she'd never heard before.

Celina had made the ultimate mistake, in leaving the nest, but she didn't want to pay with her life. *Magic! Maybe it will help me escape?*

She called on the power deep within. Celina reached for it desperately, in the hopes that she could make it release her. But only a thin trickle curled deep inside of her before it subsided. She gave an incoherent sob, searched again, but the harder she tried, the more the magic shrank away, and thinned in her mind.

The animal holding her prisoner breathed harder, its hot breath washing over her face as if excited by the tiny sliver of magic she'd managed to call forth.

Claws sank deep into her thigh. She screamed as pain careened through her. The creature tore at her clothing. Her thin trousers no match for the sharp nails resulting in shredded flesh. Agony stole her senses, and she tugged and twisted, while the warm blood spilled onto the floor.

"Let me go!" Her screams bounced and echoed as she thrashed madly. The creature fought to hold her. Each move accompanied by another flash of the on-going torture and the floor grew slick and wet. The scarlet ribbon of blood hideously bright against the dirty concrete floor.

She slid and slipped while the scent of copper wafted.

A mouth fastened over her leg, sucking at her, and she tried to twist, but weakness stole along her limbs. Her body began cooling and calming while the wild fluttering of her heart slowed.

Black dots invaded her vision.

This was it. Somewhere, deep in the recesses of her mind, she accepted these were her last moments being played out. She bitterly regretted the decision to leave without at least telling Javed goodbye.

"Javed!" Though she screamed the sound was little more than a whisper, and was lost in the greedy grunts of feeding.

His heart pounded. The long day stretched longer than a century ever could. He'd tossed over everything he'd said.

At each turn, he wondered where she was. Who had her? He'd even considered that she might not be alive, but each time the thought invaded, it nearly brought him to his knees. So he thrust it away.

He'd been unable to rest, while thoughts of her in a place unknown clawed at him.

His stomach turned into knots. He'd rung Cressida in a panic, knowing that he was trapped here until sunset, leaving him feeling like a caged lion that needed to hunt. Every human from every nest was pressed into service searching for Celina.

He mentally promised retribution to whoever had taken Celina.

"Everyone is looking for her, Javed. It's only a matter of time. Now we have found a likely location. One of our sources says there is a place, a little to the east of the gallery."

"Give me the details. As soon as we can, we'll be on our way."

His pen scratched across his notepad in jagged slashes. *The old section of town.* It made sense, He pinched the bridge of his nose while his blood pounded in his ears.

The instant sunset came he was out the door, his nestlings having prepared everything in readiness. He moved, his long legs in a swift distance eating stride while his mind cast over the plans he'd already laid in place.

The flying vehicle thrummed as he hurried inside. Kharisma climbed in beside him.

"We'll find her Javed. We'll get her back." Her hands covered his and he glared out the window, controlling his urge to throw her off.

He growled, unable to formulate the words as terror seized him. *What if I'm too late?*

The car rose into the sky, its engines screaming a vicious whine. He sat still, all the while his soul screamed at them to go faster. To find her, now!

He knew time was running out. Kharisma rubbed her hand up and down his arm, and he had to hold the flinch deep inside.

"Master, down there!" The driver pointed at a long building at the end of the street. Lights blazed but no smoke emitted from the old stack.

He nodded, unable to be sure that his voice wouldn't crack.

Their transport hit the asphalt with a thud and even before it stopped, he wrenched the door open.

"Slow down, Javed. You won't be helping her if you are injured trying to get to her."

His blood thrummed, but he nodded. *Kharisma was right, damn her!*

He hitched a breath, then another.

He turned in the direction of thudding footsteps as they caught his attention. "Master, this way." The young man stared at him, before pivoting. Javed bounded after him, toward a small industrial building.

A muffled scream tore through him and he careered, running faster than ever before. Between him and the sound was a door, but the heavy metal proved no defence as he let his inner predator loose. It screeched as he peeled the portal back, using every ounce of preternatural strength at his disposal.

"Let me go!" He heard the words and his blood fired to an incendiary point. She was alive, but the sound of struggle and the scent on the air told him she was in a desperate way.

Another door loomed. He backed up and rammed it, one shoulder taking the brunt. He didn't feel any pain as he rammed it again.

This time it groaned and snapped. The door buckled beneath his onslaught.

Once within he sniffed the air and followed the smell of copper. A small open doorway lay ahead and he stilled as he heard the near-silent words, "Javed!"

The creature attacking her was the one he'd seen before. It appeared to him like a cross between a werewolf and a human. He released an inhuman cry as he lurched forward. The animal or whatever it was jerked in his direction. Its eyes widened with shock.

His people hurried by, but he didn't notice them. All he saw was Celina, lying on the concrete.

Javed lost his taste for the fight. Half leaning on the wall she slumped, pale and still. Her lips tinged with blue and the beat of her heart was little more than a sluggish *ka-thud* followed by a stutter.

Blood pooled on the floor and ran in long ribbons across the concrete.

"Celina!" He called to her, voice hoarse with fear. He didn't remember moving or releasing her, just the hot trace of tears on his face as he cradled her broken body in his arms.

Near death, she barely breathed. He knelt in the pool of scarlet liquid. He'd seen how it congealed as it cooled.

He breathed deeply, knowing what he had to do. Dimly, he registered Kharisma's "Oh Javed! No!"

With slow deliberate motion, he extended one arm and allowed his teeth to descend. A nick of the artery would be enough. The razor sharp edge sliced through his flesh, calling forth a bubble of blood. He had to change her. "I have to do this, Celina. Heaven forgive me."

He hoped he wasn't too late.

TWENTY-ONE

Celina came to awareness slowly. The unrelenting pain that wracked her body melted away as she woke. She heard sounds. The soft shuffle of feet and voices in the distance impinged. Her throat now remained the only part that hurt. It was dry. Parched.

Thirst. So thirsty... She gave the sensation a name.

A touch broke her introspection and she opened her eyes.

Javed smiled, his face was drawn and pinched, but so beautiful to her. She noted the exquisite clarity of his complexion, the way his eyes sparkled.

"Where am I?"

He leaned forward thrusting a goblet into her hands as her rasp died away.

"Cressida's. Don't talk, just drink."

The scent of copper teased her nostrils. It smelled like the most delicious of nectars, and she glanced to Javed. "What is it?"

He made a moue of distress, and it twigged.

"It's blood, isn't it?" But no matter how much she might not want it, her body demanded the sustenance.

"Drink, Celina. Then we can talk."

She lifted the cup to her mouth, taking a cautious sip. It didn't taste as bad as she'd imagined, and she chanced another tentative taste of the thick liquid. Then she gulped, draining the goblet quickly before handing it back.

He took the goblet, turned and she studied his back. "What happened, Javed? The last I remember was that thing..." Horror filled her, her stomach revolted for a moment. She glanced away, eyes on the covers as she fought the nausea. Celina laid her palm over her belly, willing it to stop churning. One breath then another later she finally stared back at him. "It was... It was going to kill me, wasn't it?"

"Yes he was. He'd slashed you..." He broke off, spun around, and for a moment she was sure she heard him sob.

"Javed?" She put a hand on his arm. The crispness of the material covered the steely strength hidden below. He didn't turn around. "Javed, I'm here. You made me better somehow. Please?"

When he did finally turn, pink tinged of his eyes and told her of his pain. She moved closer, slipping one arm around his waist and laid her head against his chest. She was amazed at how much better she felt. No aches or pains existed where previously there had been horrific slashes. "Why am I naked?"

This time he pulled away and grinned, before breaking into a watery laugh. "Trust you to ask that question. By the time I got there, your clothes were shredded and there was so much blood." He stopped, faltering once more. "I had to turn you. You do understand, don't you?"

She nodded. "I do."

He inched towards the side of the bed. She shuffled over. One half of her mind rejoiced; now she was a vampire she wouldn't have to leave him. They could be together forever. The other half of her psyche raised its head in protest and she slammed the lid on her thoughts. What might-have-been's or nearly's had no place right now.

"So... What happens now?"

"That depends on you." His voice deepened as she leaned into him. Her gaze narrowed on his warm full lips, and she was suddenly hungry for his embrace.

Hot on the heels of that thought came a slashing pain at her mouth... "Ahh! What's happening?"

He grimaced. "Your teeth are descending for the first time." Javed dragged her close. "You will need to feed with them." A shudder slid through him and she felt it. "You need to feed from me."

His heart thrummed. The sound strangely reassuring as she considered his words.

"I... Um, I have to feed from you?" She sounded faint as if the thought hadn't occurred to her.

Her face had paled during their discussion. Then he leaned in. Javed watched her pupils narrow to pinpricks. Her focus was centered on somewhere beneath his mouth. He knew exactly what she was seeing, the hint of red that was his pulse racing beneath his skin. This time, as she shifted, he caught sight of her two very sharp teeth. Her hunger was growing. The sound of her heart beat sped up. He knew the adrenaline was coursing through her veins.

She panted, as her inner predator took control. He held out his wrist, knowing exactly what she needed. Exactly what the beast within demanded, right now.

She glanced at his face, and for a moment he caught a flash of fear before she bent. She slowly latched onto his wrist. Her tongue grazed the sensitive flesh, and his body hardened under the onslaught of sensations. "Feed, Celina."

He sat still while she pushed her wickedly sharp teeth through his skin. Then he was caught up in the web of ecstasy.

She moaned as she fed, his body already aroused had him holding onto the thin thread of restraint that remained.

He jerked away and she reached again. "More?" Celina licked her lips, catching the last droplets of blood.

He shook his head. How could he trust his voice when his body screamed from intolerable frustration?

He gasped as she touched his chest, her hand fluttering like the touch of a butterfly's wing. "Please Javed?"

He took her wrist, her skin as soft as that of a peach. Javed allowed his incisors to slide through her skin before drinking from her. He prepared for the final act that would seal them together forever, as Master and vampire. He took a sip then another before he raised his head. Her blood was heady, full and rich, just like she was.

With a single firm motion, he lifted up, taking her mouth, and she met him. The kiss was voracious.

His body reacted, firing up. He wanted her. Needed her. Hungered for her.

The predator deep inside roared its approval, bringing Javed back to himself. He wrenched away, panting heavily.

She mewled and he closed his eyes. He breathed in and out, in a vain attempt to settle his body, which clamored for more.

"Javed?"

I had to pull back. He sent the words to her, watching as she opened her eyes in confusion.

"What did you just do?" Her voice rose slightly. Not an octave, but he knew she wasn't exactly happy.

I am your sire. Your Master. When I fed from you and you from me... When our blood combined... I sealed our ability to communicate like this.

"You what?" She pushed back. Away.

Javed winced.

"No. No way..." Her face was stormy. Anger evident in her tone. Her eyes shone with what he was sure was hurt. The emotion bloomed inside his chest. "You did this with all..." She broke off and turned her head away.

"No! Celina, I have never done that with anyone else. Not even with my sire. Only the strongest of *connections* allows us..."

He was making a mess of his explanation and his stomach

curdled. *Should I have given her a chance to say no?* But the truth was, he had needed the final bond and taken it.

Hurt flashed through Celina. *Has he done this before? With others?* The inherent intimacy both excited and repulsed her.

Celina?

She heard his voice inside her head. The hunger that had filled her evaporated. She knew he'd had a relationship with Kharisma. *Had they...?* She tried to turn away from the thought, but it lay there, tantalizing her. "Did you... Did you share this with Kharisma?"

No! Believe me Celina. I have never wanted to share this with anyone else. Ever! Only you.

Javed's voice sounded sincere and heaven knows she wanted to trust him. She wanted to trust everything he said. But her mind swirled madly.

Please Celina. If you doubt what I'm telling you, ask Cressida. She is the only other one I can communicate with.

She reared back. "What? How many... No, don't tell me!" *Cressida? He'd shared this bond with her too?* She felt like some damned groupie and she wouldn't settle for that. She jerked away, tugged on the sheets. *No, God damn it! I'm my own person.*

"Stop!" His words forced her into stillness.

"What?" She turned to him and knew he saw the belligerence in the way she held herself. But that was a brittle veneer as hurt and shame filled her. What they had wasn't special enough to him. *No, he'd shared this gift with other women.*

"No." Javed's spoke the words and confusion filled her.

She scowled. "Don't move? I am allowed some freedom, *Master*." She used the word as an insult and saw the way he flinched.

Then he leaned in. "I've only shared it with Cressida and the councillors because of the investiture. Before that, I didn't have the ability."

Her stomach wobbled at his words. *Could it possibly be true? Am I building a mountain out of a molehill?*

Confusion overwhelmed her and she dropped her head to her hands. "Why? Why am I so unsure?" She whispered, not expecting any answer.

"Because I've made so many mistakes. Celina please. Let me show you our world."

She gulped as the sting of tears burned her eyes. "I want to... But I'm so afraid." A quick shake of her head flicked her hair around. "I've finally found somewhere I belong. I don't... I don't want to lose that. I don't want to lose you."

He wound his hands around her waist, pulling her closer. This time the shiver was caused by the desire running thick and hot through her veins.

"I've done this all so wrong."

"We both have." Her voice rasped as heat suffused her. "But... I think we can start again. Please?"

Her mind whispered that any relationship between them was a figment of her imagination. She might love him, but his feelings? She wasn't quite so sure. He'd said he loved her, but only in the heat of passion, and heaven knew, men said a lot of things when they were getting what they wanted. Or so she'd been told.

She banished the negative thoughts, instead, she turned to him, met his embrace. Accepted what he offered.

His lips felt firm against hers and she opened wide. Her body fired like tinder in a blaze and the heat was upon her.

She was hungry, urgent as his touch became surer. She felt hot, as arousal prepared her body for him, her core melting again. Their hearts beat in time, while pleasure spiked with each new touch.

Celina twined her body around his. He skated his hands over her skin.

She tore at the covering he wore, please to see it was little more than a robe.

She touched bare satiny flesh.

Javed jerked back. "Are you sure?"

"I've never been surer of anything."

He gave a gentle push, then she was on her back, resting her head on a pillow as he crawled up beside her. He tugged away the covers to bare her skin.

Now there were no words—nothing to impinge on their private world, except the sound of sighs and flesh on flesh in the silence.

He kissed his way over her collarbone. "The first moment I saw you... I was aware of you on that sidewalk. I wanted you even then."

Her breath caught, strangling her as he feathered his lips lower, to find a nipple. It was already distended and ready for his caress. He suckled lightly, running his tongue over the beaded tip.

His teeth descended just a short way, and he slid them into her flesh. The feeling of heat and pleasure shot through her. Zinging arousal raced from tip to core and back again. Nerves quivered and rippled and she clenched hard, as orgasm rolled deep within.

"Oh!" She arched up, wanting more.

He lifted his head. *No one will ever love you the way I do.* Her mind splintered under the onslaught.

He used his clever and wicked fingers, fondling the curve of her belly. Carefully he found the nub at her very center and touched it. Already sensitive she shuddered under the onslaught.

Celina wrapped her fingers around his shoulders and shoved. Hard. He rolled, hands catching at her hips and he pulled her with him. "I don't have any patience tonight. I want you. All of you." He grinned.

Their loving was wicked.

It was hot.

Surveying the golden flesh arrayed before her, she debated for a second where to begin.

His gorgeous pectorals caught her eye and she shifted in his direction, her breasts swinging with her movements. She found one berry brown nipple and tweaked it with two fingers. It sprang up, ready for her and she leaned forward, sucking the tiny tip into her mouth, running the point of her tongue over the tiny nub. She wrapped one of her arms around his waist, just below his ribs. She skimmed the fingers of her other hand over the silky bared flesh of his chest.

He slid his fingers into her hair, grabbing her tresses and twining them in the strands, while he pulled at her.

Celina tutted. "Not yet, lover boy."

She slid her way down his body, gazing at him from below her lashes as he thrashed beneath her careful touches. Down past his firm belly and trim waist, finding the hair on his legs before tracing her way back up. His hips jerked as she circled his erection with her fingers. He was firm and hot. Celina swiped her tongue over the rounded head, the slit weeping a small droplet. She licked it up. *Hmm, salty.*

His hiss filled the air, and she smiled before slowly closing her lips around his erect length. Her long draws a parody of his suckling at her breast.

Celina burned but kept up the sensual torture until he stilled her with shaking hands.

"No more. Not like that." With one firm haul he jerked her up, slanting her mouth over his as he positioned her above his cock. She was slick and ready when he slowly penetrated, the sliding sensation eased by her moisture.

Her core stretched to accommodate him and she whimpered at the sensation of fullness. The friction toyed with her senses and he pushed up—hard and urgent.

Javed cupped her breasts, toying with her nipples, plucking and tweaking while she arched and cried out. She opened her mind, wanting him to know how much pleasure he wrought on her. The pace increased and the beat of her heart reached fever pitch.

Together, they rocked faster in the most intimate dance of all.

One last thrust was all it took. She cried out, eyes closed as her orgasm crashed through her senses. Their cries mingled. Then they stilled, holding onto each other.

TWENTY-TWO

Attar stalked from one end of the cavern to the other. He was ready to leave his stony tomb, but he was no fool. He needed Jelani to show him how to survive in this new age. After all, the last time he'd hibernated much had changed. That had been a single century. This time three had passed.

He growled low in his throat. A scuttle sounded followed by a sobbing hiccup.

He spun around to see his servant, Jelani slunk through the stone entrance. "Master, I bring information."

He bowed low, but Attar could see something had happened, something he tried to hide. Obviously Jelani had lived too long without him to oversee his actions. He would soon become a liability. "What news?"

Jelani shoved a large woman to the floor in front of him. "I have found one of the descendants, Master." The words filled Attar with elation. Finally, he could carry out his mother's decree on his sibling's progeny.

"This one? She is not one of the descendants. I cannot feel the power that they would carry in their veins." Anger filled him, and Jelani quaked.

"No, Master. But she knows where one is." Even as triumph filled him, Attar stilled. He could not afford to be cocky. He had been thwarted before. In the past, he had come close. But all three needed to be destroyed for him to mete out justice.

"And?"

Jelani scuttled away, and Attar advanced.

"Master, this one knows the red-haired girl." He indicated the cowering woman, the ripe stench of fear clung to her body. He shifted away, from her, her very presence offending his nature.

"What do you suggest I do with her?"

The tension in Jelani dissipated, and Attar watched him, wondering what infraction he'd committed, to have him skulking in this manner.

"Master, I could find out more about the nest that shelters her."

He wanted to query his servant's manner, but right now the woman had taken the opportunity to creep some distance as if to escape. He pounced, catching her with one hand. She cried out, Attar smiled.

He flicked her away with a casual wave of his hand. "Fine. But do not kill her until I am ready to feed. It would not do to be hasty." Jelani bowed low and Attar got an impression of fear and relief. His servant grabbed the woman's hand and made to tow her from the room.

"But... " Jelani stopped.

Attar had to contain the grin that nearly spread across his face. "You have done something you may or may not regret. I will know soon." Now fear emanated from his servant as well. It wouldn't do for Jelani to be too sure of himself. After all, he was still a servant. *Replaceable.*

The quiet "Yes Master," filtered through the air.

"And one more thing."

This time, Jelani did not turn back to him, though Attar could see his rigid stance. "Yes Master?"

"You may bring me my sustenance now."

With that Jelani forced the openly sobbing woman from the underground grotto.

Yes, it was definitely time for him to leave these walls and venture aboveground.

TWENTY-THREE

Javed held Celina close. Their lovemaking had been wild
and uninhibited.

Javed? Her tone was unsure, weak even, but he grinned.

Thank you, once more. He gazed into her eyes, marvelling at the bright emerald green. *We should rise.*

What time is it? With each thought she directed at him, her voice strengthened, and he smiled.

"Well after sunset. Cressida will be awaiting you downstairs."

Celina huffed and made to rise, but he reached over and caught her against him. Kissed her. The contact was scorching hot, at the end they were both aroused. "Cressida will demand you make an oath of allegiance."

Her glance was questioning. "Why? Didn't I do that at the investiture? Why do I have to do it again?"

"It is a way of showing that you will be true to our laws." She agreed, but he wasn't sure she understood. How could she? She had no history with vampires. She'd received none of the induction prospective vampires received.

"There is so much you need to learn. I really don't know what you understand or don't." Only now was it evident that he'd been hell bent on forming this union that he hadn't done the right thing.

He hadn't told her enough to allow her to make an informed decision. His pride stung, but the truth was, though he'd changed her to save her, he'd made no attempt to explain their rules and responsibilities in the weeks they'd been together. He damned himself for that now.

"While you dress, I'll give you a rundown of our rules. They are few but none are negotiable."

Celina looked at him stricken. "But Javed... What am I supposed to do for clothing?" She seemed genuinely concerned, even when he started laughing. Now she appeared upset and angry.

"I had Kharisma pack clothing for you, while you were unconscious. She brought them here." He indicated the large walk-in wardrobe.

She flushed. "Why didn't you just take me back to the nest?"

For a moment, he was surprised by her question, but he shrugged. "Cressida's was closer, and time was a vital commodity."

Celina stalked to the door and peered in, but instead of the wardrobe, she'd found the bathroom. "Maybe...?"

"Sure. That will give me more time to explain things to you." He followed her into the too large room, dragging on his clothing. Then he leaned back against the counter while she showered.

The water sluiced down her lush curves, the same ones he'd laved, and there was the familiar tightening at his groin. *Would it always be like this? Will I always experience the instant flash of desire when she's around?*

"So go on, you haven't explained anything yet." Her voice was peevish and he grinned. His woman didn't like to be kept waiting.

"As with any government, there are layers in our world. You know a little of the Council, having observed the investiture. They handle the day-to-day governing of our nests and the justice for our continent. We have one Overlord on each continent and the head of the Council acts as an adviser to the Overlord. Our Overlord is Gianna and Cressida is the head of our Council."

"Yeah, so what does that have to do with anything?" He waited as she ducked her hair under the spray, displaying her rounded buttocks. His body heated again and he closed his eyes, concentrating on settling the mad pumping of blood through his veins, willing his body to relax.

Did that help? Amusement? He cracked his eyes open to see her peering at him, a broad grin on her face.

"Not really," Javed muttered.

She turned off the spigot and climbed out, her red hair plastered against her alabaster curves. He swallowed, then handed her a towel before he turned away. The mirror in front of him showed her movements, and he gritted his teeth.

She snickered. *You probably shouldn't have followed me in here, then. Should you?*

He rolled his eyes and opened the walk-in wardrobe door for her as she strolled, naked, into the bedroom. *So young, yet already full of sassy attitude.* He wouldn't have her any other way.

"I...uh, put all your clothes here." He indicated the top drawers and the few hangers. The clothing consisted of jeans and light blouses. She laughed as she tugged the underwear from the drawer.

"So, go on."

He breathed deeply, trying to clear the fog from his brain. "Each nest has a Master or Mistress to whom all other vampires are either placed as guards or staff. We are only allocated so many new vampires, or changelings, each year. Our nest was not allocated any, however, Cressida gave me a dispensation after..." His voice trailed away.

"After what, Javed?"

"After I told her I couldn't... After I turned you." He gazed at her.

She stilled, her eyes shadowed. "What do you mean?"

He frowned, unsure how to declare his emotions to her. "I love

you, Celina. I was going to raise this once everything settled. But..."
He turned away, unsure how to continue.

"Well, it's about damned time you told me then. Because, I honestly didn't know what you wanted, you dumb man." She stalked over to him, dressed in only bra and panties, flinging her arms around his neck and kissing him thoroughly enough to leave him light headed.

"You'd told me you loved me in bed, but it's kind of hard for a girl to know if that's honest emotion or just lust. And you never once mentioned a possible future for us. You just kept saying you wouldn't let me go. It's not quite the same, you know."

He blushed, a deep hot hue before she tugged away. "Now keep talking."

He closed his eyes, gathered his scattered wits and continued. "There are two kinds of vampires. Those attached to a nest and those considered rogues. The untrustworthy and unaffiliated, who sell their skills and abilities to the highest bidder. We also don't feed off the public at large, unlike rogues. There are easier ways to fulfil our needs."

She nodded slowly. "Okay so 'nested' don't feed off humans, and rogue do feed off humans. So far, that all makes sense."

"We also never take the death drop. To do that is to call the demon that exists within us to the surface. If we must feed directly, we only take what is required. Most of us now only drink decanted blood mixed with wine."

"So, in short. We live in nests, are civilized and drink wine mixed with blood. The others, the Rogues feed direct from humans and will drink to the dead drop, whatever that is."

He laughed before sobering up. "The death drop. The very last drop within the human body."

"Ewww!" She tugged the denim over her hips and pulled on the shirt she'd grabbed from the hanger. "Thank heavens I don't have to feed like that."

THE SHORT WALK DOWN THE HALL WAS A BIT LIKE STEPPING back in time. For all the bravado she'd put on, she still had another major hurdle ahead of her. *What if Cressida is unimpressed? What if she says no?*

Celina's knees wobbled as she made her way over the ceramic tiling to the statuesque blonde who waited below.

"It's nice to finally meet you properly, Celina."

Celina bobbed her head nervously at the Councillor's words. *What am I supposed to call her?*

"Councillor Cressida, it is a pleasure." Javed took the Councillor's hand, and Celina seethed for a moment until she saw the laughter in their eyes.

"It's okay Celina. Councillor Cressida will be fine. But Masters or Mistresses and their partners usually just call me Cressida." She waved her arm towards a finely carved seat and indicated they should sit.

Celina lowered herself to a chair and waited.

"So, Javed. Have you had time to explain our world to Celina?"

"There is much she doesn't know, but I've explained about the hierarchy and rogues."

Cressida scowled for a moment before speaking again. "Well, we don't have the luxury of time. It has to be done now. Celina are you ready to take the oath? Knowing that there is still much to learn?"

Her stomach tumbled and yawed but now she understood some, she was sure the rest would come. She gave a cautious nod. "I think so."

Cressida stared at her. "You must be very sure, because if you aren't then you will still be bound, forever. This isn't something to be taken lightly or without careful consideration."

Celina cast a questioning look at Javed.

I will help you.

"Yes."

"Then hold out your hand, Celina. Can you and will you uphold our hierarchy, our way of life and our commitment to the common goal of a peaceful existence? Will you give your future service to those who would guide and protect you? Will you give your life for your brother and sister vampires, and for the protection of the nest you are assigned to?" She chanted the words as if she had memorized them while a scent filled the air.

Vanilla.

Celina's body jerked as an electric shock passed through her. She gasped.

"Will you, Celina?" She stared into Cressida's eyes, noting a swirling pattern deep within.

"Yes. I will and I do." The air around them skittered and her skin itched a little. "What was that?"

Cressida winked. "I'll let Javed explain it all later. But right now, we should get the other things done. Tomorrow is the full moon and we have nearly run out of time." Cressida turned to Javed. "So, what do you know?"

Javed ran a hand over his face and Celina noticed the fine shake, the lines of weariness. "Professor Anderson has been working on the information she found in the glyphs on the tomb wall." He shook his head, "I have a copy of her email here in my pocket."

He pulled it out and started to read. "I need to ask about a scroll. I can't find very much information, but my investigations tell me, it holds the answers to defeating the evil God. A guardian was charged to protect the princess and her offspring. When the evil one became aware that this information existed, I have learned, the guards were divided and later slain when the princess raised concerns regarding the safety of the child. The mother too was slaughtered, and the child disappeared. What I have gleaned is that the Princess's personal guard escaped and kept the scroll, hid it and their descendants ensured its safety. Where the child went, remains a mystery. I believe the scroll holds the key to both questions."

Cressida blanched. "Oh..." She stood and turned away, wiping her hands over her black pants. "Oh dear. Well, I'd say this necessitates a visit to the vault." She stumbled over the words and Celina wondered what could make this woman so concerned.

"You both should stay here. It's not something..." Cressida blinked suddenly. "Damn, I hate it when she does that." She cleared her throat noisily. "Gianna is rather unhappy. She has told me of her plans to visit the Council and nests."

Javed stood and stalked towards Cressida. "You have our support." Cressida nodded absently, placing her hand on Javed's.

"I know, Javed." Her decisive nod indicated the moment of uncertainty had passed. "Now, you must wait here. I have to go to the vault. I think I know what you're looking for."

Cressida spun on her heel and Celina gazed at Javed as the sound of footsteps died away.

CRESSIDA RETURNED AN HOUR OR SO AFTER SHE'D LEFT. HER face pale, but she waved away his query. In her hand was a large pot. The elaborate decorations in dark browns and blacks reminded him of Greek antiquities that he'd seen unearthed.

"Cressida?"

She turned to stare at him, her blonde hair moving fitfully in the night breeze. "I need to open this." Her fingers curved gracefully, and for a moment she allowed her nails to sharpen and lengthen to claws. With great care, she inserted, first one then another into the old cork stopper and with a small tug she pulled it free.

Celina gripped his hand as he peered within.

What can you see?

He nearly snickered at her demand. *Just a rolled up piece of parchment.*

In the silence, Cressida gripped the old dry paper and lifted it. "This was entrusted to me decades ago. I have always kept it in a vault, at Gianna's request. Now..." She stopped, carefully laying it on the sheaf of acid free paper she had demanded be laid out. "I think it would be best to have Professor Anderson here, when we unroll it."

Javed gripped his phone, flipping to a social media site. "I believe Professor Anderson is awake now." He handed it to Cressida who peered at the screen.

"Ring her then." She held herself tense and he wondered at the implications of Cressida's actions.

He dialled, the phone rang three times.

"Hello?"

He heard the bleary tones and felt a moment of guilt before brushing it aside. "Professor Anderson. It's Javed. I was wondering if you would be willing to come and do an urgent reading on a scroll." He gripped the handle, aware of the seam in the plastic device and the way it bit into his flesh.

"Oh, Master Javed! Uh, yes, I can do that... I might take a while to get there."

He frowned at the scattered tones of her answer. It must be tonight." A long silence was punctuated only by the sound of her breath over the line.

"Of course, it's just that..."

"Yes?" He gripped the phone harder to his ear and ignored the glance Celina and Cressida shot his way.

"Can you send someone for me?"

"Of course." He exhaled, placed the handle in the cradle then turned. "I need to send someone for her."

He strode out from the room.

Idris was there, melting out of the shadows and Javed felt a moment of shock at the man's presence. "Yes, Master Javed?"

"Send a car for Professor Anderson straight away. We have found what we seek."

He caught the glint of satisfaction in Idris' eyes before he turned on his heels and was gone.

So close! Find the clue and unravel the mystery. His stomach churned, the movement heavy in his gut. It had all seemed so easy at the investiture.

Still very ill at ease, he headed back to the room where Cressida and Celina waited. Now they had taken seats.

"Something has changed lately. First the attack on Hope and Xavier and now this. I wish we knew what was going on."

He shot Cressida a searching glance, which she returned. "I don't know Javed. But you're right. There has been a change. One that I will raise with Gianna when she arrives."

"When is that likely to happen?" Celina slipped her fingers into his grasp. They fluttered like the wings of a hummingbird.

"Soon, Celina. I can't tell you when, just that it will happen soon. Gianna is the most responsive overlord vampires have ever had. While no one is quite sure how old she is, it is accepted that no one remembers a time when she didn't exist. But that also means I can't tell how long her 'soon' will be, as her grasp of time is different from ours." Cressida leaned back into her chair and closed her eyes. For the first time, Javed got the impression of tiredness. Something he had never seen her show before.

In silence they waited, the ticking of a clock indicating the passage of time.

The sound of an engine filled the air and they stood as voices and footsteps heralded an arrival.

"Master Javed, Councillor Cressida, Celina." Professor Anderson stood before them, dark smudges under her eyes and clothing rumpled. "The umm... The scroll?"

Cressida indicated the table and Professor Anderson drew white gloves from her pocket before she spread the parchment out.

She glanced up, shock on her face.

"This... This document talks about the existence of the First Ones."

Shock rocketed through Javed's system. *The First Ones? The ones who made the first vampires?*

"See, here is the story of the princess." She pointed to the glyphs. "And here is the prophecy that you spoke of, Master Javed."

She dragged her small tablet device from her bag then opened a screen, making notations. Some words left her humming, but she worked quickly.

Time ebbed and flowed. They paced and watched as the professor worked in silence.

"Right. Here it is. Thankfully it was written in a language common during their time, and preserved." They converged on the table, all eyes on the single human in the room.

"Witchling young, power unknown
A bold partner to a throne
The one of blood who embraces night
These three alone can make it right

Late one night as moon is bidden
A treasure found one most forbidden
The evil rises to banish light
And now to them evil shows its might

Three as one and three united
Strength from partners uninvite
And when the battle it is done
A curse is lifted for all bar one."

Javed grunted. "What does that all mean?"

"You must find the third partnership. They alone can save us from whatever is coming our way." Cressida muttered.

"The three?" Javed spoke sharply and Professor Anderson blushed.

"That is what I would also assume, based on what I have read, of course."

"The first two are...?" Javed eyed the woman.

"I believe it would be Hope and Xavier, yourself Javed, joined of course, by Celina."

Javed slumped down on the seat, his hand sliding over his eyes. *What more could possibly happen?*

TWENTY-FOUR

This time when Celina woke, it was in Javed's arms. *Good evening.* She wasn't sure how long it would take to get used to talking to him this way, but waking in his arms was sheer bliss.

She nestled for a moment, inhaling his scent, musky and tinged with frankincense. "You smell so good."

Javed's laugh filled the room, warmth stole through her. "I haven't laughed so much in a long time." He gazed in her direction and she reached out, tracing the hard planes of his face and his full lips.

With careful movements, she leaned in to him, capturing him with a kiss, watching his eyes. *I don't think I'll ever get enough of you.*

The embrace shifted subtly as he deepened it. He pushed his tongue within her mouth and she moaned in her throat, pressing herself closer against his body. The rock hard flesh felt warm and welcoming to her touch. She skated her fingers over the satiny skin of his shoulders as she straddled him, his waking erection hard and ready.

Her own body was warm, damp at the core and she opened herself to him, willing him to see everything that lay deep within her head. *I love you.*

Javed's eyes burned with hunger. She didn't attempt to control the shiver that ran through her body. *Forever, my love.*

Down her neck he grazed her with open-mouthed, drugging kisses that pulled at her senses. She tangled her fingers in his hair. "Javed." She arched up, gave into the sensations rippling through her body. He found her collarbone, laved it as streaks of fire rushed through her.

When he found her breast with his mouth and his hand, the pressure building within her belly made her buck. "Oh God, don't stop!"

Like that, do you? I'm going to savor you. Your taste is so sweet. She felt him pierce her breast carefully before taking the merest drop of blood, but it was enough to push her through orgasm.

He gripped her hips with firm hands, lifting her over his body. He settled his cock against her core as the final ripples enveloped her.

Again!

His harsh demand stole her sanity. She scanned his features, graven and hard against the white satin sheets. "Yes."

This time, she lowered herself slowly, feeling her folds part for his invasion.

When she would have started to undulate over him, he held her still. "Wait."

She needed to move, but he held her tight, rubbing against her now hard nipples and she gasped.

"Did you know, in my culture, sex is one of the ways to achieve enlightenment?" His voice was liquid and velvety, and she swallowed involuntarily at the promise in his words.

Let me show you.

With slow and careful touches he shifted her so that her knees sat under his armpits. *Lean back.* She did and gloried in the sensation of him, deep within her body.

She grasped his knees before she rubbed, gently back and forth, straining. Her engorged breasts jutted forward and his eyes gleamed. She made to brush against him and as before, he stopped her. *Not yet, my beauty. I am fascinated by every inch of your body.*

Without touching, he gazed at her body. That alone ignited her senses, leaving her heated and more than ready by the time he let go of her hips.

This time she shifted, sat up before she slid up and down over his flesh. He hissed, his body as damp as hers and the scent that rose in the air was musky and smelling of sex. It left her mouth aching and her entire body trembled with need. The sounds of passion, gasps and flesh moving against flesh echoed in her mind. Teased her with the innate eroticism of the moment.

The coiling spring deep inside her belly wound tighter.

Just as she was about to reach the pinnacle, he stopped her again, his chest heaving and his eyes shining a deep golden color. *Wait!*

Celina stilled. "Javed, I don't think..." the thought splintered and broke away as he carefully tugged her forward so that she lay over him again. Now, when he undulated, her body dancing in time with his, it was as if they were indeed one.

"Forever you will be my love." He chanted at her. *"Bahebek aktar kol youm."*

The waves washed over her and she danced, lost in pleasure. They rocked together as consciousness splintered.

"I love you, Javed!"

His grunt of pleasure followed and he thrust one last time, holding himself still against her body, panting filled the air as fingers gripped the flesh of each other's bodies. The violent thudding of their heartbeats slowed before finally settling into an even rhythm again.

"You've changed." His lethargic words cut through the silence.

"What?" She cracked open an eye to stare at him. "What do you mean?"

"When you came... there was a glow. Something has changed in your power."

"Really? No, I don't think so!" She brushed away his words, resting against him as her body settled. Her eyelids drooping.

She let sleep lull her. In fact, she was nearly asleep when Javed stiffened beside her. He radiated anger as it burned brightly inside her mind. Now that she was aware and understood how his body reacted, she opened her eyes and noted the horror dawning on his face.

Javed?

I'm so sorry Celina. A package... Cressida just let me know. He turned and the feeling of well-being melted away in an icy rush as fear bloomed.

Bertha?

"Her hand was delivered to the house. We must go home."

Now anger swirled, deep and cold. "You're sure?"

He nodded without a word. Tingles spread through her, waves of pure power. "They must pay. Nothing else is acceptable." Her voice boomed, and Javed's eyes opened wider. The gold deepened, but she ignored it, allowing the power to surge.

He smiled, but it was tight. "Then come with me. We will deal with this together." They rose and prepared for the journey home.

THE TRIP BACK TO THEIR NEST WAS RAPID. KHARISMA CLIMBED into the car with them.

"We will find her, Javed. I already have people checking. I think they have a second hidey hole. We stormed where they had Celina previously. There was evidence of habitation since our last visit. But they've left it. If it's any consolation, I'm sure they are still nearby."

Javed scowled into the night. Cressida had promised them aid, but he wasn't so sure it would be in time to save Bertha. Celina had been silent and white faced since her outburst.

He'd been stunned as her eyes flashed golden, and the air in the room had arced with her power. Something she certainly hadn't shown before. He'd wanted to question Cressida about what he'd seen, but they'd had to hurry to make it home before sunrise.

Now as they turned into the drive, he could still feel the vibrations filling the vehicle. Kharisma kept casting glances in his direction, but he wasn't going to say anything until he had the information to explain it.

Until they knew what had changed exactly, he wanted to keep news of the growth of Celina's abilities to themselves.

"We've arrived, Javed." Kharisma's voice intruded on his thoughts and he realized he'd lost track of where they were. The car had stopped, and he was still watching Celina.

The enervating sense of imminent sunrise pulled at him and he ushered Celina from the car before the shutters of the house started rattling their way to the ground, shutting them off from the outside world.

He could see Celina fighting the weariness that all new vampires felt as the sun rose into the sky. "You should retire." He touched her arm, but she glanced at him, her lips flattening into thin white ribbons.

"No. I'll remain with you. Do what I can." She turned away and he knew she was wrestling with deep emotions.

A large body of nestlings awaited him, the anger on their faces disconcerting.

"You should all retire."

A female stepped forward.

He wracked his brains trying to bring her name to mind. "Yes, Alison?"

Her eyes glinted in the half light. "She's one of us. They took Celina and those of us who were with you saw what they did... And now Bertha." She paled and gulped before continuing. "We stand by our own. Tell us what you need and we'll do it."

Barely a month since the investiture had passed and they had become a cohesive unit. He'd been so invested in building a nest and grappling with his personal issues he'd somehow missed it. It humbled him.

"The best thing then, is to get on your phones, ring anyone you can think of in the area of the original incursion. Get them out there looking. Search yourself, but only if you have the skills to stay safe. Kharisma?" He turned to her in wordless entreaty.

He knew the instant she understood what he wanted.

She stood beside him, taking control of the room. "Those of you with weapons skills, come see me. I will arrange teams to go together into the old district. These creatures are not to be taken on lightly. They will sacrifice anything, kill anyone, so you must be careful and stay together."

He scanned the room as a full-suit of emotions crashed down. Concern, anger, and fear all washed over him.

"At all costs, we will not lose another. That is not acceptable." Nestlings nodded but he continued. "We find our own and bring them home."

They scattered, those who would meet with Kharisma formed a line outside her office. Others took up positions, preparing rations and getting cars ready. But even as the guards of the nest prepared to rest, for the most part, the humans took lead positions.

"Javed?" Celina touched his arm, the brief caress noticed by many assessing gazes.

Finally everyone melted away, leaving them alone in the corridor. He cupped her cheek tenderly. "You should rest."

"I can't." She swallowed and her eyes filled. "It's Bertha. How can I rest when she's still out there?"

He could feel her swirling emotions. "I know. But you are still letting vampire DNA work its way through your system. Rest is essential." Javed gathered her against himself, allowing her scent to calm the nerves that were stretched thin.

"I need to do something useful."

He sighed, perhaps there was something she could do, for an hour or two? Then he could send her to bed. He cast around thinking of anything. "Fine. Man the phones, noting location time and details." She hurried to the small alcove where the house switch was located. Once he was satisfied he headed for his office.

With care, he lowered himself into the chair and turned to his computer. Several minutes later Daniel entered. "Since you are awake we can go through these reports and projections." It really wasn't what he wanted to be doing. He'd rather be out there, searching for the lost nestling. He chafed again but the nest had to grow and provide for itself.

So he and Daniel settled in while waiting for news, spreading the files over the table. At some point, Kharisma entered.

"I'm sending Celina to bed. She's asleep in the chair." He started, but she waved him away with an, "I'll see to it."

The hours ticked by. From time to time, the phone rang and was answered. Information was ferried to him and orders given. Finally as the sun reached its zenith, Daniel left him. Fatigue pulled at his mind and he made his way to the secured suites, letting himself into his room. Celina laid face-down on the bed. He stripped and climbed up beside her. Finally satisfied he'd done all he could for now he allowed himself to drift away, wrapped around her.

THE LAYERS OF SLEEP PARTED AND HE CAME TO AWARENESS. His sleep had been dreamless, but he didn't feel rested. Agitation coursed through him. Bertha was still absent, the vampires had worked themselves to exhaustion. His nestlings were out, prowling the city.

Javed rubbed the grit from his eyes and yawned, looking at the empty spot beside him. He rose and headed in the direction of Celina's voice in the room beyond. A tray with two goblets had been delivered and Celina seemed shocked to see him. "I thought you were still asleep."

With a smile, Javed accepted the proffered goblet, Celina sipped at hers. "It's getting better?" He indicated to her blood wine and she gave a nod, the deep gold starting to lessen as the green of her eyes peeked through.

"Yeah." She swirled the drink, her gaze on the movements of the liquid. "I'm really scared, Javed. What if she isn't found? Or it's too late?" He heard the anxiety in her voice. He took the drink from her wobbling hand. "What good is it to be a vampire if I can't help my first friend in this world?"

Her words cut through him. He couldn't promise her a miracle because he wasn't sure there was one. Instead, he held her close, running his hands slowly over her back. Finally, the rapid beat of her heart slowed.

"We will do everything we can. Everyone is searching. News will come soon, and we will follow it." Javed smiled. "But first, we should dress."

She giggled, the sound thin, but he pulled her towards the bedroom with him.

Since her change, he had contemplated asking her to join him as his Life Partner, the one who would remain by his side for the millennia of his life. The thought caused his stomach to curl as it had every time in the last few days when he allowed the thought to rise.

Would she be like Anisa? Stay with him until something she couldn't deal with happened? He doubted it. But the niggle of uncertainty nipped at him.

He should wait until after they found Bertha. He was evading commitment. He knew that.

He scanned the western clothing he usually wore, stopped, then pushed them aside. Tonight he would wear his traditional garb. It seemed somehow appropriate to return to his roots now as Master of his own nest. His basic *sirwaal* and *thawb* would suit his needs. He dressed with an economy of motion and donned his *gutrah* and *agal*.

A knock came at the door and he glanced at Celina. She stood dressed in black—leather pants, long sleeved jacket and thigh high boots. She nodded as if asking him to argue the point.

Before him stood not a fragile witch-woman, but a warrior and the thought elicited a broad grin. Even her red hair had been tamed into submission, tied back into a tight bun at the top of her head.

"Javed? We've found her, we think." Kharisma called from the other side of the door.

He looked in its direction and strode to the door, before wrenching it open. Her eyes glittered a deep icy blue, her hair coiled away from her face. She was ready to fight. Whoever had taken Bertha would rue the day.

"Where?"

"In the same section we found Celina. It is well guarded though. I have already called on Cressida and Xavier. They will come to our aid.

"The other nests?"

She screwed up her face. "Some will give their people the choice. Others have stated she is only a witch. They will not order their people to help."

Savage fury lashed at him. *Damn the politics of the nests! After this is done, I will raise it with Cressida and the Council! Perhaps even Gianna, if she will allow me an audience.*

"Have the guards assembled?" Kharisma fell in beside him as he marched to the door of the secured section. He knew Celina was behind him, could hear her footfalls. He made a mental note to find somewhere safe for her. Her magic had returned since she'd become a vampire. Indeed it had even strengthened as he'd seen at Cressida's as if had been waiting for something to boost her abilities, but for all that, he wouldn't risk her.

His people waited for him in the foyer, a sea of black, their eyes glinting with gold fire. Instead of watching them mass and being one of the many, here he stood, as Master.

He waited for the hubbub to settle down.

He noted how the human nestlings had taken to the stairs and banisters to observe the massing of the warriors. "You would fight to save a missing nestling?" His voice rang out. For a moment not a sound could be heard bar the echo of his demand.

Then a wild cry broke out.

He silenced them. "We will find the missing of our house. We will bring her home. Tonight is ours!" The wild huzzahs and chants grew louder while their feet stomped the floor. He raised his hands, calming those who waited before him. "Tonight will not be easy. We may see things that will test our resolve, make us wonder at our own humanity. But no one..." He paused, all eyes on his face. "No one takes one of ours."

He gave a short and curt nod. It was done. *Time to go find Bertha.*

TWENTY-FIVE

Attar stared out of the box on wheels. That it moved so quickly amazed him. Just like the stories his mother had told him. They flew through the night, flashes of illumination on long poles amazed him. "Where will we be going?"

"To the place where I keep your sustenance, Master. I have the woman chained and many more for you to feed from."

His fangs ached, hunger gnawed at his innards. He growled.

With difficulty, he turned his attention to his dilemma. Jelani had become brave or was it just that his servant had become cocky? Either way, his usefulness had nearly reached its limit. He was hiding something he'd done, Attar was sure.

No one hid anything from Attar. He was a God! Just as his mother before him.

"Tell me more about this age." He waved to the world beyond the glass and Jelani talked of travel, communications and time saving devices. He listened dimly while taking in the sights before him. The buildings lit up like sparkling obelisks, and the sky was a black matte, not a star to be seen. Had they winked out during his long hibernation? "There are no stars."

Jelani stopped his monologue. "I'm sorry Master?"

"Why are there no stars?" The fact worried him. The stars had been his guide since his first days of life. His mother had taught him about constellations and her travels. Of the ways she'd used the lights to guide her path to this place. *Had they disappeared? Winked out while he slept?*

"It's all the lights, Master. They obscure the stars. If we were somewhere without as much light, you'd see them."

He stilled. A simple explanation. It calmed the nerves for now. "Continue telling me about the age."

Jelani nodded but eyed him with suspicion.

Something about tonight was wrong. His instincts warned him of danger, but he brushed them aside. *I am invincible!*

The vehicle slowed and came to a stop outside a drab gray building, little more than an oversized box. "What is this?"

"Master?" Jelani bowed deeply and indicated he should precede him. Within the ugly building, two or three dozen vampires massed. His followers, Jelani told him. They parted like the ancient seas for him to proceed within and bowed to him as he passed.

Doors stood ajar and the scent of fear on the air reminded him once again of his hunger.

"You have done well." He strode forward, heading in the direction of the nearest entrance.

TWENTY-SIX

They climbed into the cars, Kharisma in the front of Javed's personal vehicle. Celina sat next to him in the back. He held her hand tightly.

"Promise me you'll stay safe."

She glanced in his direction. "I will do my best, but I won't be kept wrapped in cotton wool, Javed."

He frowned.

She sighed. "My magic is stronger, I can tell. I feel it. I can use it to help." She leaned in, cupping his cheek with her hand. "I do understand your fears. But now I have something to offer."

He made to speak but she laid one of her fingers against the soft pads of his lips. "My friend is there. I need to help her. Please, let me."

His eyes clouded. She understood his fear. She felt it for him. For so long she'd been alone, the thought of losing him gutted her, but she wouldn't ask him not to fight. That would be cruel. Just like the long-gone wife he'd told her about. Anisa had wanted a tame warrior, but the man beside her wasn't that. He'd never be able to step back. It wasn't in his makeup.

They travelled quickly and the vehicle halted in an alley, near the gallery. "Here?"

He nodded and she gulped. This place carried only bad memories for her.

The leather of her pants creaked slightly as she alighted from the car. Javed followed her out, laying a soft hand on her shoulder. The car drove off, no doubt to some well-hidden location. The warriors waited uncertain.

Stay close. If you get in trouble, call. If I can't come, I'll send someone.

She indicated that she understood and sucked in a deep and unsteady breath. He handed her a gun. "Point and shoot. Just make sure it's one of them first." He dropped a quick hard kiss on her lips, pushing away a stray red curl before straightening.

Now here's my warrior!

His eyes took on a deeper hue, seeming to be flat and emotionally detached. Javed's face seemed like granite. She shivered, gripping the butt of the ultraviolet gun in her hand. In silence, using only hand motions and the occasional whispered word, his men and women positioned themselves in readiness for the attack. The sound of an engine filled the air and they melted against the walls, as a car pulled up to the building.

Out climbed the creature that had attacked Celina. This time it was joined by a man. He was lean and copper-colored, wearing a loin cloth and collar that reminded her of the ancient Egyptians. He might have been spare framed, but he carried an air of danger and fury. He stretched and glanced around him, rather like an emperor surveying his kingdom. It stole the oxygen from her lungs .

An aura of hate filled the air. His eyes glowed. He glanced around as if he could sense them.

Fear curled for an instant before she thrust it aside. She was no longer a frail human. Vampire blood pulsed in her veins.

Javed curled his hand over her shoulder. *Wait and watch. We'll see what he does first.* A door opened, a crack of light escaping but the sound of moans and wails split the night. When it closed with a clanging rattle she knew they had to enter.

We are going in there, aren't we? She turned to see Javed's face. It was grimmer than before.

Yes. With a single fluid movement he pulled away from the wall and time slowed to a crawl. He gave a single urgent but silent command and they formed around the building. She scurried in behind him and they surged forward.

Several vampires, large men with battle scarred faces, battered at the doors, pushing and thudding until they gave beneath the onslaught. The vampires flowed forward and Celina followed.

"In there!" The vampires fanned out.

She hurried, stopping as she felt the touch of a claw at her shoulder. She turned.

In front of her was a creature of nightmares. Teeth bared and eyes red with hunger.

She shoved the open mouth of the weapon into its belly and pressed the trigger.

Its eyes blanked. Then it slumped to the floor while the stench of burning flesh filled her nostrils.

She hurried, her feet slipping a little but she didn't glance down. She didn't dare as she made her way farther within the building.

The scent of copper rose, thick and pungent. Hunger raged but she fought it off. In the middle of the melee, Celina kept her gaze on Javed's back.

Sounds battered at her as individuals fought, some cried and others screamed. She peered through one doorway, then another. A voice called to her and she turned. She knew that voice.

She widened her eyes in shock as she peered within a large room.

The dog-man held Bertha. Her face was pale and strained, the wound in his center seeping.

She stopped. Javed was across the room. *Stay where you are. Do not engage this one.* The other, in loincloth and collar stood beside Bertha.

The man's gaze had zeroed in on her. The knife he held under Bertha's chin wobbled slightly before a manic smile cracked his face.

"Finally." There was a wealth of satisfaction in his tone.

With one fluid motion, he slid the blade along Bertha's throat, cutting deep. Blood spurted.

"No!" Celina loosed a howl of fury, raising her arms, channeling her power as Javed pounced, catching Bertha inches from the floor. He tugged Bertha along the floor, but Celina already knew that her friend was dead.

As the creature turned to Javed, she called on the well of anger, planning only to create a barrier between them and the animal that scared the bejeezus out of her. Instead, he was too close, and that terrified her. Something about him read as evil incarnate and she'd already seen that he was willing to kill indiscriminately.

The air around her sparked and arced wildly, blue green fire flashing from her hands. "You will not touch us." She projected everything into the words, which boomed outwards.

He gaped, before laughing. Her body strained as she fought to push more power into the ward that glowed between Javed and Celina, and the others.

The animal with razor sharp teeth, advanced on Javed, sliding through the magic before they grappled on the floor. Sweat trickled down her face as his gaze locked with hers. The other man, with red eyes searched her face. She gritted her teeth. She didn't know if she could hold him off.

"You cannot defeat Attar!" He lunged in her direction, lurching against the wall of her magic and she shoved back.

He gave a cry of pain and she pushed further. Attar, as he seemed to call himself scowled and fought against her power. She felt him hunting for a chink so he could negate her ward. He shoved back with his own, and she lost ground.

"You can do this, Celina." She muttered as she thrust forward again. This time Attar was thrown back. He frowned and an expression of fear descended as she advanced once more. He howled in pain, jerking backwards away from the magical flames that rose and licked at him.

Her strength was failing but she wouldn't let him see. She closed her eyes and forced him back using the last vestiges of power.

The sound of feet echoed but she concentrated on her opponent.

It hit her from the back, her hands dropping as she fell to the floor with a heavy thud.

JAVED WAITED AS CELINA'S HANDS ROSE, THE WARD THAT SHE wielded springing to life between him and the large man that attempted to advance toward her. The heavy weight of Bertha in his arms, told him she was dead already. The ribbon of red at her neck slowing to a dribble as her life blood seeped away.

The other creature stared, its hungry eyes locked on Celina. Then it glanced at him, pounced. They fought for several moments until the animal pushed him to the floor, winded.

The battle raged around them, both in this room and the ones nearby. He could hear it, until now.

With a start, Javed turned back to see Celina close her eyes. She was low on power now, he realized. Attar gave a roar and lumbered away shoving through the half open door and out into the night. Javed rose. Even as he made his way towards Celina, the dog-man jumped her.

She gave a cry, falling to the ground.

Javed roared, lifting his scimitar high while he loosed his inner predator. It pounced on his unsuspecting quarry.

He had a fistful of fur in his hand and he hauled back. At the last second, it turned his head toward Javed, and clamped onto his wrist with its powerful vampiric jaws. His prey now assumed the shape of a dog.

Javed howled and shook the hybrid off, his fangs descending in a rush. The need to destroy and defeat rode him like an avenging angel.

He tore the thing from his arm, uncaring of the damage to his own flesh.

"No one harms her." His voice was guttural. Javed's nails grew long and he used them, sinking them deep into the flesh of his assailant.

The scent of blood filled his nostrils and he welcomed it. One quick savage flick saw the animal fly through the air, where it collided with a wall. It lay slumped but Javed stalked towards it. He would end this now.

He raised his arm at the dog once more. It pounced and Javed feinted, avoiding the raking claws and razor sharp teeth. His vision had narrowed to a pinprick as he followed the trajectory. *Exhaust it. Let it wear itself out.* The teachings of his past slid into his mind and he straightened, his mind now calm.

"You will not stop Jelani and Attar." It had assumed the half human half dog shape again. Javed filed the knowledge of the shape changing creature away to consider later.

He turned in circles, watching as his competitor made a swipe at him, the whole time aware of where Celina lay, once more aware and observing the battle in silence.

Each pounce of the one called Jelani was weaker than the last—noticeably so. He caught the hybrid under a rib, slicing through fur and skin, a splash of scarlet spattering on the stained concrete floor.

On the next pass he cuffed it across the head, the room silent bar the grunts and sounds of impact of flesh on flesh. Javed weighed each action. Here he moved to the left but his arm signalled he would head to the right.

Javed countered every motion until finally it surged forward. He was ready. Jelani opened his mouth, claws fully extended as he launched. At the very last second Javed thrust his scimitar forward and with a wet sucking sound Jelani impaled himself on the blade.

"You will not defeat him. My master is strong." The final words were slurred by the blood spilling from his lips, the red of the eyes dulling at the onset of death, its claws reaching and sinking into the flesh of Javed's hand.

He stood still for an instant, uncurled the claws then with a slow and careful maneuver he pushed the body off the blade. He turned and Celina stood, a little unsteady on her feet, her eyes shadowed.

He avoided her gaze. Would she think him a monster now and turn away? She had seen the ugly inhuman side he hid. His heart stuttered in his chest.

Celina touched his arm. "That needs to be cleansed and wrapped." Her voice was soft and he gulped, the adrenaline washing away. His body ached as abused muscles made themselves known. He glanced at her and saw the sadness on her face. She turned toward Bertha's body. "She accepted me. Just as you did." This time when she turned back to him, he saw love and tenderness.

He closed his eyes, sending a prayer of thankfulness to whoever watched over him as he pulled her against his body.

"Javed?" The voice of Kharisma intruded and his body stiffened.

"No damned privacy."

He heard Celina give a muffled laugh at his complaint and turned to his second, Kharisma.

HER BODY WAS HEAVY AND ACHING, BUT SHE'D DONE HER BIT, though sadly she had been unable to save her friend. Kharisma had taken control of Bertha's body, arranging for it to be conveyed to the house.

Javed had attempted to send her home too, but she'd been stubborn, standing her ground. So now she stood in the darkness, followed him as he'd made his way through the horrific building. Seen the sight of bodies piled in corners where they had been slung after they'd been drained dry.

Men, women and even children cowered, chained to walls. Some showed signs of having been used in innumerable ways—both to assuage hunger and sexual urges. "What will happen to them?" She jerked her head in the direction of the holding cells.

"I have sent for Cressida and members of the human government. Decisions will need to be made. But first we need to know if any are nestlings."

She glanced at him, his shoulders slumped and his face pale and drawn. "You couldn't have known. This does not look like a facility that has sprung up overnight."

His eyes flashed. "No."

They moved from room to room as Javed surveyed the layout and number of victims. On the second floor she turned to him. "Let me gather them in one room, collect their names and status. That should make it easier for you to track them."

He stared at her. "You'll find stationary in the vehicle. But don't go out yourself. Get some of the guards to go as a pair, in case we missed anyone. Remember Attar is still out there." His words were like a dousing of ice. She hurried off, searching for two guards she knew. Her request was fulfilled and she searched for a room free of bodies, but none existed. Celina ordered for the removal of Jelani's body.

She instructed the guards to bring the survivors to the room where she had confronted Attar, reasoning it was large enough to hold them all. Her request was met with a quick nod and she cast a glance at the door leading outside. That he might return scared her totally witless, but right now she had to focus on those who needed her help.

They shuffled in, some sobbing quietly, others silent. Their eyes found the pooled blood on the floor and they skirted it, clutching each other's hands and casting her wary looks.

As the last stragglers entered the two guards returned and she indicated the door. "Keep an eye on that. I don't want that Attar guy surprising us."

"Are you going to kill us?" A girl, probably no more than fourteen called out and Celina's heart cracked.

"No. I just need to collect your details so we can ensure you get the help you deserve."

There was a ripple as some derided her words. But, she reminded herself that was to be expected. Instead she squared her shoulders and faced them. "I'm going to collect your names and where you were when taken. I also need to know if you belong to a nest. Where possible, we will attempt to send you home if that is what you want."

"You're going to separate us?" Another, not quite a child spoke up, her fingers twined with that of other two children. Fear painted their faces. "Cause I won't let you. They need me." Celina glanced at the teen. Beneath the grime and caked on blood, she was probably a pretty thing. Her lank hair was likely blonde though right now it was little more than a dirty rat's nest. The other two, whose hands she gripped so tightly were younger, though given how dirty they were it was hard to guess much else.

"Do they have a family?" Celina inclined her head toward the two standing beside her, sobbing in silence.

"They're runaways. I told them I would protect them."

"Then you three come first. Tell me your details and I'll do my best to keep you together."

Her spokesman didn't like the answer, though. She flattened her lips and her eyes flashed. "It's together or nothing." The bravado on her face was both frustrating and heartening.

Javed? I have three girls who must stay together. Is there any chance we can make that happen?

The teen cocked her head. "You're talking to someone. In your head. I've seen that happen before."

Celina smiled. "I am."

Javed strode into the room and some of the humans on the floor cowered. "We'll make it happen."

Celina didn't question his words, just turned to the three. "His promise is his bond. We'll keep you together, if it's possible."

Then the older girl stepped forward. "I'm Lucy."

As the car pulled up in the driveway, Celina ushered the three from the car. "You need a shower and a good meal." She hustled them into the house.

Kharisma hurried down the steps toward him. "You're going to have your hands full there." She nodded to the door and he grunted. Kharisma's smile melted away. "Cressida is waiting inside with some visitors. You're going to want to meet them."

He made his way slowly up the stairs, his feet dragging. His arm stung, his head ached and his ears rang. But that was the privilege of being a Master he told himself. He limped down the corridor, Kharisma following him closely. "If you stop, I can clean your injuries before you meet with them."

He shook his head. "No. Get this out of the way then we settle the nestlings in for the day."

The door to his office slid open smoothly and Cressida strode forward, assessing them, Javed was sure, for injuries. "We were on our way, when Kharisma let us know it was over. She also informed me about Bertha..." Her voice broke off.

He sighed. "Celina is naturally upset. Which reminds me, I need to meet with the *Conclave*..."

"Before you do, I need to make some introductions." He frowned at Cressida, her face was drawn tight. She gripped his hand and he hissed, she let go and winced. "Sorry."

He followed her to his desk. An exotic woman sat, pushed back in his chair. Her eyes glinted. "You are the Master of this nest? Javed I believe?" Her voice was liquid, just like her eyes, reminding him of molten pools of gold. Her full ruby lips matched white skin, grabbing his attention. Her flame-red hair tumbled around her shoulders.

She rose, the movement sinuous and he knew in that instant this was the Overlord, Gianna. He gave a deep bow and as he rose she smiled. "You should have allowed them to care for your wounds.

However, we won't keep you long this time. I would introduce you to these women."

She indicated to the three who sat at the meeting table. He stared at them. They all seemed familiar. He started and pointed a finger at the dark haired woman. "I know you."

She inclined her head. "Indeed you do Javed. I am Jemima. You know me as a survivor of the massacre at the manor when Hope was abducted. These are my sisters." She pointed to a red haired woman. "This is Danicka. Familiar isn't she?" She stopped for a beat and his mind whirled. She also appeared familiar. "She is also Professor Anderson." At the woman's words, the younger woman aged and now he could clearly see the professor in her.

"The other woman is my other sister Selena." He didn't recognize her face but he acknowledged that really didn't mean much, given what he'd just seen. "We are aunt to Gianna—your Overlord."

The final pronouncement was too much as his mind churned over the facts that pounded into his brain. He staggered for a chair and slumped into it. It squeaked and squealed as the cushions absorbed his weight.

"Aunt? Aunts to Gianna?"

"Well, by your standards, technically Great Aunt."

He rolled his eyes. "By all means, let's be technical." His tone dripped with sarcasm.

The woman shot him a steely glance and he quietened, sure that much was about to change. Cressida took the seat beside him. "If it's any consolation, I didn't know any of this either."

The spokeswoman nodded. "There are some things we need to share with you."

He waited in mute silence.

"Let me see where to start? Well, Attar is our nephew. He was one of four children born to our long dead sister, Aliana. As is our way, we separate from the collective once our children are born to raise them in solitude. They were...close." She blushed deeply and turned away.

Javed felt sickened by the implication, but also understood. It was the way of ancient times.

"Our sister struggled particularly with Attar, he was very...*intense*. But I digress. The one thing they were all forbidden was to procreate with the humans. All except Attar took human lovers, but when one of the sisters fell pregnant, Attar was enraged. The Princess, as you know gave birth and the child was sent away. Attar came searching for the child, but it was gone so he took his frustration out on the princess. Her guards... They saw and recorded her slaying."

"I know most of this." He waited. There had to be more to this story.

"The information about the scroll wasn't in the crypt. I added that to the copies I made after the trip to Egypt." Danicka took up the tale now, her face earnest. "You had to find the prophecy, because the time was right. It was foretold not long after the death of the princess. That the time would come when we could join forces with someone able to defeat Attar. In him, we saw the worst of our race—the hunger and the rage. It's why we left our home in the first place. As you've probably guessed, we are not human." Javed nodded.

"Anyway, we sheltered the child long enough to find a trusted warrior to care for and train Gianna. He kept her for many years while she grew. We gave the instruction that she should be turned, then we ensured she was placed with a nest. We knew that at some point, we would need help. The kind only vampires and humans can give us." She shrugged. "We can't directly fight him, for there is a biological imperative that forbids it. But the children of the children can."

"For centuries he has survived with his servant, Jelani. I understand the servant was slain tonight?" At Javed's jerky nod, she sighed. "Good. That leaves him weakened. Now, all we need to do is find the last of the three. Hope was the first...she is the one of blood. Your consort, Celina? She is a witch I understand. She is the witchling.

Now we must find the sorcerer. For it is only as the two stand as one and the six are three that he can be overcome."

"What?" He sat forward. "I have no idea what you are talking about."

The blonde woman smiled. "What they mean is that there are three couples. A couple is two who become one. So three couples are six." She gazed at him enigmatically and he groaned.

"We have watched over the children of the children for centuries. Taking on different personas and bodies. But, don't worry. I know who the third consort is, and I know he is nearby. He doesn't know it yet and one among your number is the Vampire who will help him to become what he must be to complete his part in the prophecy. These two will fall in love, but to complete their role, they must make a choice. Only then can the circle be complete."

"Why don't you just tell us?" He waited hoping for an easy answer.

"Because magic doesn't work that way." The blonde reclined back in her seat as Javed reeled at her comments.

TWENTY-SEVEN

ANGER SUFFUSED HIM. "HOW DARE THEY STOP ME FROM feeding?" He roared his dissatisfaction. They had hounded him out of the building like some mangy dog. *He was a God! Did they not understand that?*

He would visit retribution on everyone who had participated. *But the witch...* He would keep her, for a while. He could feed off her for some time. She was so like his sister.

His grimace was followed quickly by pain—powerful. She was far more powerful than any witch he had ever seen. That made her dangerous.

He looked around for somewhere to wait out the day—somewhere safe from the rays that would cook his bones. In the distance, he saw an outcropping of rock. Perhaps that would give him suitable shelter for the night.

He'd left the sounds of the city behind. Now he could see the stars, and that settled him. They always had.

Hunger was building, gnawing at him. He could stave that off for a little while longer while his body repaired itself. Attar kept moving forward, but his feet ached and he longed for a servant to call upon—

to arrange his transport. But he had no idea how to find one here, in this time. "Tomorrow night, I will find one. Change them and make them serve my purposes."

By the time he arrived at the rocky outcrop, his breath came in pants, his heart hammering madly beneath his breast bone. He spied a small cavern and hurried within. A growl split the air, and satisfaction filled him.

A large cat lumbered towards him. It wasn't perfect. He would prefer the blood of a human, but animal would do for now. He could slake the immediate thirst. His teeth descended as his claws lengthened.

There was no necessity to take his revenge in haste. He had time. And he needed an army if he were to find and dominate the offspring. He coiled his muscles, prepared then pounced. A shrill cry rent the air.

Then there was silence.

TWENTY-EIGHT

SHE WOKE SLOWLY, STRETCHING HER ARMS ABOVE HER HEAD.
She was warm and squished... "Squished?" Celina opened one eye.
Two of the children, Rachel and Marian had slipped into bed with
her and Javed. "Thank God we wore something to bed last night."

A rumble started under her head. *Yes, otherwise they'd get an
eyeful.*

She rolled her eyes. Javed was awake. He wiggled a little, and she
felt the ever-present waking erection digging at her back. *Down boy!
You'll just have to wait.*

The laughing rumble came again and she smiled, running her
hands through the little Eurasian girl's hair. Rachel had been a street
kid, living on the streets after being dumped at a shelter. She'd
teamed up with Marian, who had escaped after vampires had killed
her family. Together they'd lived under bridges and in abandoned
squats until Jelani had found them. He'd lured them with promises of
food and warmth in the bitter winter that had passed.

They had been held for months in the squalid conditions. Her
heart broke for them.

Rachel started. Celina stilled her movements, understanding that she had little trust for people and less for vampires.

"Where... Where am I?" She shrank into herself and Celina couldn't help but wrap her arms around the child.

"You're safe. Marian and Lucy are here too. See? There's Marian, asleep. And Lucy is probably still in the other room."

Rachel shook and shuddered in her arms as Celina held her. She knew the girl was shedding silent tears because the hot drips were landing on her arm. "We will look after you. We will be your family now. No one will ever hurt you again." Tears burned in her eyes and she felt Javed rubbing his hands up and down her back.

I won't let them go, Javed. The protective instinct had risen, driving her to claim these children as her own. *Lucy is too old, she probably won't let me mother her, but these two... Javed?*

She felt rather than heard his sigh. *If there is any way, I will petition the government, the council and even Cressida to allow us to keep them. If they want to stay, that is.*

She jerked a nod. "Now let's get the two of you back to Lucy. If she wakes, I doubt she'll be impressed to find you two missing." Marian was yawning and stretching, so she hustled the two children from their bed. *I'll be back in a few minutes.*

The light touch of his mind on hers was both reassuring and arousing. She had to gulp as her body tingled. *Not like that right now!*

He laughed and she wandered behind the children into the living area. Marian and Rachel held hands. She noted the way they twined them together. They climbed into the makeshift bed beside Lucy who woke. "What... Where?"

The younger ones cuddled into the older girl and Celina sat opposite. "Javed said if you want to stay here, we'll petition everyone to make it happen. It's your choice. But we need to arrange somewhere safe for you to live."

Lucy curled her lip. "Why would he do that?"

"Because he's a good man."

"He's a vampire. Vampires kill humans." Lucy's eyes flattened just the way Celina had seen Javed do.

"No. We live in a nest with humans. We protect them, they help us. It's symbiotic." The teen stared at her, uncomprehending. "It's for everyone's benefit."

"What would we do?" Rachel spoke quietly.

"You'd go to school, so you have an education. You would live here with us. We would help you find your family if you want, or anyone who is left."

"What if I want to learn something else? Magic for instance?"

Celina stilled, gazing at Lucy, where she sat in front of her. "Then I will personally find you a mentor, who will find out what skills you have. We mean what we say. Not all vampires are ugly creatures. Not all feed off the unsuspecting and unwary. There are some who are good."

Lucy relaxed in the made-up bed.

"Now the best thing you three can do is go back to sleep."

She waited while the three dropped off to sleep. She would have liked children, but knew realistically that without Javed's interference, she'd probably be dead by now. His actions had given life. Now he'd given her this chance at a family too.

Suddenly she needed him. Needed to tell him how much she appreciated all he'd given her.

She swept into the bedroom, where he waited for her, sitting on the side of the bed. "I heard you. I heard what you said. Not all of us are monsters. It's only taken me eight hundred years to find a woman who can make me believe that."

Celina stopped as he raised his head to look at her, stretching out both his hands, and she gripped them firmly. "I should have asked before. Be my Life Partner, Celina? Since you've been here, the gray of night is alive. You are the stars in my darkness." He framed her face with his hands. She felt the shake of them and saw the uncertainty in his gaze.

"How could you doubt that I would accept? I've told you I loved you. From that first moment I saw you on the street. It was like a bolt to my heart." She let him see the joy that radiated deep inside her. "I will be your Life Partner. I can't think of anything else that I want more."

She couldn't say who moved first, but now they mashed their lips together, wild and hot. He tugged at her clothing and she wanted to cry out her delight. "Oh God! We have to be quiet! The children!"

He laughed against her collarbone. The zing of desire overtook her. Her body reacted instinctively. Celina's knees felt weak and she slid her hands into his midnight black hair. She played with the silken strands as he kissed his way over her neck and shoulder freely.

With an arch of her spine, she tugged him toward the bed. *Wait!* She stilled her body taut like a bow at his thought and he shut the door with a swift motion.

Her breath escaped in a whoosh. *Great thinking!*

A gentle push from his hand had her falling to the bed, still warm from his body and he leaned so gently over her, his breath a subtle caress on her heated skin.

"Well, since we have to be quiet, we'd better be inventive." The impact of his words sent a curling heat spiralling deep within. Javed brushed away strands of red hair, pushing them out of the way.

"A halo of red. The angel that saved me from my own darkness."

She reached for him once more, savoring the touch of skin as she toyed with his pajamas. "Your angel wants you to get naked."

He gazed down at her and she grinned. "Truly my lady? And what boon would you give me?"

She stilled. Wanting to tell him how much she treasured him. "Forever? Every night that comes? Because all of them are yours."

They kissed. It was harsh and greedy, tearing away the thin tissue of urbanity. Now he clawed at her clothes, tearing them from her body while he nipped at the tender flesh he uncovered.

Celina returned the act, pulling the pajama shirt from him, uncovering his muscled chest and planting her hand against his pectorals, savoring the smooth warmth. The beat of his heart beneath her touch told her plainly of his arousal, in the way it beat a rapid tattoo. She lifted her hand to take his, placed it beneath her generous breast. "Feel that? Feel how much I need you."

The slide of his hand curved upwards, taking the weight of her breast. He flicked his thumb over her nipple so that it quickly distended. His gaze turned fiery as he continued his sensual ministrations. "Such bountiful breasts, tipped with the most exquisite nipples.

He rubbed over the nubs and each touch ignited another little flickering fire in her core. "Javed?"

At her cry, he released her breasts. "There is more bounty though, my lady." He gave a lopsided grin, but his face was flushed and damp, like her skin. He hooked his fingers in the elastic waistband of her pajama bottoms and she raised her butt, allowing him to slide them off.

With care, she scooted back to the center of the bed and he climbed up before prowling along it. She saw his nostrils flare, smelling the heady scent of musky arousal on the air.

He stopped at her hip, lowering his head towards her belly. The touch was electric. Her body clenched as he slid his fingers over the sensitive flesh of her mound. He traced over the slit at her center, back and forth with aching tenderness. She worked to contain the moans that rose in her throat.

The next pass saw him dip one finger within so that it grazed over the sensitive point between her thighs. She couldn't contain the hiss this time.

He pulled back. "Slick, warm and ready. " He raised the moisture to his mouth and licked, watching her. Her breath fled and she arched as his hands returned again to their pleasurable torture.

"Javed, please. Now."

But instead, he dipped his mouth down, covering her and running his tongue between her legs. She mewled and bucked, the pleasure streaking like fire through her.

Her chest heaved and she twined her fingers in the cotton of the sheets as she sucked in air, staring blindly at the ceiling. The torture continued as a spring wound tightly within her belly.

She bit her lips. *Javed! Please! Please, now! Don't make me wait.*

He surged up and she released her grip on the bedding, grabbing at his shoulders. He toppled to the bed as she rose. Celina kissed her way along his belly, flat and lean. She tasted and laved, mad with need, while she played her fingers across his sweat slicked flesh. She found his hips and gripped before following the small line of hair from his navel, with her mouth.

His cock was proud and erect. She slid her lips over the bulbous head, teasing it with her tongue before pushing down. This time he groaned as she glided up and down.

Javed tangled his fingers in her hair, tugging. *Now! I need to be in you.*

She crawled up his body, noting his graven features and the golden shine in his eyes. One movement of her legs and she straddled him. *Forever.*

With exquisite care she lowered herself, until she was impaled on his length.

The ride was wild.

Fast.

The gyrations mad as he rose up, kissing her. Their combined tastes mingling. The coil snapped and she arched. Celina gave in to the pleasure, aware that he too had achieved orgasm. Their bodies entwined still and finally quiet.

Then she slumped, safe in his embrace.

EPILOGUE

Javed followed Celina into the communal area, the three children lagging behind, still desperately unsure of the others. They stayed close to Celina. He made a mental note to have Kharisma assess them in case they required psychological assistance.

Waiting for them were Hope and Xavier. Hope had dressed in her favored uniform of jeans and peasant shirt. She smiled as the small unit moved as one, but Xavier just quirked an eyebrow.

One of the nestlings, an older lady came forward and Celina introduced them. "Lucy, Marian and Rachel, go with Jean. She will get you some food and organize what things you will need so we can order clothes. Then Kane wants to talk to you about school."

"We don't want to." Lucy jutted out her chin, though she checked the reactions of those either side.

Javed felt frustration at her words. "I can come with you if you'd like." He had little experience with children, but if that gave them comfort, then he would do it.

"We want Celina."

Javed shook his head. "She has meetings now. People have come to talk to her. When they are done, we'll make arrangements." He saw the mutinous expression on Lucy's face and leaned forward. "They are all human. You'll be safe with them."

Lucy's gaze was distrustful but she finally nodded. "We stay together, okay?" Then she looped her arms through the other girls' and they followed Jean to the kitchen.

Celina welcomed their visitors to the nest. He grinned at the easy way she talked to Hope and Xavier. They were his closest friends beside Kharisma and he wanted her to feel comfortable with them.

The door swung open and Cressida arrived, Gianna following her closely. Daniel was descending the stairs. "Fine. We are all together. Let's head to my office."

They filed in and took up spots at the conference table. In deference to the fact that it was his nest, Gianna sat beside Javed, who was directed to the end of table. Celina accepted Cressida's instruction that the other end was hers.

"After all, you accepted him as Life Partner haven't you?" Celina blushed and Cressida shot him a glance.

"You did ask, didn't you?"

"Not that it's any of your business, but I did."

Cressida sat back smugly in her chair, fingers steepled. "So?"

"I accepted." Congratulations flowed at Celina's quiet words.

Finally the room quieted, Cressida cleared her throat. "We are, however, not here to discuss your union. Last time I was here I asked Kharisma for details of Celina's test results. After it threw up that Daniel was her half-brother, it reminded me that Hope is his cousin, on the maternal side. As she's now a vampire, her results were excluded from the trace. So I gave instructions that they should be. They matched."

"How do they match?" Javed sat straight in his chair.

"Hope and Celina are cousins. That leads me to think there is more still to this than meets the eye."

"Well damn." Celina put a hand to her forehead. "That would explain it then. Attar looked at me like he knew me." Her eyes were wide. "When I held him back, he sort of stared at me. I'm sure there was recognition in his eyes.."

"How did you manage to hold him back? Your magic is from the sun." Kharisma leant forward. "What changed?"

Gianna sighed. "That's easy to answer. Our strength comes from the stars and the night. I'd say her body has finally adjusted to her new state. That her affinity has settled to the night."

Celina smiled, the sight breathtaking. "You have no idea how pleased I am to hear that." She laced her fingers together and he breathed deeply.

"But back to Attar?" Her eyes flickered, her gaze lowered to the tabletop as if she were thinking over a great puzzle.

"Celina?" Gianna stared at Celina and Javed while a ripple travel through the room. "I know what you're thinking, and it's excellent. There is no reason that some kind of latent DNA could be present still in your blood." She inclined her head to the newest vampire in the room.

"I don't get what you mean?" Adrenaline spiked through Celina again.

Gianna shrugged. "Blood. The prophecy was about blood. Either our mixed blood that created the vampire race or shared blood... History. I pondered it all day. Four siblings. But one survived, meaning three descendants to beat Attar. Family connections. Descended from one. Me. My children before I was turned."

Everyone gazed at her. "Well, I was hardly likely to share that last night. Hearing that procreation was banned? But yes. I did bear a child. A daughter." Gianna smiled, then settled with a smug and satisfied expression on her face.

He rose, shoving away from the table, and his stride ate up the distance. "If that's true... Kharisma!" He bellowed, knowing she would hear him. Her footsteps clattering on the tiles.

"Javed? Are we under attack?"

He brushed her words of concern aside. "How soon can you run a DNA trace on blood samples?"

She screwed her nose up at his question. "Well, probably overnight. I know someone…" Kharisma searched his face as she obviously started to put the information together.

"Get your kit. Four samples. Whatever it takes I need the results by tomorrow evening." Her face blanked, but she hurried from the room.

He regained his seat. "Right, so if this theory is correct…?"

"We need to find Daniel's mate. The sooner that happens, the better."

He chanced a look at his *Yeux Secondes*. He'd barely got to know him, but was happy with his services so far. Surely he wasn't about to lose him just as the nest was finding its feet? Then he castigated himself for his shallow thoughts.

Gianna rose. "I would suggest for now, we leave Daniel, Hope and Celina to get acquainted." As she spoke, Gianna looked at Javed, Xavier and Cressida meaningfully.

As one they rose. Kharisma rushed into the room to take her samples from the three waiting, then did the same with Gianna. She sealed it in a specially marked bag and nodded to her partner who took the bundle.

Javed and the others left the room. They waited in the dining area, waiting while the nest settled into its now familiar routine.

Then he waited, impatient. One hour then another ticked by.

Finally, Daniel, Hope and Celina entered where they waited, with an air of togetherness and he stood, his gaze searching hers. She was smiling. His heart beat resumed its normal rhythm as she took his hand.

"We'll leave you now, Javed and Celina." He bent forward as Hope brushed her lips over his cheek. "She's lovely."

As a group they made for the front door, where Cressida stopped as the others filed by, into the night. "By the way, the three children? Lucy, Marian and Rachel? The government has agreed to allow you to have full and unconditional custody of them. There is no contest." Then she walked away, leaving them open mouthed.

The tail lights glowed red in the darkness and he thought of the glow of Attar's eyes. "He's out there. Waiting for his chance."

Celina shivered and he pulled her against his chest. "We'll beat him. All of us together. I can feel it in my bones."

Right now though, we have it all. Home. Family. Commitment. I never thought to have any of them.

She chuckled. *And three kids. Don't forget them.* He chuckled, then they headed inside, ready to embrace their next adventure.

If you enjoyed this book by Imogene Nix why not check out some more of her titles by scrolling through to the following pages?

THE BLOOD BRIDE BY IMOGENE NIX

Hope just wants to be an ordinary nestling. She went to college and escaped, but now she's back and there's a secret everyone is keeping from her.

Xavier is the new master of the nest, ready to welcome home the daughter of the house who he has never met. He's unprepared for the woman who steals his breath and enchants him.

Now Hope and Xavier must fight for lives and those of the innocents. After all, it is only by overcoming the rogues that they will have a chance of a timeless future together. But will it be in time?

PROLOGUE

As silence descended on the house, the shadows grew—dark grays and blacks that bled into each other. First one figure then another broke away, making a run toward the house. Silent as the grave, they moved swiftly over dew-slicked grass. Then they stopped still. Waiting. Not a movement betrayed them until a signal propelled them back into action and they started crawling upwards. The walls damp coating no barrier to the intruders that ascended in the darkness.

The sound of each window breaking shattered the quiet—the figures were inside. Screams echoed through the night. Yet, in this area of large estates, heavy with noise-absorbing shrubbery, no one could hear those within. The blood-curdling screams went on and on before finally dying away.

Just one sound echoed through the night: The sobbing of a child.

The front door opened and figures trooped out—ghostly specters against an inky night sky, broken by a single outline. A child in white, carried at the center of the pack.

No sound broke the silence as they moved toward the trees surrounded the house.

Flames now licked at the manor: A deathly glow of oily smoke rising.

All that remained was a single person—wrapped in a cape of midnight blue beyond the house—watching them melt away.

Jemima moved toward the burning structure, breaking into a run as she breached the threshold. Vainly she attempted to enter, but the heat drove her back.

Now dashing tears from her face, she raced across the graveled driveway toward the gates, where the guardhouse was located. No sign of life existed within the building and some instinct of survival slowed her pace to a careful creep. Out of breath and heaving from exertion, she nervously checked within.

Small puffs of white vapor colored the glass. She darted from one window to another. Her cloak drawn tightly around her body, hoping it would camouflage her from sight.

Satisfied, Jemima entered through the heavy, wooden front door and moved toward the phone she spied on the floor. Her eyes darting here and there she dialed, listening to the rotary motor as it returned to the proper position. Time was short and if *they* came back, she needed to have shared the message.

The phone rang once. Twice. With a brrping sound it connected.

"Hello?" A male answered and she felt a warm flush of relief at the voice. A voice she knew well.

"The manor has been breached. The girl child taken." The words erupted and her hand trembled.

"On our way." The click of the receiver being replaced echoed loudly in the stillness of the room.

Copper. She smelled copper.

Her stomach soured, knowing it meant more deaths. Jemima looked around for the gun—a gun with deadly, holy water-infused copper bullets—she knew was hidden somewhere in the room. A gun she couldn't find. *No divine intervention exists here*, she thought.

Hopefully *they* didn't remain. Feeding. If they were still here, that's what they would be doing. She found a corner and scrunched down, hiding from sight.

Crouched low, she tried to stay as still as possible, listening for sounds of the vehicles she knew would be coming. She dug her fingers into the flesh of her arms; remaining aware enough to stop before drawing blood. That would surely bring them out. Jemima dragged the cloak around her to capture the warmth, yet there was little to be found.

The sounds of engines roused her from the corner of the room. Jemima inched toward the window, the lead of the old glass distorting her view, hearing raised voices she knew Mistress Cressida had arrived.

Jemima retreated. Remained hidden from the woman because if she knew, all may well be lost. From the shadowed room she listened to the conversation…

"It smells like Estersham." The Mistress' eyes closed. "If it is, we have a problem." She turned once more, her face set and eyes now glacial in intensity. "James?"

The man nodded as if he knew what was to come.

"If I take those steps, I cannot return. Another must stand in my place." Her voice hardened while her eyes glittered in the dim light, piercing in their intensity.

Then the Mistress' voice called out in the near silence. "You and yours have been my loyal servants for so many years. I took an oath to protect you long ago. I renewed it with marriage and births, over and over. Now, my home and yours have been breached and this child taken from us. The girl child, who will be the hope and salvation of our kind, was ripped from the bosom of our nest. I will repay your loyalty and I will get her back." The words of power rippled in the night and licked at Jemima's skin.

Available in Ebook
books2read.com/BloodBride-Nix

Direct Autographed Copy
https://bit.ly/TBB-Nix

emotionally fragile Jane and Davis, a famous author. The task is more complicated, with the existence of Carstairs her could-be ex-husband and teenage daughter, Frannie.

In **Revenge on Cupid**, Diocail must take the ultimate chance and find his own happily ever after with Simone. Sometimes the past gets in the way and HEA's don't come cheap though.

The dusty, dingy little diner was full, even with its current state of cleanliness—or lack thereof. People from the surrounding offices didn't care about anything except the incredible, well-prepared food at a reasonable cost. They flooded in, like waves to the shore. As one tide left, another swept in.

"Honestly, Simone. I'm going to try getting his attention one more time. If that doesn't work, I'm out of there. I mean, how long can I keep trying?" Cara picked at the caramel tart she hadn't been able to resist with the cheap metal fork and flicked the blob of fresh cream that sat on top to the side of the plate.

"You've said that tons of times before. Besides, what are you going to do to get his attention? Hmm? Walk naked through the typing pool?" Simone bobbed the straw in her smoothie as she eyed her friend with a frown. "It's been what? Eighteen months since you saw him, and you've mooned over him from a distance ever since you met him. You need to move on, Cara. That is, unless there's something you haven't shared?"

The query was arch. Cara shivered even as she shook her head. "No."

Simone quirked an eyebrow, obviously unconvinced with the answer. Cara let out a deep sigh of frustration. "There's a position...it's only temporary, for a PA reporting directly to him." She speared a forkful of tart, chewed quickly and swallowed, before continuing. "In his office, full-time for the period of the engagement. I saw the memo yesterday. I mean, I have the skills, right? I can type, answer phones, make coffee, file, greet people. What's more, I can probably do it better than all those size eights in the typing pool that

Ms. Jackman seems to prefer." She nodded thoughtfully. "All I have to do is get past the ogre in Human Resources."

Simone stared at her, disbelief clear on her face. "Girl, I so remember that woman. If you think you can get past her, you're doing better than I ever did. That's why I left Veha Industries, remember? Maybe it's time to haul out your resumé and consider some other options. Look for something better." Simone shook her head and billows of her crimson hair swirled through the still air.

Cara understood Simone only had her best interests at heart. But this time she knew the outcome would be different. Hell, she could feel it in the air. The tingle of expectation.

"Cara, the HR ogre will hang you out for breakfast before she offers you anything like a position in that office. Remember her mantra? Good looks and good work make for a positive workplace!"

Simone didn't sugar-coat anything. It was another great reason for their long- term friendship. Honesty. But Cara didn't want to hear the truth in the statement. Even if it was exactly as her friend said.

Cara nodded quickly. "Yeah, I know, but if I don't try, then I won't know how close I can get to him, right? And the only way to catch his attention is to get past *her* and see him in person." Cara quaked a little at the information she needed to share. The favor she needed to ask. "Anyway, I tidied up my resumé and dropped the application into a memo envelope yesterday, so it's too late to back out now. I mean, fortune favors the brave. Doesn't it? If I don't snag an interview, I'm going to visit the career advisor across the street and register with them." She shrugged. "I'll look for temp work until something more long-term shows up. I can see what they have on offer and well...who knows? Maybe a job with the right boss is just waiting for me. But I'd rather this worked out, to be honest." Her voice trailed off into a whisper. "I really wish he would notice me."

Simone took a long slurp of her banana drink, and Cara noticed her questioning gaze even as she squirmed. Finally, Simone nodded. "It's your funeral. So anyway, you'd better show me this memo if you want me to be a referee for you. I'm guessing that's what you need, right? I'll have to know what I'm supposed to say about you before they ring."

Cara smiled. "Thanks, Simone. I knew I could count on you." She slipped a piece of paper out of her handbag and handed it over. "Sorry it's a bit creased. It was in the bottom of my bag, I stashed it so none of the others from the pool would see. You know how it is."

Available from Love Books Publishing
books2read.com/CelticCupid

Direct Autographed Copy
http://bit.ly/2vs7wtS

BIOCYBE BY IMOGENE NIX

Can a cyber-enhanced warrior and a ship's captain find love together?

Levia Endrado never wanted to be a warrior, but at seventeen she was deemed suitable for battle. After intense training and multiple enhancements, which gave her superior strength and healing ability, she was sent off to defeat the enemy—a killing machine with a mission.

When the war was over, she had to find a new life. At twenty-seven she's a washed-up veteran without a future. Or she was, until she met Sandon Daria.

Serving as a pilot aboard Sandon's spaceship the *Golden Echo* makes Levia long for a different and gentler life. But old hurts and even older enemies aren't so easily forgotten. Particularly when they come back for her.

Sandon is determined to show Levia that she's more than just a BioCybe...she's the woman who completes him. Getting close is just the first step, keeping her alive is an even bigger challenge, but one he's willing to take because the prize is their combined future.

Levia scanned the long line of other hopefuls entering the chamber. The large building in the center of town was cold, and she dragged her wrap around her body, even as she craned her head, looking to the high ceiling. She'd never before had an occasion to enter the testing complex, yet she'd seen the lines of teenagers every time they passed the building.

Once she'd asked her parents why the teens were lined up and her mother's face had shuttered. Her stepfather had just shaken his head and growled. They'd stopped her questions with a carefully uttered, "You'll know soon enough, Levia." The pain in her mother's eyes had been enough to shush her questions. For endless months afterward, her parents had traveled different routes to the educational facility she attended and Levia lost interest in the puzzle of that building.

Now, as she looked around, remembering that long ago spring day, it was her opportunity to find out. But she felt a surge of concern at what lay ahead. She likely wasn't the only one, given that there were probably two to three hundred seventeen-year-olds gathered in the one place. Ahead of her, she caught sight of a couple of girls, their arms linked together and wide smiles on their faces. Scanning the crowd, she became aware that, by far, a majority of those gathered displayed both fear and trepidation.

"All female subjects will enter through doors three, six, and seven. All male subjects will enter through gates four, eight, and ten." The speaker above her was loud, and she jumped before checking the numbers etched on the black metal sign over her head.

The massive doors beside her swung open, and now an uncertain silence reigned. Many of the youngsters hung back, clearly discomforted by whatever testing regime lay ahead. This was where they'd been told their futures would be determined.

"Oh gosh, I hope they only have an aptitude and psych eval. I don't think..." Levia turned to see the white face of the girl behind her. The girl had uttered what many must silently be thinking.

Levia dragged an unsteady breath in, her hand resting flat against the plane of her belly as she looked around. No one had entered yet. It was clear many were on the verge of taking the step, but still they hung back.

She straightened her shoulders. "I'm not afraid." It was always wiser to approach things head-on, she believed. When her biological father had died, she'd been one of the few to view his capsule before it was sent into the massive gray structure built to accommodate those who'd moved onto the next life realm.

Her legs shook as she wobbled toward the entrance. Beyond the doorway, she spied sealed cubicles and her heart stuttered. Why cubicles? Usually testing—med and psych—were in eval-units, hidden only by billowing white curtains. She glanced back, noting that others had taken the first step.

"Move along, subjects." Once again, the androgynous voice of the address system blared.

Of course, given it was her seventeenth anniversary of birth, she was technically considered an adult now.

She thought longingly of baby Rald and her half-sister, Elda, waiting at home for her to return, and the celebrations to be held that night. That made her smile. She would need to make them proud of her.

She entered a row and the tall Educational Specialist, the edu-specs as her peers laughingly called them, stopped her. "Present your credentials to the scanner."

She'd done this many times since the tiny implant had been slipped below the dermal layer of her skin at birth. The small unit in her wrist heated as her details were checked.

"Enter the first cubicle, Levia Endrado, and follow the instructions to complete your assessment."

Thus dismissed, Levia moved to the first unit, laid her palm against the scanner, and the door slid open soundlessly.

"Welcome, Levia Endrado. Take your place in the eval-unit." The soft contralto of the voice echoed after the door closed silently behind her.

"What are you evaluating?" Her voice was breathy, and she peered around.

"Your skills—physical and psychological. Your emotional and medical status. Your educational attainment levels."

It was an answer that shed little insight into the many things she was hungry to know. "Why do all seventeen year olds—"

"Take a seat, Levia. Then we may begin your testing."

If she'd expected an answer, she was sadly mistaken, she considered sourly. She dropped into the seat, the soft leather-like surface molding to her body.

"Levia Endrado, you are required to remove all non-specified apparel."

She jolted in the chair. "It's cold."

"The temperature will be amended. Remove the non-specified apparel."

Her misgivings grew as she dragged off the light wrap she'd brought with her, and then threw it to the floor at the side of the unit.

"We will begin, Levia Endrado. At any time, should you experience any malfunctions of the unit, simply depress the red button." It glowed and she grimaced.

Levia reclined against the chair and waited for the testing to begin.

The first examination was based on her understanding of the political system, where she saw herself, and her knowledge of the rights and responsibilities accorded through citizenship of both her planet and the commonwealth.

The second test was mathematical and scientific proficiency. It felt like hours had passed by the time she'd finished, and she lay limp on the seat, exhausted.

"Levia Endrado, you may rise. The sanitary unit will emerge once you trigger the yellow button at the door. Should you require refreshment, press the blue button and a restorative will be made available."

"Can I leave?"

"Negative, Levia Endrado. Your needs will be catered for in this capsule."

"Why?" Her voice hitched and true fear rose for the first time. Why did they keep her in the alcove?

"All will be revealed at the end of the testing cycle."

Levia looked at the now empty screen before hurling a curse word. It was met with silence.

The urgent throb of her bladder reminded her that she needed to use the facilities, so, with

a sigh, she rose and clambered from the seat. After attending to the needs of her body, she walked around the unit, peering at the door, but it was obviously programmed remotely. She poked and prodded, but it made no difference. With a huff, she headed back to the chair.

The moment she'd settled in, the viewing screen shone bright. "Welcome back, Levia. The next sequence will evaluate your psychological reflexes, then that will be followed up with the general knowledge portion of the evaluation."

"When can I leave?" It seemed better to ask bluntly, she told herself.

"Once the examination is completed. After the next set of evaluations, you will be subjected to the physical aspect."

"Then I can go home?"

"Levia Endrado, you will now complete the psychological test. This will be undertaken by one of the center's personal evaluators."

She frowned. Personal evaluators? She bit her lip, and the sting reminded her that this wasn't something to joke about. In her seventeen years, she'd only heard of personal evaluators being brought in once before, and that was when one of the girls at her academy had been in a serious accident. Both legs were amputated and her body's ability to keep her alive had been gravely compromised. Her peers had been informed that the girl had requested the assessment before she could request her support systems be disconnected.

"Levia Endrado, are you ready to recommence processing?" The emotionless voice echoed once more and she gulped.

"Yes."

Available from Beachwalk Press
http://www.beachwalkpress.com

Direct Autographed Books
http://bit.ly/BioCybe

ALSO BY IMOGENE NIX

Warriors of the Elector

- Star of Ishtar
- Starline
- Starfire
- Star of the Fleet
- Starburst
- The Star of Eternity

The Star of Ishtar & Starline - Print

Starfire & Star of the Fleet - Print

Starburst & The Star of Eternity - Print

Blood Secrets (Re-releasing 2020)

- The Blood Bride
- The Illuminated Witch
- The Sorcerer's Touch

The Search Duology

- Miss Elspeth's Desire
- Miss Isabelle's Craving

Reunion Trilogy

- War's End
- The Assassin
- Executing Justice

The Reunion Trilogy in Paperback

Sex Love & Aliens

- Tangled Webs
- False Webs
- Covert Webs

21st Testing Protocol

- Cyborg: Redux
- Children Of A Greater Evil
- When Evil Came To Stay (Not Yet Released)
- Finis: The War To End All Wars (Not Yet Released)

Celtic Cupid Trilogy

- Blame The Wine
- A Stranger's Embrace
- Revenge On Cupid

The Celtic Cupid Trilogy in Paperback

Zombieology

- The Reset (2018)
- I Dream of Zombies (2019)
- The Six Million Dollar Zombie (Not Yet Released)

Knights of Pleasure

- Silken Knights (Not Yet Released)

Single Titles

The Chocolate Affair (also in Print)

Falling In Love Again (Previously A Sapphire For Karina)

BioCybe (also in Print)

Hesparia's Tears (also in Print)

Tomorrow's Promise

A Bar In Paris (also in Print)

Inheritance Of The Blood (also in Print)

The Plan

Loving Memories (also in Print)

Hero of Heartbreak Hill (also in Print)

Raspberry Dreams (Not Yet Released)

Non Fiction

Self Publishing: Absolute Beginners Guide (With Suzi Love)

Written as Ciara Cave

25 Curated Ways To Get Rid Of Telemarketers

Book Signings for Absolute Beginners

ABOUT THE AUTHOR

Imogene is published in a range of romance genres including Paranormal, Science Fiction and Contemporary. She is mainly published in the UK and USA.

In 2010, Imogene Nix (the pen name not Imogene herself) was born. Imogene sat down and worked tirelessly for 3 months culminating in the book Starline, which became the first in a trilogy titled, "Warriors of the Elector." Since then she's had over 30 titles published and is now focusing on hybridising herself - with a mixture of traditionally published and self-published works.

In fact, she's taking control of many of her back catalogue books, which are slowly re-releasing as self-published titles.

Imogene is a member of a range of professional organisations world wide, and believes in the mantra of mentoring and paying it forward and is actively involved in mentorship (through NaNoWrimo and her vlog: In The Chair With Imogene Nix) and tutoring of new and upcoming authors.

In her spare time she loves to drink coffee, wine & eat chocolate and is parenting her spoiled dog and a ferocious cat along with her husband and 2 human daughters and looks forward to weekends away with her husband in their caravan "The Seven Year Hitch!" Do look forward to her caravan romance at some point!